D0166876

L. MARIE ADELINE

S·E·C·R·E·T
REVEALED

A NOVEL

DOUBLEDAY CANADA

Doubleday Canada and colophon are registered trademarks of Random House of Canada Limited

LIBRARY AND ARCHIVES OF CANADA CATALOGUING IN PUBLICATION

Adeline, L. Marie, author
S.E.C.R.E.T. revealed / L. Marie Adeline.

Issued in print and electronic formats.
ISBN 978-0-385-68243-5 (pbk) ISBN 978-0-385-68244-2 (epub)

I. Title. II. Title: SECRET revealed.

PS8563.A253155S44 2014   C813'.6   C2014-900858-9
                                                 C2014-900859-7

ISBN: 978-0-385-68243-5

This book is a work of fiction. Names, characters, places and incidents are products of the author's imagination or are used fictitiously. Any resemblance to actual events or locales or persons, living or dead, is entirely coincidental.

Cover images: (bed) Larysa Dodz/Getty Images, (bracelet) Peter Locke
Printed and bound in the USA

Published in Canada by Doubleday Canada,
a division of Random House of Canada Limited,
a Penguin Random House company

www.randomhouse.ca

10 9 8 7 6 5 4 3 2 1

For Lisa Laborde, with love and gratitude.

TEN STEPS

Step One: Surrender

Step Two: Courage

Step Three: Trust

Step Four: Generosity

Step Five: Fearlessness

Step Six: Confidence

Step Seven: Curiosity

Step Eight: Bravery

Step Nine: Exuberance

Step Ten: Liberation

CASSIE

Had it been only a week? A week since I put on that black-and-white lace camisole with the matching panties? My ear pressed to the door, I listened to him take the steps in twos, forcing myself to count to five after he knocked lightly, trying so hard to appear a little less excited to see him than I actually felt. I only made it to three seconds and then whipped open the door.

There was my Will, with a fistful of scurvy flowers clearly stolen from a vase at the Café.

"For you," he said, holding the flowers under my nose before tossing them over my head onto the floor behind me. "And for me," he said, scooping me up and carrying me backwards to my bed.

He threw me down on the bedspread. I squealed, delighted, as he pushed my camisole up over my breasts to kiss my stomach. Then I went lax, watching as the mere taste of my skin inflamed him, making him hungrier, rougher, which I found agonizing and thrilling. The sound from his throat as he worked off my camisole and threw it aside . . . I can still hear it.

"Are you real?" he asked as he gathered my breasts in his hands.

"Well, I thought about implants, but I'm just not that kind of girl, you know?" I said, lazily running my fingers through his thick, dark hair.

But he wasn't going to be distracted by my joke. We weren't "just friends" anymore. We were lovers. And he was lost in me, in my body, my hair, my skin. I was an ocean, allowing desire to wash over me, my blood pumping, sending small shudders through my legs, making me ache in places he would soon be touching. He pulled off my panties and whipped them over my head. They hit the window and fell to the floor. He regarded my body as if it were a banquet, unsure where to kiss first. His hands knew where to be, his fingers especially, as they traced along the curve of my pelvis, gracing where I was wet and waiting.

"I want you so badly," he said, his hot palm on my skin, urging a finger inside.

There were more words, but I don't remember them. My eyes were shut, the blood now pounding in my ears, my anticipation so great I threw my arms over my head, presenting my body to him like a gift, just to see what he would make of it. And that's when he flipped me over onto my stomach, lifting me, sinking his teeth into a cheek, not too hard but hard enough to mark me as his. I heard him yank his clothes off. Then his hands squeezed my hips and he arched me farther, opening me up to him, my arms stretched to the sides, my cheek against a pillow. I felt his prodding erection and I writhed to let him in, heated now, hungry for him to fuck me. I was like an animal, my fingers now claws pulling on the duvet. His own hands pushed their way down my back, caressing the skin before him.

"Oh god, Will."

I couldn't explain hunger like this any more than I could the fullness I felt as he began to inch inside me, his palm on my hip for leverage, since it was clear there'd soon be madness. But at first what I remember was this perfect, slow slide in, then this gorgeous ache as he pulled out. Over and over he thrust, and I began to match his fucking to my moans, or my moans matched his rhythm—it was hard to know. My thighs widened, my back bowed farther. I felt his thumbs press into my hips and then I looked over my shoulder at his face, so determined, so astonished. I think I wanted to snap him out of his trance, because why else would I say it? Why would I ask him to spank me? He paused.

"Do it," I hissed, my hair in my face.

This had never occurred to me before. But we were in a different place, an animal place, and then I felt it. Will gave me a swift, sweet slap—just like that—followed by a mellow rub, and I loved how it felt, the way his skin on mine sent vibrations straight to my core, now wrapped so tightly around his thrusting cock.

"*Yes.* Do it again," I commanded, my face now pressed into the duvet, eyes closed. *What is happening to me?*

But by then he was lost in the fucking. He was driving so hard into me, I couldn't have changed the direction of things if I tried. I sent a dizzy finger to my tight clitoris, greedy to come, but he roughly pushed it away, his own finger finding me—and feeling far better against that knot. All I could do was grab the duvet, hold on, and buck backwards as white stars crowded my vision.

"You're so hard," I said, and then it happened, the hot wave of my orgasm sneaking up on me, sending me up, up and then over the side, as I sighed, *Oh, yeah, yes, oh god, oh Will,* just as he was saying, *Jesus, Cassie, I'm coming,* and pulling out just in time to release across my spine, both of us knowing condoms were essential, but *man,* at a certain point there was just no looking back, no way to stop it, and no need to either. He was mine and I was his. I picked him, he picked me. We were each other's. If there were consequences, we'd accept them. After a few seconds of shuddering joy, he collapsed across me, pressing into me, pulling me to him, gasping and laughing at so much good fortune.

"Holy . . . holy . . . *fuck,*" he whispered, his mouth at my ear.

"I know," I said, shutting my eyes for a second and thanking the gods of sex for this man.

"So . . . where did *that* come from?"

"Where did what come from?"

I had already forgot that, ass in the air, I had asked my sweet Will to *spank* me.

"The 'spank me' stuff," he said, still a little out of breath but now carefully peeling himself off my back to collapse next to me.

I flipped over to my side to face him, my hand going to the part of his stomach I loved the most, the part still sticky with us. I thought of how the embers of friendship had so long been stoked that I had once worried we'd never be able to generate enough heat between us.

I no longer worried about that.

"I don't know," I said, shrugging. "I guess . . . I was over-come with desire." I laughed into the pillow. I sounded ridiculous!

"Why are you asking me?" I asked, coming up for air. "Did it bother you?"

"*Hell* no. I just never took you for a spanking enthusiast."

"I don't know if that's what I'd call myself, but yeah, in that moment, it felt, I don't know . . . like it was just the right kind of spice to add."

"I'll keep that flavor on hand in the future," he said, holding up a wide palm to high-five me, the punctuation to a lame, sweet joke.

Just as I was thinking, *How lucky am I that my friend Will is next to me in bed*, he pulled my whole head to his face for a long, deep kiss.

His mouth on my mouth—that's what I'll remember the most about that day.

"Who knew you were some kind of *sex* goddess," he whispered, cupping my chin.

I threw my head back and laughed, because he had no idea about S.E.C.R.E.T.

But less than a week later, Will would discover from whence his so-called sex goddess learned to be so goddess-y—and I would be left standing in a dark hallway at Latrobe's. He'd think of me as some dirty slut, covered in another man's scent, another man's pleasure, eight different men not counting Will: all from S.E.C.R.E.T—nine if you count Mark Drury, my recruit.

Soon I would no longer be a sex goddess to Will but rather a dangerous woman.

Soon this man who once could not get enough of me would not be able to get away from me fast enough.

SOLANGE

I grew up in this house so I knew every plane and corner, every nook and cranny; the cracks in the tile roof from hurricanes that failed to do more than bruise the siding; the grouting that needed tending to on the only stone porch on State Street. These flaws always drew my eye when I pulled my Volkswagen into the cobblestone driveway. My dad had bought this Craftsman-style house from its original owners, and for a time we were the only black family for two blocks in Uptown. So I was still conscious of keeping it looking as pretty and pristine as he had. But lately I'd let things slip. What can I say? I'd been busy. And I'd never been the obedient type.

Still, when I pulled up that warm fall day, I knew something was not quite right. Or that something was *very* right, depending on how you looked at it. The broken roof tiles had been replaced, the newer ones now a little more vivid than the old ones surrounding them. And the grout was dark where it had been newly filled in around the porch stones. My ten-year-old son, Gus, was with my ex, Julius, for the weekend. These were jobs he had said he'd help me with. When he got around to it. I said, *No. I'll do it. I can take care of myself, thank you very much.*

But between ten-hour shifts with grumpy news crews chasing breaking stories and weekends anchoring, I had no time to properly research the right maintenance company or to ask around at work if anyone could recommend a good contractor. They were so hard to find in New Orleans, so many were booked up on the Warehouse District condo boom or on big government reconstruction jobs. And Julius was never any good as a handyman. My ex-husband was an entrepreneur, a creative type, or at least that's how he saw himself. So how the hell had these repairs come about? Surely if Julius had tackled them, or found someone who could, he'd have told me.

It was only when I threw my car into park that I noticed the white utility truck in front of my house, a long ladder jutting out. Someone was here. I quietly exited, not fully closing my car door. Just then I heard a metal on metal clanging sound coming from my backyard.

My journalist instincts were on high alert. *Leave your purse in the car. Just take your keys. Be prepared to throw them. Don't go into the house. Observe from the outside in.* I was wearing heels so I padded on my toes, navigating the side drive, noticing as I did so that the leaky hose had been repaired. *Wow. Nice. But still. How? And who?*

I looked across the street. Dr. Franz in the brick Colonial was washing his car. Okay, good. There'd be a witness, someone to hear me scream in case whoever was in my backyard tinkering and hammering was actually breaking into it my house.

Ding, ding, plink, plink. The sounds continued. Feeling bolder, I made my way to the gate and raised my hand to unlock it, but the lock was completely gone, removed by the screws! My heart leapt. *Should I stop here and call the cops?* I padded around for my phone, but realized it was in my purse in the car. *Damn it.* I stepped onto the grass, my heels sinking into the moist lawn. *Who watered it?*

Carefully peeking around the corner, I saw him: a young man bent over a portable sawhorse, hammering away at something. It was 73 degrees, a hot day for November, so he was shirtless, an expanse of muscled back deeply browned by the sun. When the police asked for a description I'd say he was probably Italian, Greek or Hispanic, lithe, with more of a dancer's body than a construction worker's. No. I wouldn't use the term *dancer's body* with the police, would I? I was five-eight, shoes off, so I put him at five-eleven. Full head of curly black hair. Sinewy forearms. Not that I would describe them to the cops as *sinewy*; I wouldn't say that. Thick, maybe. Ropy? No. Wait. Why would I even describe his forearms? Well, they were remarkable. He looked to be twenty-five, thirty tops. Faded khaki work pants, naked torso, a white T-shirt hanging out of his back pocket.

He continued hammering at something finicky resting on a platform strung between the sawhorses, his tool belt hanging crooked around his lean hips. More tools were neatly laid out on a portable worktable set up on the back patio. (*Yes, Officer, that's when I came upon a young, lithe Italian man with a dancer's body, brown rippled skin, black curly hair, lean hips and incredibly sexy forearms—he was doing repairs on my place. Arrest him.*)

The man looked relaxed. At home. At *my* home. Maybe police weren't necessary.

"Ahem."

He didn't hear me.

"Hello," I said a little louder.

That sent his hammer flying out behind him, landing just a foot in front of me on the grass.

"Holy shit!" he exclaimed, turning around. "You scared me!"

"*I* scared *you*? This is *my* backyard you're hammering away in."

I finally took in his face, full on. He was seriously handsome but with gentle features: soft brown eyes, full lips. He gave me an easy smile and rested a hand on his hip, his other hand pulling the T-shirt out of his back pocket to wipe his brow.

"How long have you been standing there?" he asked.

I realized I was holding my car keys so hard they'd pressed grooves into my skin.

"I just got home. How long have you been working here?"

"All day. I fixed the broken tiles on the roof, reset some of the stones on the porch, watered the lawn—"

"I know. I saw. Who hired you? I certainly didn't."

"—and I was just fixing the fence lock, but this here's

just going to be a temporary fix. You'll have to get a new lock. One with a dead bolt, I think. I mean, this is Uptown, it's pretty safe, but you never know."

He had a very slight accent, not from around here—maybe East Texas? For me as a journalist this instant awareness of details was an automatic skill, one I was known for. I took a step closer to him as he thoughtfully tilted his head; he was taking in my shoes, my legs, my waist, my breasts. I was wearing a blue silk blouse, a deep jewel tone, the same one I had worn to anchor the news that morning. I felt a current dance through my body, instantly warming me. *Solange, this is a very young man. And you are a professional, a divorcée, with a young son and a high-profile job in the city. It would not be fitting to flirt. With this man. Who is trespassing on your property. Who is fixing your house. Who is younger than you.*

"Who are you and who hired you?" I repeated, a hand moving to rub my neck. Nerves.

"I'm thirsty. I'm wondering if I can get a glass of water maybe? Then I can tackle the leaky dishwasher—that is, if you'll let me into the house."

Sexy man, this one. He had swagger; he had a bit of game.

Sounding firm but not angry, I said, "You will remain thirsty until you tell me who sent you and what it is you're doing on my property."

"Well, I'll tell you . . . if . . . you accept the Step."

As he said it, literally as the words were coming out of his mouth, I knew. Finally, it was starting. The thing. The S.E.C.R.E.T. thing.

My guide, Matilda, had said it would begin within the month, that'd I'd be warned about some of my fantasies but that others would simply . . . unfold. God, how many times had I thought to pick up the phone and cancel all this sex-fantasy nonsense before it started. I didn't have time for this. Sex used to be important. Certainly it was a big part of my life with Julius before things turned sad for us. But I was forty-one years old, for crying out loud. I had a kid. I had no business gallivanting around town, or even my own back-yard, having sex with strange men, even if they *did* have a dimple in the left cheek and wore pants that kind of draped around their lean hips. Did I mention that?

He walked over to the garden hose. Actually, he saun-tered. *Damn.*

"If you won't quench my thirst, I'll have to do it this way," he said, raising a cool arc of water to his lips.

I held up my hand.

"Wait, you can come in."

"And?" he asked, letting the water run onto the lawn.

"And . . ."

My mind was scrambling. *How will this go? Oh god, what if I am bad at sex? It has been a while . . .*

"Will you accept the Step?" he asked, taking in another mouthful of water, letting some of it splash across his bare shoulders and chest.

I almost burst out laughing. "Do you know how old I am?"

"Do you know how *hot* you are?"

"Are you guys told to say those things?"

"Yes. We are . . ."

I felt my face drop. *Do I look crestfallen? I'm too old to be crestfallen.*

". . . but we're also instructed to say only things we mean."

He dropped the hose and shut off the water, standing stock-still in front of me, his expression calm, cool, his beautiful arms relaxed at his sides, one hip cocked, his stomach muscles contracting.

I closed my eyes.

"All right."

"All right what?" he asked.

"All right." I shrugged, waving my hand. "I accept . . . the whatever. The Step."

"You accept?"

"Sure, why not? What do I do now? Am I supposed to go upstairs and put on some lingerie? Or should we just do it back here?"

His mouth fell open. I could hear Julius in my head: *Why do you have to be like this, Solange? Can't you turn off the defensiveness? Can't you just relax and be a woman?*

"We could do it here if . . . you want . . ." he said, casting his eyes around the yard, thinking. "But I should take a shower first."

"Okay. Yes. Fine. Good idea. I'll show you where it is. Follow me," I said, about as seductively as a librarian taking someone to a stack of books.

He stood behind me as I tried to unlock the back door, the keys shaking in my hand. Covering my trembling fingers with his, he turned my whole body so I was facing him and pressed my back firmly against the siding.

"Solange," he said, looking at me sternly.

"Uh . . . ye-yes," I stammered, swallowing hard. I looked over his shoulder at the backyard.

"If you want me to, and *only* if you want me to, I'm gonna do some things to you," he whispered, boxing me in with his hands, his eyes taking in my body.

I could feel his breath on my clavicle, my back growing warm against the hot siding.

"At first these things I'm gonna do to you might feel . . . awkward. But then I think it's gonna start to feel really . . . good."

I nodded nervously.

"That's what I'm here for, to make you feel good. That is *all* I'm here to do. That's my job."

"What's your name?" I asked.

"Dominic," he said.

"Where are you from, Dominic?"

"Tyler, Texas. My parents are from Colombia."

"I knew it!"

"Knew what?"

"Your accent . . . forget it." I giggled. Nerves again. *Solange, relax, just let him do his job. He's been good at it so far. Don't kill the moment with your brain.*

He stopped my nervous laugh by pressing his lips to mine, waiting a second to part them with his tongue. He kissed with the depth and flourish of someone who knew what he was doing. He kissed older, like a more experienced man. He kissed well. He kissed like he wanted this. Really wanted this. This kiss was going a long way towards convincing me that this was the right thing for me to be doing right now.

His hands grasped my rib cage, a thumb boldly traveling over my nipple, which was hardening through the silk, his mouth moving from my mouth to my ear. He smelled like a *man*—musky, woodsy, soapy. *When was the last time I smelled this smell, this glorious man-smell?*

He pulled his lips away from mine and commanded me, quietly in my ear, "Gimme the keys."

I dropped them in his hand and he leaned across me, unlocking the door. The house was bracing cold. I had left the air conditioning on again. He dropped the keys back into my hand.

"Brrr. I hate when I forget to shut off the air," I said, rolling away from his body into the house, feeling dizzy. I walked over to the thermostat, moved the needle from 67 to 71 degrees.

"If it were up to me," I said, "I would just get rid of the air con—"

When I turned around, Dominic was gone. The kitchen and dining area were empty. A few seconds later, I heard the hiss of water through pipes. He was upstairs filling the bathtub! Oh jeez. It dawned on me: this was happening exactly the way I had outlined it three weeks ago as I sat at this very kitchen table. After that weird and wonderful day at that mansion on Third Street, Matilda had told me to write them down, all of them, every sexual fantasy I'd ever entertained, all the things I'd like a man to do to and for me but was afraid to ask.

For one of my fantasies, I wrote: *I would like to come home and just for once have all those gnawing little tasks and chores taken care of, by someone sexy . . . who has also drawn a bath for me.* I wrote that in the little folder they gave me. And even while I was filling it out, I had my doubts. I still thought: *This is crazy, this is a joke. These things don't happen. And they don't happen to forty-one-year-old workaholic moms.*

"Solange! Where do you keep your towels?"

My heart was pounding so hard I could hear it reverberate in my ears. I removed my watch and put it next to the fruit bowl. Then I unbuttoned the cuffs on my blouse and stepped out of my heels, leaving them side by side on the tiled floor. Then slowly, I headed for the stairs, moving towards the sound of the water, because apparently I was wrong. Apparently these things *do* happen. And they were happening now, to me.

Three stories were brewing at that S.E.C.R.E.T. charity event, which was where I first met Matilda Greene. But most journalists present only knew about two.

There was the Carruthers Johnstone story, of course. The recently reelected DA was in the corner issuing "no comment" about his new girlfriend and their even newer baby. And then there was the story of a small philanthropic organization that no one had ever heard of suddenly donating a staggering fifteen million dollars to various charities. We were told that S.E.C.R.E.T. stood for the Society for the Encouragement of Civic Responsibility and Equal Treatment, a legit charity registered with the city since the late '60s, but I couldn't find anything else about them. (It was only a while later that I'd come to know its off-the-books acronym.)

But the biggest story of the night actually staggered in a few minutes after my crew set up near the bar to interview Matilda. A very drunk Pierre Castille, one of the richest land developers in New Orleans, had crashed the party. He was generally extremely private, so to see him there at all was strange. To see him so incautious and disheveled was shocking, though I might have been the only journalist there who recognized him. Few pictures existed of him, and no video. He had never given a brief comment, let alone an interview about any of the goings-on of his company, which he had inherited from his equally elusive father. His was a name that would likely appear at the top of every journalist's wish list, if you asked any of them whom they'd most like to profile. After all, he owned half the city and was scooping up cheap land along the river near the French Market. Plus, he was a bachelor, and to look at him was to wonder why. He had to be the sexiest beast I'd laid eyes on in a long time. And he wasn't even my type. And now, there he was, weaving over to a small crowd in a dark corner near the kitchen.

A few minutes later, a drama erupted and it looked like a punch was thrown. Matilda emerged from the scuffle whispering something to a bouncer before joining me for our interview. By the time I had a chance to ask her what the tussle was all about, Security was escorting Castille out the door. As he passed us, his eyes narrowed at Matilda. He was about to say something nasty to her when he noticed me standing nearby. He smirked.

"Hey, Action News Nightly," he said. "There's a story here. It's just not the one you came for."

Then, before the bouncer shoved him out the door, he yelled over his shoulder, "Good-bye, whores!"

It was a vivid moment, but one that Matilda Greene did not care to expound upon when I asked her how it was that she knew Pierre Castille and why in the world he was talking that way.

"Actually I don't really know him," she said, brushing imaginary lint off the straps of her evening gown.

"You just had the Bayou Billionaire forcibly removed from your party, he called you and your other guests whores, and you say you don't know him?"

"A good hostess would have anyone that inebriated removed, billionaire or not," she said. And with a wave of her hand she expertly changed the subject, launching into a smart interview about her charity's goal to help women. Minutes later she ducked out of our conversation to comfort a teary brunette in a black satin dress who was also leaving the event in a hurry.

It was a perplexing, dramatic night.

Afterwards, Matilda and I exchanged cards. Even if nothing mysterious was going on with S.E.C.R.E.T., the fifteen million dollars, an agitated billionaire and an upset brunette, I filed that party away as a strange story to revisit. So when Matilda called me a couple of weeks later to ask me to lunch, I was thrilled, determined to poke around a little more.

We met at Tracey's, a strangely masculine place for such a feminine woman. But they seemed to know her there, as though she were a regular at a sports bar. Matilda was prettier than I remembered, her red hair pulled back into a thick ponytail, the tension of that evening completely absent from her face. Seconds into our meeting, however, it was clear Matilda wasn't there to talk about Pierre, her charity, or bawling brunettes. On the contrary, she was completely (and strangely) fixated on me, namely on a recent profile *New Orleans Magazine* had done on me after my port lands story broke and I was promoted to weekend anchor.

"Thank you so much for meeting me, Solange. Or should I say 'The Formidable Solange Faraday'?"

Ugh. Matilda was referring to the magazine's headline. The article itself was not really about my career. Instead, it was focused almost entirely on the fact that I was a single mom who hadn't dated much in the eight years since my divorce.

"I cringe every time I see that magazine at the checkout lines."

"I should think you'd be thrilled for the coverage," she said.

"Normally you'd be right, but the article . . . it was a *joke.* Yes, I am divorced, but my parenting relationship with my ex-husband is good; he's a great dad. We work hard at that. Calling me a 'single mom' is an insult to women everywhere who *are* actually raising kids alone, and to divorced dads who *are* doing their half of the work."

And then I unleashed years of bottled-up indignation, the depths of which even I was unaware of until just then.

"They said it would focus on the hours, days, weeks and months my whole *team* spent on my port lands story, the one our network broke last year. We put some local politicians in jail over that graft scandal. But instead they portrayed me as some lonely, workaholic divorcée!"

I could almost see the ends of Matilda's hair getting singed by my diatribe, but I didn't care. I couldn't admit to her or anyone else that almost a decade had gone by since I'd been in a serious relationship. There had been dates here and there. I'd had sex. But it was usually lousy, furtive and just not worth giving up the rare night I had to myself. I wasn't really looking to get married again. I certainly wasn't looking to introduce a new man into my son's life. Besides, raising him was so deeply fulfilling it didn't leave much room for anything or anyone else. And it was true, I loved my work. If anything I was married to that. But oh man, to feel a pair of warm feet in a cold bed every once in a while . . .

"How was the sex? With your ex-husband?" Matilda asked, blithely stirring her coffee.

To this day, I do not know why I was able to discuss my sex life with a complete stranger, but Matilda had a gift, a way of making it easy for me to tell her everything, even though she herself seemed to be a closed book.

"Julius and I were very compatible in that arena," I said. "Then I gave birth to Gus, and everything . . . changed. I changed. He changed, or rather he didn't. And sex kind of just fell away. At first it was because I had a baby to take care of. Then it was because he took care of the baby while I worked. A lot. Then I got ambitious, and really busy. And he . . . he didn't. It took a toll on him." My mouth wouldn't stop moving! It felt like being hypnotized.

"Sounds like he had a crisis of confidence," Matilda said.

"Yeah. That's exactly right."

I told her how Julius had been fine being a stay-at-home dad. At first. But one failed venture followed another and sex went the way of his self-esteem. Despite counseling, we drifted too far apart to ever really recover what we'd had.

"Was it a bad split?"

"Not really. I mean, my dad died and my mother had a stroke. So I moved back to my childhood home to take care of her. We took it as an opportunity to separate. But after she died, I never really left that house. Like I said, we co-parent well. He's the best dad. And Gus has never seen us fight. Because we don't. Anymore. But, yeah, it wasn't acrimonious. It was just . . . really sad . . ."

I suddenly felt choked up. I hated to think about what our divorce had done to our sweet, sweet boy, whom my whole body missed when he was at his dad's. On the one hand, our separating before he turned three was good. He didn't remember us together, all tense and crabby. On the other hand, he had never really seen his mother in a loving, affectionate adult relationship either. But maybe I was reading too many of those post-divorce parenting books.

At that moment, desperate to change the subject, I noticed Matilda's bracelet and reached out to touch it. The gold was warm, heavy; the charms had little inscriptions on them that I couldn't make out without my reading glasses.

"This is a beautiful piece of jewelry. An heirloom?"

"You could say that." She smiled.

"Where did you get it?"

She tugged her arm back.

"I'm sorry to hear you hated that article, Solange," she said, completely ignoring my question. She could teach a master class on evasion. "But in a way, that focus is what got me to call you."

So there *was* a purpose to this lunch.

"Fact is, I came here to talk to you about that article *and* about your sex life. Or lack of it. And how I might be able to . . . help."

Her utter directness made my face heat up. *Oh dear. Now I understood.* I wiped my mouth with my napkin and placed my hand on hers, clearing my throat.

"I should tell you, Matilda, I am deeply flattered, but, the thing is . . . I'm straight. Though if I *were* a lesbian—"

"*No-no-no.* Oh my god. That's not what I meant!" she said, smiling. "Forgive me, I'm not usually this blunt, but my approach changes for each woman and I have a feeling being direct with you is the best way forward. I'm talking about having sex with *men*. And not relationships per se. Just . . . *relations*."

"Oh."

She scooted forward in her chair, suddenly taking on the demeanor of someone offering up a great deal, the kind you cannot turn down.

"These relations I speak of are purely sexual," she added. "Fun, free, safe, anonymous encounters. Ones you're entirely in control of. Ones *you* define. They don't define you. Sexual scenarios you come up with, executed exactly the way you want them to be executed. How does that sound to you?"

"You mean . . . you're talking about sexual fantasies. About making them . . . real?" I glanced around the loud, boisterous bar filled mostly with loud, boisterous men completely wrapped up in the game or their own conversations. This *was* the perfect place to have this kind of conversation.

"Yes. Now, you're a journalist, Solange. So what I'm about to tell you next has to remain off the record. Permanently. It's highly confidential. So confidential that if I were asked to go *on* the record, I would have to deny this conversation ever happened."

I looked around the restaurant. My interest was beyond piqued; my whole body was on *Holy shit* alert, making me feel dizzy with anticipation. But I did my best to retain a cool facade.

"Okay. Agreed."

That's when she laid it all out: what her philanthropic group, S.E.C.R.E.T., really stood for, its history and her role as one of its founders and chief guides. S.E.C.R.E.T. didn't stand for the Society for the Encouragement of Civic Responsibility and Equal Treatment after all. It was an acronym that stood for *Safe, Erotic, Compelling, Romantic, Ecstatic* and *Transformative*: conditions for sexual fantasies her group arranged and executed for women. Women they selected. Women like me. Women in need of some help in that arena.

I was incredulous.

And shocked.

And completely riveted.

"Let me get this straight. You helm an organization that grants women sexual fantasies? Why are you telling *me* all this? As you said, I'm a journalist."

"I know. But I trust you. And . . . well, we would like you to be our next candidate. And quite possibly our last, for a while anyway."

"Candidate? Why me?"

"Well, in recent years we've selected women who were sexually numb, and others who were deeply broken. This time, for our last candidate, we want someone who just stopped making sex a priority. Someone with more life experience. Also, why *not* you? You're beautiful, accomplished, and busy. As you mentioned in that article, dating is not something you 'waste a lot of time on.' You no longer bother, as you stated. What I'm proposing is that you let us do something for you that you'd never do for yourself. It's what we're best at."

I was speechless for a few moments, then asked, "What do you mean 'last candidate'?"

She seemed to drift away for a moment before shaking off what looked like sad thoughts.

"Well, S.E.C.R.E.T. has run its course, I'm afraid. It's been a lovely run, but after our next candidate, we're closing up shop, whether we want to or not," she said, changing the subject again and motioning for the bill. "If you decide this is something you want to do, call me. I'll bring you in to meet the Committee."

"The Committee?"

"Yes. Other women like you, who've been changed for the better for doing this. Some are prominent members of New Orleans society—doctors, lawyers, performers and the like. Names you'd recognize. Others are waitresses, hairstylists, teachers. The men we recruit to fulfill fantasies are chefs, construction workers, entrepreneurs, business leaders. Still others are among the most famous men in the world."

That's when it hit me!

"Pierre Castille! That's how you know him. He's one of these . . . recruits, isn't he?"

Matilda Greene would have been an exceptional poker player. Her expression didn't change one iota. She didn't flinch, and when next she spoke, she weighed her words carefully.

"Even if he were, Solange, I would never answer that question. We are nothing if not discreet, something I hope you will find very reassuring if you do consider us. And I hope I can be assured of your discretion as well."

I looked down at the backs of my hands, feeling a little bad for my accusatorial outburst. Turning forty had started showing up in the oddest places: the way my skin puckered around my knuckles, that skin flap on my elbow, a stiff lower back in the morning, a gray hair or two in intimate places. I could still turn a head, but Matilda was right, I no longer bothered. I didn't care about sex. Maybe a date here and there, sometimes enough dates with one man to get naked, lights off. But more and more, the idea of giving up one of the very few relaxing nights I had to myself to go on yet another go-nowhere date, the idea of not sleeping in my own bed, of not having my own toiletries, of having my routine disrupted, well, it just wasn't enough of a lure to make me want to bother.

"I'll give it some thought," I told her, nervously pocketing the card she gave me. I was surprisingly reluctant to say good night; she was the kind of company you didn't want to leave.

That night, the house was empty. Gus was at his dad's for the weekend, something that suddenly gut-punched me. Where I once looked forward to my solitude, my couch, my book, my glass of wine, my cozy pajamas, I suddenly dreaded all of it. When I was younger, I used to love going out. I used to love the ritual of it—dressing up, putting on makeup, hitting the hot clubs and never being the kind of girl who waited in lineups. For chrissakes, I paid part of my tuition with singing gigs, closing down jazz clubs where Julius DJed, slow-dancing with him until the sun came up.

Not anymore.

Despite his own career struggles, Julius's sex life seemed to flourish after the divorce. The man had had at least two serious girlfriends in the last eight years. And if those women hadn't been so kind to Gus, I'd have banned him from introducing any new ones into his life.

Still, vulnerability was not my thing; I had a phobia about asking for help. So it took everything in me to pick up that phone two agonizing days later and call Matilda. Mostly I said yes because it would make one hell of a story. Not one I'd be able to tell, but then again, not all stories are meant for prime time.

I was a ball of nerves approaching the Mansion on Third to meet this Committee. But Matilda was right: the women, they *did* all look like me. I don't mean because several of them were also African American, though it was a relief to see the Committee wasn't all white. But rather, these women were of an age; not pretty young things, not girls but *women*,

women who looked me square-on, who glowed with a kind of sexy allure I had long abandoned for professional polish. They wore their femaleness fearlessly, comfortably, proudly.

After my nerves calmed, introductions were made and they assured me that all of this would be anonymous. Obviously, I had questions. If I change my mind at any time, can I stop? *Yes, absolutely.* I have a child. Would you work around my parenting schedule? *That's the plan.* I'm not looking for a relationship. *Good, we don't promise one, though they've been known to happen.*

In the end I was more intrigued than scared, which, because I'm a journalist, is always a good sign.

So I said yes, blushing at the resulting applause.

"With that 'yes' comes a symbol of our bond with you and with one another," Matilda said, placing a purple box in front of me. Inside was a bare gold chain, the same color and texture as the ones the other women were wearing, except theirs were covered with tinkling charms.

"This is mine?" I asked, holding the heavy eighteen-karat gold chain up to the light.

"It's yours," Matilda said.

After hugs and congratulations, they sent me home with a folder I was cautioned not to open until Gus was asleep.

That night, I paid the sitter, double-checked to make sure my son's light was off, made some tea and turned up some classical music. I checked on Gus one more time before I sat at my marble-topped kitchen table, the one I had eaten my meals on as a child, and opened that folder with shaky hands. Inside was a long list of fantasies and scenarios, some shocking, some common, a sexual wish list of sorts, with several blank lines to improvise ideas. Matilda had told me to be specific and to be honest, that no fantasy scenario was too dull or too off-the-wall to be considered.

I sharpened a pencil and proceeded to give this task more thought than the guest list at my own wedding. My first scenario wasn't hard to come up with:

Just once, I'd love to come home from a long day at work, and all the nagging chores and jobs would have been tackled by a very attractive man, someone sexy, who has also drawn a bath for me, and for whom I do not have to cook and clean or even talk to if I don't want to. We would just— this was where I hesitated—*we would just . . . have sex?*

I included the question mark at the end. The sex was not a foregone conclusion, at least not on my part.

And now, three weeks later, this scenario was unfolding exactly as I had written it. Here he was. My first fantasy man.

⁓

The sound of running water grew louder as I neared the staircase. My hand seized the balustrade and I noticed my bare S.E.C.R.E.T. chain peeking out from under the sleeve of my blouse. Quietly I climbed, careful to keep my feet on the carpeted part of the stairs. Then the sound of water stopped, and so did I.

"Dominic?"

"I'm in the master bath!" he yelled. "I found the towels."

I slapped my hand over my heart to calm it some.

"You can come in, Solange. I'm decent."

Oh dear lord. I made it to the top of the stairs and turned down the hall to my bedroom, feeling my stomach clench. *I've never had sex with a complete stranger. What am I doing? Am I crazy?* The ensuite bath had both a shower and a tub, and Dominic was just stepping out of the shower, a towel secured around his sculpted waist. The dusky light from the glazed window blurred the room, or maybe it was the steam, or the fact that I was vibrating. But this bronze Adonis was dripping water all over my tiles and I'd never minded anything less. I realized my breath was shallow and I tried to force it lower into my system to prevent fainting at the sight of him, his taut skin, his thick arms, his bare feet planted solidly on the floor. I pulled oxygen deeper into my lungs, the way I had learned how to in Lamaze classes . . . *Lamaze! I have a kid! I shouldn't be . . . STOP thinking.*

Dominic was smiling the smile of a man who understood his effect on a woman. *You're going to get yourself naked in front of this man, Solange. And you're going to be okay with it.* The tub next to him was full, bubbles floating on the surface, a row of lit tea candles along the back ledge. It was very pretty.

"I took a quick shower and ran a bath at the same time. I probably used all the hot water in the house. My apologies." That smile again.

"That's all right," I said, massaging the back of my neck.

"I think the water temperature is okay. Wanna check?"

His eyes stayed on me as I crossed the room. I leaned over and dangled my fingers in the sudsy water.

"It's nice," I said.

"Why don't you get in? And . . . I'll get you something to drink," he said, perhaps sensing my shyness about undressing in front of him. "Any requests?"

Oh thank god.

"Yes. That would be nice. Some water, maybe? Glasses are in the dining room hutch. Or wine. Maybe wine? There's an open bottle in the fridge door."

I watched him disappear. *Doitdoitdoit.* I quickly slipped out of my skirt and blouse, piling them (neatly) on the vanity. I slipped out of my bra and underwear and slipped them under the pile of clothes. I tested the water with my toe, *Ouch,* a bit hot, but fine, no time for inching in.

I sunk to my collarbones, my body neatly concealed beneath the bubbles, my knees now brown mountains with soapy snowcaps sliding off them. I loved my tub—a beautiful white oval model, one I'd picked out when I realized Gus and I were going to remain in my childhood home and I renovated the master bedroom and ensuite. It had seemed so decadent at the time to install a whirlpool tub, but I did use it. It was often my only means of relaxing.

A few minutes later, Dominic came back up the stairs and into the bathroom, a sweating glass in one hand, his towel still clenched in the other. I leaned forward to wrap my arms around my knees, concealing my breasts, and averted my eyes from his seemingly airbrushed abs. He *was so . . . this was too . . .*

"Here you go," he said, handing me the glass.

I accepted it.

"Are you comfortable?"

I nodded, took a sip and carefully placed the glass on the tiled corner of the tub. He kneeled next to me on the floor.

"Because if you're not comfortable . . ."

"No. I'm fine," I said, choking a little on the wine. I knew the smile on my face was a weak one. "Really. This is just . . . I'll get used to it."

I'll get used to it? Wow. So sexy, Solange.

He returned the smile and I felt almost like crying. I don't know why. I wasn't afraid; I wasn't sad. Quite the opposite. I was . . . grateful. *Moved* even. His torso was inches from the rim of the tub. I could have stretched out a hand and touched it; I so wanted to. He wasn't just beautiful, he was kind.

He took a folded white washcloth from the rim of the tub. Dipping it into the sudsy water and squeezing out the excess, he placed it on my shoulders and eased them down. I let him make long, slow circles with his cloth-covered hand, my head easing forward, relaxing. *A hand on me, this human touch. I have been lonely. How have I not noticed?*

The scratchy fabric, the warm water, his hand so near my skin, all served to calm me. I closed my eyes.

"How does that feel?"

"Good," I murmured. Moments later I felt the cloth pull away to be replaced by his soft lips on my shoulder blade.

"How does that feel?"

"Good too," I said.

He placed another kiss on my back, wiping with the washcloth as he traced a path from one shoulder blade to another. *Oh god.* I was melting into the water. How long had it been since I'd been handled so tenderly?

"It's getting a little chilly out here," Dominic whispered, pressing his mouth behind my left ear. "May I join you?"

It's happening! Breathe. I scooted forward in the tub to make room for him behind me. Out of the corner of my eye I saw him drop his towel, and I glimpsed a thatch of short dark hair, a semi-aroused penis, a *nice* one. He stepped into the water, his knees bracketing my hips as he lowered himself in. He gently pulled my torso back against his warm chest. I could feel his erection against my lower back, getting harder as his hands moved from my shoulder caps down my front. My own hands still covered my wet breasts, and he curled his fingers around my wrists.

"Let me," he said, coaxing my hands apart.

"Let you what?" I asked, stifling a nervous giggle. *You are forty-one. You mustn't giggle.*

"It's time to surrender, Solange. Just . . . let me."

After a brief hesitation, my arms went slack, and he . . . well, he *unwrapped* me, opening one then the other arm, placing them around the outside of his strong thighs. It was fascinating, an experience that I was both enjoying and observing. He trailed his hands up my smooth arms to my shoulders and then down again, this time cupping both breasts, now slick and wet and bobbing out of the soapy water. I watched him circle my nipples with his thumbs, sending a sharp bolt of arousal straight behind my belly button. I inhaled quickly, pressing back into his torso, his erection now fierce against my spine, my head tucked under his slightly stubbly chin. I was careful to keep my hair dry. I was game for a lot of things, but getting my hair wet was a no-no. My hands curled around his as they kneaded my breasts, his thighs firm against the outside of mine. I swear it was like being held between two tree trunks.

"Mmm . . ." I said, my eyes closing as his hands loosened around my breasts, then slid down between my legs, plunging under the water. Would he be able to tell how wet I was? He let his fingers gather and tug my short hairs and it was all I could do not to scoop out of the water to give him easier access. I was so turned on by then, I was pressing him back into the tub. I *wanted* him. I let my arms drift up and wrap around the back of his neck as he teased and tickled me, both of his hands now spreading my thighs as wide as they would go against the sides of the tub.

As his fingers traveled along my folds, he sunk his mouth into my neck, his lips covering his teeth, sucking, kissing my skin hard. I felt devoured as two fingers slipped between the most tender parts of my flesh, then inside.

"*Ohh,*" I said, my back arching, the water between our torsos gently slapping. I raked my fingers through his thick black hair. His other hand massaged up my side, cupping my breast again, this time harder, more urgently, as his other hand worked me, his fingers thrusting a little deeper now, a little faster. He would stop and circle as I engorged under his touch. His other hand moved from my breast and cupped me under my chin, turning my head slightly so his tongue could tease my ear. He was moving me this way and that and I had completely surrendered to him. Then he stopped what he was doing, shifting away from me, leaving one hand reassuringly on my back. I looked over as he pulled out a condom packet from beneath a stack of washcloths, ripped it open, then slid it over his hard cock.

"Turn around, Solange, so I can look at you when I fuck you," he whispered.

With strength that surprised me, he lifted me out of the water and flipped me around, his magnificent erection just below me. I took a hand to guide him deep inside, sighing as he entered and pulled me in tight to him, holding me there as I felt him pulse deep inside of me, my legs wrapped around him. It was an exquisite sensation. Then he began to rock beneath me, his arms around my waist.

"Lean back on your hands," he said. "I want you to watch me fuck you."

I did so, both of us fixated on his cock easing in and out of me, slowly at first, the water lapping against the sides of the wide tub. His fingers had only to grace my clitoris, which was so fat I knew I could come like *that*.

"Mmm," I said involuntarily, one of my hands grabbing onto his shoulder, the other holding the side of the tub until I could find and match his rhythm. His dark eyes on me were too much to bear. I threw my head back and squeezed my eyes shut. *I cannot believe this is happening to me, here, in my own tub!*

"Oh, Solange . . . you are so fucking gorgeous," he moaned, thrusting into me, his thumb circling my clit, the muscles in his upper arm flinching with precise effort. We were splashing bubbly water between us and over the sides, extinguishing a tea candle, then another one. Then, leaning forward to cup the back of my neck, he placed his lush mouth next to my ear.

"Come for me, Solange," he whispered. "I want you to come. For me . . ."

Then I felt it—my tense core melting, giving way. My legs braced the sides of the tub as it rippled out from my center through to the tips of my limbs. I fell back onto my hands, his gaze now ardent. He continued to push his cock up and into me, fucking me hard, while gently massaging my clit, a masterful combination that finally made the ache all too much to bear and suddenly I was letting go, I let it *all* go, and I came hard and fiercely, his pumping still relentless, as I moaned into the ceiling (*Oh yes, oh yes . . .*) and he came then too (*Yeah, oh god!*), his whole body emptying into mine, and no one could hear us with the windows closed, not the neighbors out back on the other side of the pine trees, not the ones across the street washing their cars, not the pedestrians walking their dogs past my cozy house on State.

Gasping and spent, I fell forward, draping my wet body over his torso, my arms dangling over his back, pulling in breath like a drowning victim. He wrapped me in a tight embrace, kissing my shoulder cap. We stayed tied in that damp knot for a few moments until my breathing subsided and the water began to cool. Then he carefully peeled himself away from me and stood up in the bath, water rivulets dripping down his magnificent thighs. He stepped out of the tub and unhooked my robe from the back of the door, hanging it from his fingers, inviting me in.

"Madame, your robe," he said.

I stood up, feeling dizzy, a bit sheepish, happy.

I stepped onto the bath mat and turned around, putting my hands through the robe's arms. He enveloped me with it and did the sash up from behind, rubbing my arms and sides vigorously to dry me.

"Thank you." *Was that a silly thing to say?*

As he bent to wrap a towel around himself, he said, "Check the pocket, Solange."

I reached inside and pulled out a small purple box. Inside was my first charm, a golden raindrop in the center of a puffy cloud. *Surrender* was spelled out in cursive on one side, a Roman numeral one on the other. It was just like the ones on Matilda's bracelet, and on all the bracelets the women at the Mansion had worn that day.

"Would you mind?" I said, handing him the charm. My heart was pounding.

"Of course," he said, his talented fingers easily securing the charm to the chain.

I walked over to the vanity to get a look at it in the mirror.

"It's lovely," I said, dangling it in front of my eyes.

"As are you."

I turned to face him. "Thank you, Dominic, for . . . tackling all these odd jobs. And for that . . ." I said, pointing to the tub. "Now what?"

"Well, now I suggest you rest a bit. And let me take care of that dishwasher and anything else you might want me to fix before I go."

"I can think of a few things on my to-do list," I said, throwing a shy smile at him from the mirror.

He plucked his clothes from the floor and left me standing very still in the bathroom, my legs quaking, the windows all steamed up. *I did it. I did something I've never done before: I just got laid by a beautiful young man I will probably never see again. And I'm . . . I'm proud of myself.*

I made my way over to my bed, peeled back the duvet, dropped my robe to the floor and slid naked between my cool sheets. Closing my eyes, I let my hand travel down to where I was just starting to feel a little sore. *Ow.* Wow. I heard him downstairs as he started and stopped the dishwasher. Then I heard the *plink plink* of tinkering and repairing. *Nice.*

Drifting off, I was thinking of at least one more thing he might be able to tackle before he left. Just one more thing . . .

CASSIE

I t had all happened so fast. Something had told me not to bring Will to that S.E.C.R.E.T. charity event. But I didn't listen. Something had also told me to pull him away from Pierre Castille the second he opened his mouth to reveal the truth of my involvement in S.E.C.R.E.T.— the sex, the fantasies, the men—using the vilest of terms, *slut, bitch, whore.*

But I froze in the dark corner of Latrobe's that fateful night. I said nothing when Pierre told Will that S.E.C.R.E.T.'s mandate was to "use and discard men." When Pierre spat out that I'd do that to Will, too, if he let me, it looked like Will believed him.

How many men, Cassie? How many? And since when?

Secrets and lies now surrounded me the way they'd surrounded his ex, Tracina, a woman who had convinced Will for the better part of a year that the baby she was carrying was his. It had been only a month since he heartbreakingly discovered that that wasn't true, that the baby was the product of her affair with Carruthers Johnstone, the once-married-now-separated DA she really loved. Not that Will had loved Tracina. He hadn't, but he had so loved the idea of the baby. I had hoped our blissful reunion would help heal his wounds over that, but they were gaping once more, and I was the one who had ripped out his stitches.

"I—I'm sorry I never told you everything before, Will, but I was worried you'd react like this," I stammered.

My hands on his chest, I tried to explain to him what S.E.C.R.E.T was about, what it had done for me. But he wasn't listening. He was glaring at Jesse Turnbull, my ex-lover and now friend, who had come to find me, to see if I was okay.

"Was he from this year's roster or was he last year's model, Cassie?" Will hissed. "Maybe you're into having *him* spank you too."

Jesse took a step forward. He had already decked Pierre and I had no doubt that if necessary he'd do the same to Will.

"I've had enough bedroom drama to last me a fucking lifetime," Will said before storming out of Latrobe's, leaving me in a pile for Jesse to gather up and carry home.

And just like that, Will Foret was no longer in love with me.

On the way home from Latrobe's, I was inconsolable. Jesse tried to explain that Will wasn't rejecting me, he was rejecting the duplicity. I listened, watching the city smear past me in the passenger window. He pulled the truck up to the curb in front of the Spinster Hotel, shutting off the engine. He turned to face me.

"Want me to come up?"

When the love of your life tosses you over because of your past, it's easy to imagine running into the arms of the man who accepts everything about you, especially when those arms are warm and taut and welcoming. But while I did invite Jesse upstairs, I didn't so much as kiss him.

While he boiled water for tea, I slipped out of that awful, beautiful black satin dress and pulled on my sweats. While the tea steeped, I sobbed for a few minutes on the futon couch, pushing away my cat Dixie's attempts to comfort me. Jesse sat beside me and listened. From time to time, he'd lay a reassuring arm on my forearm, telling me everything would be okay, that Will would come around, that I had done nothing wrong, and that I just had to be patient.

"You heard him tonight, Jesse," I said, tossing another ball of spent tissue onto my coffee table. "He's *done*."

Jesse studied my face for an opening. He was going to be honest with me and I could already tell I wasn't going to like what he was about to say.

"Well, here's the thing, Cassie. I'm a man . . . and I'm thinking . . . after the year that guy's had, I'd be scared too."

"He's not scared, he's *pissed*."

"Let me tell you something about men, Cassie. When we get scared we don't show 'scared,' we show 'angry.'"

Maybe there was some truth in all that, but I wasn't ready to let Will off the hook, or myself.

"Nah. He's thinking, 'What a fucking whore, glad I found out now.'"

It was a tossed-off statement, but Jesse leaned towards me, peering into my face like a concerned doctor. "Why would you *say* something like that, Cass?"

"You saw him, Jesse. He hates me. He is repulsed by what I've done."

"No he doesn't, and he isn't. He hates that the woman he loves has been leading some . . . I don't know . . . strange, sexy double life . . . And he has no idea what to do about that but feel scared and threatened. You following me?"

"I am. I just . . . I've made such mess of everything. Will and me. *You* and me. I mean, why are *you* even here being so nice to me after the way I treated you?"

We hadn't seen each other in about a month, not since the day Tracina's baby was born, when it became evident that Will's heart was mine, and mine his, and whatever I'd had with Jesse wasn't going to amount to much more than sex.

"There you go again with the self-fucking-loathing. You need to cut that out, Cass. I'm serious. If Matilda was here, she'd slap those words right out of your mouth for good."

"It's true. I'm sorry."

Jesse's face softened, concern giving way to kindness.

"Don't apologize to me. You never did anything wrong to me. Apologize to yourself."

My eyes felt hooded and swollen from tears. I rested my head on my upper arm, outstretched across the back of the futon. I let my fingers glance Jesse's shoulder. I looked at him through my damp lashes. Was I flirting? No. Maybe.

I was looking for comfort, connection. Jesse responded by moving close to me, then by placing a soft, sweet kiss on my temple.

"Bye, doll. You sleep. I'll call you."

If he had reached under my chin and drawn my mouth to his, would I have resisted? I think so. Maybe. No. Yes! Who knows? In truth, I had no idea what I wanted that night. But ambivalence, blurry lines, confusion and sadness, these were not aphrodisiacs to the men in S.E.C.R.E.T.

Jesse rose and stretched, his taut stomach peeking out from beneath his T-shirt. I had never thought I was a visual animal, but since S.E.C.R.E.T., I had discovered that I had been wrong about a lot of things.

Too tired to get off the couch, I waved good-bye to Jesse from my spot. He gave me his trademark two-finger salute and left, quietly shutting the door behind him. Then I glanced down at my arm, down to my glittering bracelet, the one covered with ten charms, each one loved and earned. Suddenly it seemed to weigh heavily on my wrist.

The next morning, I dressed carefully for my regular breakfast shift at the Café Rose. I wanted to look pulled together, calm, adult, not like I'd been crying all night. Not that Dell would notice. She hadn't paid much attention to Will and me kissing in the corners of the Café this past month, so I figured she'd barely register that we'd broken up.

Then I was slammed by another memory from the night before! Yesterday, in the throes of deep affection for me, Will had not only asked me to manage his new, fancier restaurant upstairs, but also had said he was naming it *Cassie's*, after me, a gesture that had moved me to tears. Now, I wasn't even sure I wanted to work there anymore.

Maybe what I needed to do was walk in and quit. This time for good. Maybe a long break from seeing each other, being around each other, hurting each other, was what we both needed. Then cold dread snaked up my legs: *Will could fire me.* I'd have a wrongful dismissal case of some kind, but I wouldn't spend my savings on lawyers. Knowing me, I'd just leave, tail between my legs, taking Angela Rejean up on that hostess job at Maison.

When I got to Frenchmen Street, I made a right. The autumn sun felt comforting on my shoulders. I began to walk a little taller. If only I could make Will understand all that S.E.C.R.E.T. had done for me, not just sexually. But I could also stand up for myself. I could go after what I wanted. I was bolder, surer, no longer clingy and afraid. I wasn't one of those women who would rather be with anyone than alone. Alone was not scary anymore. Alone was challenging, but it was also deeply satisfying. Alone was not lonely.

By the time I reached the Café Rose, I was certain today was the last day I'd work for Will Foret. And I was also certain I'd be okay. I looked upstairs to the new restaurant, its freshly installed windows still sporting the manufacturer's stickers. I would be sad, but I would survive. Resilience was one of the many things S.E.C.R.E.T. had given me, and today it was the only thing I needed.

⌒

Breakfast was a blur. Dell and I passed each other going through the swinging doors, her emerging with platters of eggs, me punching in with dirty dishes piled in two arms, both of us at various times tapping our fingers while waiting for the coffee to finish brewing. It wasn't until the late-morning lull that Will snuck in through the kitchen while my back was to him. I was grating lime rinds while Dell was prepping crust for one of her famous pies. When I turned around, my heart took a second to catch up to what I saw: Will's handsome face now drawn, his dark eyes bloodshot, his lids heavy with grief.

"Hey," he said, eyeing both of us as he deposited a crate of oranges on the metal prep table.

Dell ignored him, knowing that greeting was for me.

"Hey," I said, mimicking his deadpan delivery.

"You got home okay?" he asked, his voice hoarse.

"I did," I replied curtly, not turning fully around to face him, refraining from telling him that Jesse drove me home, *but nothing happened.*

"Good. Good," he said. "I'm sorry I stormed out of there. But I figured you were in good hands."

There it was, a dig about Jesse.

"Will, I—"

Dell wasn't interested in overhearing any more of what wasn't really being said.

"If you kids need me, I'll be at my job, working," she said, heading through the swinging doors back into the Café.

Will turned to finish unloading the fruit and vegetables. I went to follow him out back, to help, like I always did.

"No!" he said, turning around. I took a step back. "I mean, I can unload myself. Just take care of the customers."

Claire, Will's niece, who must have accompanied him to work that morning, came bounding into the kitchen, her blond dreads piled on her head in a tight nest. I'd begged her to contain her hair, as too many customers were finding her strands in their omelettes. Finally she relented when her uncle jokingly threatened to send her back to live with her folks in Slidell, something I knew he'd never really do. He was thrilled to have her live with him while she went to art school. And I was becoming as smitten with her as he was.

"Hey, lovebirds, get a room," she singsonged, shrugging off her jacket.

It was a phrase she'd been overusing over these past few weeks, because we could barely keep our hands off each other. She plucked a fat strawberry from a pile in the strainer and shoved it in her mouth. Our flat expressions, our dense silence must have given off a palpable tension. She glanced at me, then Will.

"O-*kay* then. I'll just . . . go find Dell," she said, slinking out to the dining room, rightly afraid of the storm brewing over our heads.

I looked into Will's haunted eyes.

"Is this how it's going to be?" I whispered. "Everyone tippy-toeing around us. Because if so, I'm happy to hand in my resignation. Today. Now."

I was astonished at my own resolve. But I meant it. And he knew it. He raked his fingers through his sleep-flattened hair. Was he grayer than yesterday?

"Please don't do that," he muttered. "I'm sorry."

"For what, Will? For *everything*?"

"No. Not for everything, but definitely for the way I behaved last night. I know I left you feeling bad about yourself. I'm so sorry. That wasn't my intention."

I took a step toward him as though it were the most natural thing in the world to throw my arms around him, to accept his apology. He put up his hand as a barrier, keeping his voice even, calm, as though talking to a scared animal.

"Wait. No. The thing is, Cassie . . . I've been thinking . . . I've been up all night thinking . . . and I realize that I probably rushed into things with you. Clearly you still have some loose strings to tie up, maybe with that guy, maybe with that . . . *group* you're in."

"There are no loose strings, Will. There is no guy. Jesse is a friend. And there is no group. I left that . . . group once I realized you and I were . . . that we could—"

"That we could what? Finally be together? Right. As if you were pining away for me."

Indignation flooded in. "Is that what you wanted me to be doing?"

"No, I mean . . . I *meant* . . . that's what *I* was doing."

"Ha. Wait. You're telling me you were *pining away* for me while living with and sleeping with a beautiful young woman who was about to have what you thought was *your* baby. Meanwhile, I was supposed to stay celibate, not date, not have sex with anyone else, but instead sit around waiting for your relationship to die so that I could finally have you?"

"Fuck," he muttered, rubbing his face furiously, trying to dig out a better answer. "I'm an asshole."

"No argument from me on that," I said. "Because yeah, you're right, Will, I *wasn't* waiting around. And frankly, now that it's looking like it's over *again* between us, I'm *still* not waiting around."

We were a foot apart now, both incredulous at the things that were coming out of each other's mouths. We seemed to be marinating in speechlessness and shock.

"Seriously. Tell me now, Will. Should I hand in my resignation?"

He straightened up, and when he spoke his voice was gentle, insistent.

"Cassie, as I tried to say last night, but couldn't, you are one of the best employees I've ever had. I don't want that to change. I want you to continue working here and training your replacements at the Café so you can manage the restaurant upstairs. It *is* going to be named Cassie's, since that's the name I registered, that's the name on the liquor license, that's the name that's going to be on all the invoices and menus I've printed, and on a sign that's going to be delivered any minute now," he said, checking his watch. "I haven't changed my mind about that."

I'd been staring at his lips the whole time he spoke, wanting to kiss him, wanting to slap him for the words issuing from them, willing myself not to cry, not to stammer. I placed one hand over my stomach and with the other I braced myself on the counter.

"Will, tell me something."

"What?" His shoulders dropped. He knew what was coming.

"Did you ever love me?"

He looked down as though the answer were scribbled on a piece of paper balled up in one of his fists.

"I . . . did. And I still . . . think the world of you, Cassie. I do." He pinched the bridge of his nose with two fingers before continuing.

"I still feel . . . very deeply for you, Cassie. But I can't be in love with you. I won't be. I won't let myself. Because I want—no, I *need*, I seriously *need* my life to be more uncomplicated from now on. I've got Claire to look after now, and she's going through some shit at school, and I've got a new business to run. Tracina and the baby are behind me now. And I just have to focus on having a quieter, simpler life. I need that. For my sanity."

The silence that followed said everything.

It was over between us. Completely.

"I see."

"But we *can* work together, Cassie. We're not children. And good jobs aren't easy to come by. Don't punish yourself out of pride. Stay. I need you."

What do you say to that? What do you do? Do you beat on the person's chest, demanding that the heart let you in because the heart knows better than the brain? Or do you just nod and say, *Okay. Fine. I will stay. For now.*

That's what I said, while a rivulet of liquid mercury entered my veins, solidifying and steeling me against any further rejection, or from ever opening my heart again. It happened so automatically it would have been almost awe-inspiring if it didn't signal doom. This man had doomed me for love. I had shown him some of my true self, the parts I felt safe showing. But when my deeper secrets were revealed, he rejected me. And it wasn't just rejection, it was denial, of everything I was and of everything I had been through.

"So that's it then?" I asked.

"I think so," he said. "We were friends for a long time. I hope we can be friends again. I can be yours, I think, with time."

He held out his hand. He wanted me to *shake* his hand? I looked at it like it was on fire. *Don't cry right now. Cry later.*

⁓

And that's what I did. I worked like a dog for the rest of my shift, training both Claire and our new hire, Maureen, a bartender we stole from the Spotted Cat across the street and who'd eventually replace me downstairs. I hoped, despite their style clash (Claire was a hippie, Maureen a punk) and slight age difference (Claire was almost eighteen, Maureen, twenty-three) that they'd eventually get along.

I cashed out and left just as a truck pulled up in front of the store and parked. A huge canvas-covered sign jutted out of the cab, casting a shadow over the car behind it. I could make out the top of the big red *C* of *Cassie's*, and that's when it became all too much. I fled down Frenchmen, past the bike shop, past the Praline Connection and Maison, cutting a hard left at Chartres to the Spinster Hotel, marveling at how much life can change in twenty-four hours. Yesterday at this time, Will and I were heading to Latrobe's dressed to the nines and looking forward to a future together. Today, I was in sneakers and a stained T-shirt, unlocking my door and running up the stairs leading to my third-floor apartment, barely holding back my tears.

Inside my little apartment, I stripped on the way to the bathroom, turned on the shower, stepped in and let the hot water hit my skin. I stayed like that for a long time, forehead against the tiles, not able to feel my tears. I must have scalded my skin a little because when I finally got out, it hurt to dry off. As I was throwing my hair in a towel, my phone rang in the next room.

Maybe it was Will and this was all a big misunderstanding and he was on his way over because while unloading the Cassie's sign, all he could think about was how much he loved me. Or it was Jesse checking up on me while a beautiful girl lay napping next to him. When call display showed it was Matilda, I felt relief before I even heard the sound of her calm voice.

"Cassie, you've been on my mind all day. How are you doing?"

I told her everything, recounting what Will had said last night, today and what he had decided going forward. Matilda sighed deeply. There was a longer than usual pause before she began to speak.

"This is not an indictment of Will, Cassie, but some men still don't believe that a woman's sexual appetite can be as important to satisfy as theirs. Or they don't believe a woman's sex life can or should be as varied, complex and interesting. Which baffles me, because, I mean, who are these men having sex with?"

I wasn't in the mood for sexual politics or a long discussion about Will's chauvinism or the dreaded double standard.

"I get all that, Matilda. But the thing is, my heart's just busted," I said, letting more tears flow. "I love him. And he doesn't love me anymore."

She let me blubber for a few moments.

"I wouldn't be too sure of that."

"Then what do I do?"

"Nothing. And I sure hope you didn't apologize, because you've done nothing wrong. Your sexual history is your business. Your stint in S.E.C.R.E.T. would have benefited him. It's his loss, Cassie."

"So I do nothing?"

"Well, do what I always suggest you do when you're in pain. Get on with living your life as best you can. And remember he's just a man, a human being. Don't let this stall your great progress. Get on with things. See what happens. Live your life."

"I don't know what to do with myself right now."

"The Committee could use your help."

I had quit S.E.C.R.E.T. a month ago when I chose to pursue a relationship with Will. And though I had been happy to leave, a part of me missed the camaraderie, the sheer fun I had with those women, let alone the men. But another part of me was mad at S.E.C.R.E.T.; I hadn't yet reconciled my past in the organization with my present dilemma.

I stalled. "There's a new candidate?"

"Not yet," she said, "but I met someone intriguing at the charity event last night."

"Who?"

"I haven't approached her yet. But Jesse's rejoined, so I'm sure that—"

"Jesse's back in S.E.C.R.E.T.?" Why did this slightly sicken me?

"Yes, he is."

"When did that happen? I thought he quit too."

"He did. But then he was also feeling at loose ends after you two ended it, and he decided to come back to a place that gave him comfort and distraction and a little joy. S.E.C.R.E.T. helped *you* get over lost love, didn't it?"

"It did."

"And it can help you again, if you let it. Besides, this is our last go-around. I'm afraid we've run out of money, and after our next candidate S.E.C.R.E.T. must shut its doors."

I glanced around my tiny attic apartment in the Spinster Hotel and at Dixie now lazily pawing dust motes in the sun.

"I don't have much to give," I said.

"Think about it," Matilda advised. "Meanwhile, don't quit a good job over a bad relationship. Never give any man that much power. There are opportunities buried in all this heartbreak. You just have to look for them."

SOLANGE

had spent that lazy Sunday morning with the papers, sipping coffee in bed while Gus lay splayed at my feet, playing video games, something I never let him do on my TV. I even joined him for a round of Wii Tennis.

"You're holding the thing wrong," he said, adjusting my paddle. "But that's okay. Everybody does it different."

What can I say? We lost track of time, something I don't normally do, so when noon rolled around I found myself tearing through my closet, plucking shoes and blouses and throwing them on my bed in a big colorful pile. I was late! *Again!*

The news network had scheduled our billboard photos that afternoon, citing that appointment as the only one the fancy new photographer had available. I was bitter about having to work on a Sunday, even though posing for pictures was hardly the most difficult part of my job. Luckily the shoot was in the Warehouse District where Julius lived, so I planned to drop off Gus on the way. Julius offered to keep him overnight and take him to school the next day, something I usually balked at. But this time I let him do a little extra. Why not? I told myself. He wants to. Let him.

In the weeks that followed that sexy afternoon with the handyman, I'd slacked off more than I had my whole life. Now and again I'd get lost in a daydream, but the kind that happened to my whole body, not just in my head. I also caught myself strutting, walking the halls and edit suites at the TV station like there was a pulsing, sexy soundtrack playing in my head. My heels clacked, my hips swayed. I felt a new sense of rhythm taking root in my body, a feeling I remembered from my singing days in college.

I found myself in elevators, alone, holding on to the rail behind me, singing to myself, rocking slightly while I flashed back to the tub, the water, the steam, the sweaty wineglass, the suds dripping down Dominic's arms and thighs, *my* arms and thighs. Good lord. I'd had *good* sex, and I was to have more sex, any time now, an idea that filled me with tingly anticipation. Best part? I didn't have to work for it. I didn't have to primp and flirt; I didn't have to endure agonizing dates or jeopardize my public reputation; and I didn't have to court rejection. Most important, I didn't have to introduce anyone new to my son. This was just for me, the Formidable Solange Faraday—

"Mom! You're gonna be late." It was Gus puncturing another daydream.

"Almost ready, baby!" I said, taking a fistful of blouses out of my closet and throwing them on the bed.

The Warehouse District was one of my favorite neighborhoods in New Orleans. I'd always thought that after Gus went off to college (assuming he didn't go to Loyola or Tulane), I'd sell the house and move into some kind of cool loft, but Julius beat me to it. Four years ago, he renovated a twenty-five-hundred-square-foot space on the fourth floor of an old rope factory. At first I was worried that there was no yard or green space where Gus could play. Then I worried about big windows with old sashes, the kind that can come crashing down on a curious child's little body. But I got over my fears when I saw what Julius had built in that wide-open space: an indoor jungle gym with climbing ropes and mats. Plus the place was big enough that Gus could actually learn how to cycle upright on a bike, *indoors*. After conquering circles on the floor of his dad's loft, Gus felt confident enough to take to the bike paths in the park. I was grateful Julius had done the hard part of running behind the bike at a clip before launching him. My job was now to walk behind him clutching my sweater, yelling at him to be careful.

I surveyed the pile of clothes on my bed. Jewel tones and bright colors look best on camera, so my closet looked like a storage locker for UN flags. I had to come up with six looks for the staged and awkward group shot of the network's four anchors, Jeff, Tad, Bill Rink, the weather guy (and resident asshole), Marsha Lang, and me.

Marsha was the network's star, and also my mentor and friend. As the first female African-American news anchor in New Orleans, she had won a Peabody for her editorials on Anita Hill's testimony in the Clarence Thomas hearings. But she was well into her sixties now, and claimed to be hearing the clock tick on her career. But far from treating me like her competition, she took me under her wing and considered me her successor.

Every year I wore a black skirt and black heels, from which I had no less than eleven pairs to choose, all varying heights and toe curves, some rounded, some pointed, each with a purpose. The four-inch stilettos were for when I anchored at the glass-bottomed weekend desk, the three-inch platforms for my stand-ups in front of official buildings, and the two-inch heels with the rounded toes for running after indicted members of city council or the Louisiana state legislature.

"Mom!" Gus said again.

"Listen, guy, I know!" I yelled back. "Why don't you come help me pick out my clothes for work pictures?"

Why was he so worried about my being late? He was an anxious kid. Was it because of the divorce? Julius said he had been like that as a kid, which I found a little comforting. But one of Gus's teachers once said he was a "too-serious little boy," to which I replied, "What does that even mean? Maybe that's just his character."

But that fear of being a "bad mother" was always there, hovering in the wings of motherhood, a show everyone watched and felt entitled to comment on.

Gus poked his head into my room. "You said noon and it's, like, quarter to."

The last time Julius took him for a haircut, the barber had cut it too short. It was just starting to grow out and was still unsure of what it wanted to be. An afro? Something more stylized, as his crowd became more sophisticated, more attuned to pop culture and all its awful, wonderful influences? I'd leave that to Julius to sort out.

"What do you think?" I asked, holding up the red blouse with the bow next to the low-cut gold one.

"Um, the red, I think."

"But I wore red last year."

"Then the gold," he said, his words edged with his dad's impatience.

"I'll bring all of them," I said, throwing a dozen tops into a zippered wardrobe bag, followed by a few pairs of black shoes.

"I'll carry it down," he said.

"It's heavy."

"It's fine," he said, hefting it over his shoulder.

Damn, the back of my ten-year-old boy's neck could still make my heart hurt, it was so vulnerable, so thin and bony. I imagined it coiled with muscle, strong enough to hold not just a wardrobe bag, but a head full of the thoughts and worries typical of the average young black man in this city. But those worries were nothing compared to his parents', I thought. Nothing.

When I pulled up in front of Julius's loft, Gus sprang out of my car, yelling over his shoulder, "Bye, Mom." Used to be I covered his somber face in a thousand kisses before letting him go. But he was beginning to push back, and I had to let him. He wasn't a tickle-monster anymore, and I couldn't remember the last time he absently grabbed my hand in the street. Contemplating my boy growing up could put me in a day-long funk, so I shook it off and sped away.

The photographer's loft was only two blocks away, but you could tell from its tinted windows and Art Deco–styled double doors that this building was a next-level posh conversion. This was the first time the network had veered from using its regular commercial photographer. They'd hired a guy named Erik Bando, an award-winning portrait photographer who also worked for *National Geographic*. Marsha and I had Googled his photos a week before the shoot and we were both impressed. She thought it was a sign that the affiliate was upping its game; we were currently third in the local ratings.

"Not sure how edgy photos will fix our ratings," I said.

"Ours is not to question why," she replied. "Ours is only to pose and smile."

A cool, blond assistant with big, red glasses greeted me in the lobby of the photographer's building and took my wardrobe bag from my hands.

"I'm sorry I'm late," I said.

"Oh, don't worry, you have all day," she said, punching the elevator button.

I looked at her. "Really? I thought I was scheduled for three hours."

"Well, I mean, you can . . . take your time."

Okay then. On the ride up, she was quiet, staring straight ahead.

At the top, the doors slid open to a spectacular studio, twice the size of Julius's. This was at least five thousand square feet of exposed brick and wide plank floors. Most of the walls were painted white, with small partitions carving out thematic spaces like a maze, some areas with wide, low-slung couches, some with large colorful backdrops suspended from the ceiling and unspooling to the floor. I could hear a buzz of activity in the brightly lit corner where a green-screen backdrop lay near the wall-to-wall windows. Along the outside walls were photos of bleakly beautiful landscapes, and of the awful things war does to places and people, shot after riveting shot, and a few stunning nature panoramas that no doubt required death-defying feats to capture.

The same blond now directed my attention away from the pictures to an empty director's chair next to where another makeup artist seemed to be fussing with Marsha's foundation. I took the vacant seat.

"Afternoon, my dear," Marsha said without looking up from her smart phone. "Have you heard? Apparently Madonna has been outfitted with a set of '*grillz.*' Also she is learning how to '*booty pop*,' whatever the hell that is."

Marsha proffered a screenshot of the pop star's gold mouth accessory.

"I see. Well . . . now that it's big with middle-aged white women, at least Gus isn't going to want one."

She smiled, placing her glasses on her face.

"Well, I'm off," she said, pushing up from her chair. "See you tomorrow."

"Wait! I thought . . . aren't we getting our pictures done together? Where's Jeff and Tad? Where the hell's Rink?"

"Came and went. The beauty of Photoshop. We don't have to pose together to look like one big happy news family."

"Aren't we?"

"Sure," she said with a wink.

"Have you seen Erik's work on that back wall?" I said. "Take a look on the way out. Astounding images."

"I know. But have you see *Erik*?" Marsha muttered, nodding towards where a powerfully built man, easily six foot four inches tall, stood talking to his blond assistant.

"Um. *That* didn't come up in our Google searches," I whispered, noting his wavy brown hair, almost the same color as his skin. From across the room, you could also see his rock-climber forearms flinching as he carefully polished a large, round lens.

"Born in Kenya. Dad was a half-Japanese, half-Swiss diplomat; mom was some kind of African princess. Big scandal. Grew up in Paris," Marsha whispered, peering at him over the top of her glasses. "Never married. Placed fifth in the '98 Olympics. *Biathlon.* That is the sport where you ski, my dear, with a fucking gun. He represented Switzerland."

"How did you find all that out?"

"He spent the better part of last winter documenting border skirmishes in Northern Afghanistan. Those pictures on the wall? They were nominated for a Pulitzer. He speaks Farsi. Oh, and he's a Leo."

"Bet he *never* guessed you're a journalist."

"God, if I were twenty years younger. Hell, *ten*."

"Marsha! Are you objectifying this man?"

"I am."

"But that's against everything you stand for."

"Yes. *Right up against* everything I stand for," she said, softly cackling. Then she turned to me. "Do you know what happens, Solange, to your sense of propriety after you turn sixty?"

"No, I don't."

"Neither do I, and I do not care to know. Well, good night then. And try the canapés. They're delicious."

The blond assistant slid a glass of champagne into my hand. "Here you go. To relax you."

"No thanks," I said, carefully placing the glass back on the makeup table. "I'm already relaxed."

Marsha looked at the champagne and then at me. "Oh, I could weep," she said before kissing me on the cheek good-bye. She turned on her heel and made her exit.

"Let me introduce you to Erik," said the blond assistant, leading me by the elbow across the room, the remaining assistants giving the impression of seas parting as I entered Erik's orbit.

"Erik, this is Solange Faraday. The weekend anchor."

He was directing a gaffer high up on a ladder, the muscles in his arms tensing, his voice commanding and deep.

"To the left and down. I want the spotlight right . . . there . . . where the screen creases on the floor."

"If this isn't a good time—" I said to him.

"Nonsense," he said, turning to face me, looking me up and down. "It's an honor to meet you."

Good lord, my breath actually caught in my lungs. Up close he was like an African/Asian/Nordic god, and though I hated the term *exotic*, I couldn't think of another way to describe his almond-shaped, gray-flecked eyes, his thick wavy brown hair, his crooked, bratty smile, his brown skin, which looked partly genetic and partly the result of some death-defying adventure that took him way too close to the sun. He was closer to my age than I'd thought at first, something I found a huge relief, though I don't know why it mattered. When did I start doing that? Comparing men's ages with mine? After I turned forty? After I stopped feeling noticed by anyone under forty?

"Hello. Um, so . . . where can I change?" I asked, turning into a schoolgirl. Next to this man, I felt almost petite, delicate even. *Pull yourself together, Solange! You've done important, dangerous reportage too.*

"Use my bedroom." He pointed to a door flush with a large white wall.

"You live here?" I asked, surprised.

"I sleep here," he corrected. He was smiling again,

showing one chipped front tooth, the kind of offhand flaw I'd always found terribly sexy. I felt my face heat up.

His bedroom was large and airy, with floor-to-ceiling steel factory windows, glossy white trim. The walls were white too, and the dresser white-stained oak in a matte finish. The king-size mattress was on an oak platform and covered in a white duvet and pillows. It was the kind of room where a lot of sex would take place, a room where children definitely were not allowed.

My garment bag was hanging on a bare rack in the middle of the room. I decided to throw on my gold blouse, not one I usually wore to work because it plunged a bit, but I was feeling, I don't know, like being noticed. Like being looked at, by him.

When I entered the work area again it was quiet, no gaffer, no camera assistants, just the blond assistant neatly laying out makeup brushes in front of a lit-up mirror.

I took a seat and crossed my legs.

"We'll just focus on the eyes, I think," she said, looking at me through the mirror. "Make them pop. You don't need much. You glow on your own."

She was talking about me, not to me, and yet I still blushed.

"Is this blouse okay?" I asked the assistant, suddenly feeling flustered and self-conscious, like the blouse was too low, or maybe not low enough.

"It's lovely," she said, picking through the brushes. She didn't seem to have a great handle on the tools of her trade, let alone the colors. I soon began to look a little garish. When she pumped the mascara tube ominously, I had to stop her.

"Look. I know photos require a bit more makeup than usual, but I am not sure this lipstick suits me."

Her face fell. She was clearly nervous. "Normally I do my own eyes at the network," I said. "Do you mind?"

"Yes! I mean no, by all means, I don't mind. We just want you to feel totally comfortable and sexy." She exhaled, utterly relieved.

"I just . . . want to look like myself."

"Right, totally," she said, backing away as I wiped off some of her enthusiastic work, reapplying it with my lighter touch.

Why would someone with Erik's profile hire such an incompetent makeup artist? What was also weird was how quiet everything had suddenly become. I hopped off the director's chair and poked around the partitions looking for Erik, for anybody. I found him measuring the light in front of a large green screen, onto which the newsroom and a cityscape were projected.

"There you are," he said. "Shall we begin?"

Erik expertly positioned me where I'd appear on the billboard, my elbow resting on a block, an appropriate stand-in for Bill Rink. Erik wasn't shy, placing his hands on my shoulders, moving me this way and that. And I was . . . *enjoying it*. I found it almost . . . relaxing.

"That's good. Commanding. Yes, perfect," he muttered into the viewfinder, clicking away. "Now arms crossed, that's right. Shoulder to me. Nice. That's it. Nice. Very nice. Smart. Good."

I was posing for the camera as I had done a million times before, but I was also posing, a little bit, for Erik. He was pulling a certain kind of sexiness and daring from me.

"Lovely, Solange. Let's try another look."

"Yes. Let's."

I skipped (*skipped!*) back to the bedroom and threw on my red shimmering blouse, returning to position myself in front of the green screen. This all felt so girly, heady, model-y. I was having *fun*.

I hopped back onto the stool while Erik concentrated on placing a light just so. He stepped in front of me, awfully close, to move a lock of my hair . . . just . . . so. When he was taking pictures, looking at me through a viewfinder, I felt fine. But now, standing there looking down at me the way a man looks at a woman, his hip cocked, one hand holding his massive camera like it weighed nothing, his other hand scratching the back of his head, I became wobbly on the stool.

"You're a natural in front of the camera. I mean, that's evident from your work. But you're also incredibly easy to photograph. Lovely at every angle."

Click, click, click.

"Oh. Thanks. I guess," I said. Was he stepping over a line? It felt like it and yet I couldn't help but feel flattered.

"I didn't mean to offend you."

"Offend me? No, I'm not offended," I said. "I think . . . sometimes I wrestle with compliments like that."

"Why?"

Click, click, click. He moved back and forth in front of me with the camera, crossing my sight line like a pendulum.

"I don't know. I guess I just want to be taken seriously."

He snapped more pictures, this time stepping closer. "You don't think a woman can be sexy *and* taken seriously?"

"Of course," I said. But did I believe that?

He was smiling into the viewfinder.

"It's easier doing this without my work colleagues around," I admitted.

"People on their own are far less inhibited. They're more themselves. That's why I prefer to do group shots this way. Photoshop everyone together later. Okay, I want to get a few more before we lose the sun," he said, peering over his camera, a lock of wavy hair rakishly falling over one of those gray eyes.

I noticed long shadows tracing along the wood planks. The day was drifting by. I also realized the blond assistant wasn't around anymore and low jazz music was wafting from hidden speakers. *Are we alone?* I put my hand on my stomach, feeling a little dizzy, hungry maybe. Where was that canapé table? Didn't Marsha mention food?

"Solange, I'd like to see you in something other than your work wear."

What?

"Oh. Well, I didn't bring anything else but—"

"Something that shows off your true self. Away from work."

He regarded me intently, like this was a dare.

"Like I said, I didn't bring casual clothes. Why would I?"

This was becoming strange.

"I have some things you can try on. They're hanging in my room. See if anything strikes you."

What the hell? He seemed so nonchalant, adding, "*If* you'll accept the Step, that is."

He snapped a picture of my face just then, no doubt revealing the shock registered there. The room was completely silent except for the creaks and knocks from the surrounding lofts. Oh, and my heart rattling around inside my chest.

"Are you one of the men from . . . ?"

He nodded, his face serene. He regarded me thoughtfully, his camera down, resting against his thigh.

"Don't you normally sleep with supermodels?"

"I can assure you, I never kiss and tell. So?"

"So."

"So . . . do you accept the Step, Solange?"

When he smiled, his skin crinkled around his mouth and eyes. I slid off the stool. My legs were liquid.

"Which Step is it again?"

"*Courage*," he said, his free hand now traveling under his T-shirt to his stomach. Maybe he was nervous too?

"I could certainly use more of that right about now."

"This is one way to get it."

"Okay then. Why don't I go and slipintosomething-morecomfortable?" I said it really, really fast as I made my way to his bedroom.

I shut the door behind me and took a deep breath. This was all moving fast. The first fantasy was on home turf, and that was nice. This was really close to work and it made me a bit nervous. My eyes scanned the room. Something was different. The rack that had held my work blouses was gone, replaced by a row of fancy, flimsy, sheer *things*, festooned with feathers, lots of lace, a bow or two. Closer examination revealed mostly black and nude bras and panties, with splashes of red and white here and there. It was all lingerie—elegant stuff, expensive stuff, teddies, sheer wraps, a long see-through black gown and beneath, on the white-painted floor, a pair of gorgeous black feathered mules. A thick, white terry-cloth robe lay across his bed. On the dresser was another blessed glass of chilled champagne, which I downed (impressive, for me) in almost one gulp.

What was I about to do? I was about to have sex with a sexy-as-hell war photographer, but not before he took some sexy shots. Of me. Wearing this sexy stuff!

I pulled out the sheer gown, held it up to the window. *Holy shit*, I'd never buy something like this for myself. *When would I wear it?* I thought back to Julius when we were married. If I'd shown up in our bedroom wearing this, he'd have *laughed.* Not in a mean way, but in a way that said, *Baby, you don't have to put on a show to get to me.* I imagined my hurt. Why would he laugh at a time like that, when all I was trying to do was be sexy for him, like that expensive marriage counselor had suggested way back?

And just like that, I was having an imaginary fight in my head with my ex-husband, feeling all that old familiar rage, the kind that would have sent me storming back into the bathroom, slamming the door on him, yelling, "Forget it!" to which Julius would have replied, "Solange! Come ooooon. I was just *kidding!* You looked beautiful!"

Screw you, Julius.

I snapped out of my fight. *Dammit, this is not for Julius, and truth be told, not even for Erik. This is for me!*

I tore off my work clothes, selecting the full-length, black sheer negligee, carefully slipping it over my head, surprised at its sturdiness. The gauze tumbled over my legs, the empire waist cinching tightly under my breasts. I could barely look at myself in the mirror, but I forced an appraisal.

Wow. Okay.

I not only looked sexy, I felt it.

I can do this!

A step closer changed my mind. I could see my nipples press through the material! I covered myself instinctively.

Actually I can't do this. I can't just step out there like this.

I gazed over at the rack, at all the other lovely, sexy things. I thought of Erik, his arms, my fingers running through his hair. I looked at myself again in the mirror. All those years of being single, and a mother, and a *working* mother, and a *hard*-working mother, meant I had lost the ability to just *play*.

There was a gentle knock on the door.

"Solange? Are you okay in there?"

The champagne was warming my skin.

"I'll be right out."

I slid my feet into the heeled slippers, counted to five. *Look at you in that black negligee. Are you seriously going to go through with this?* At the last minute, I reached for the bathrobe and threw it on, covering myself up.

Baby steps.

Go! Just go. Carefully in those heels, I walked to the door and opened it. I could see the light from the setting sun coming through the windows.

"I'm over here, Solange."

I followed the sound of his voice, the heels making a hollow clacking sound on the wood floors. I peeked around behind the partition and found Erik bent over the top of an elaborate-looking camera mounted on a tripod, different from the small one he had used for the earlier shots. The backdrop was different too, this one dark blue, with large colorful pillows and throws strewn about a sectional that barely rose above the floor.

"Hi," he said, looking up, his face soft.

"Hi," I said, barely cracking a smile.

"Make yourself comfortable."

Clutching the robe, I walked over to the pillows and cleared a space on the sectional, lowering myself like a big chicken settling into a nest. Definitely not sexy.

I was still in my bathrobe when Erik began to take pictures.

He looked over the top of the camera again. "What's on your mind?"

"Nothing," I said, looking around at the dark shadows, feeling horribly self-conscious. The sky was the blue of deep dusk.

"This is only my second fantasy."

"And what about this scenario had you fantasized about?"

I cast back to the day I had filled out my folder on my kitchen table. What had I written about *Courage*? It wasn't specifically about having sex with a handsome photographer, but I had written something about "watching myself, seeing myself" as a desirable woman.

"It was about being . . . watched, seen, feeling beautiful," I said.

"Why's that hard for you?"

"I don't know . . . in my business it can distract as much as it attracts. The more beautiful you are, the less, it seems, you're taken seriously."

"I'm certainly taking you very seriously right now," he said, peering over the camera intently at me. *Click, click.*

"Can I ask you something? Why are *you* doing this?"

"Why would you ask that?" he asked back, half laughing.

"It's not like you'd have any problem meeting girls." *There I go. The journalist in me is about to kill the chemistry.*

"No problem meeting girls. They're everywhere." *Click.* "On the other hand, I don't really meet a lot of *women*," he said, adding, "How about this. Instead of telling you why I'm doing this, let me show you."

My head swam with that proposition.

"Starting with that bathrobe. Let's lose it, Solange. And then I want you to just ignore me. And relax back onto the couch."

Maybe it was how commanding he was, or maybe because the light was dimming and flattering and the puffy sectional so comfortable, but I found myself tugging free of the terry-cloth robe and tossing it to the side. I rested on my side, on an elbow, in that black negligee, my hand on my still-churning stomach.

At first, I didn't know where to look, how to be. And then . . . I began to relax. I closed my eyes and lay back against the pillows. After I'd stretched and lounged for a few minutes, he stopped and flopped next to me on the sectional holding the camera. He smelled delicious, a deep citrusy musk. His warm arm brushed against mine as he positioned his viewfinder in front of me, cueing up images.

"I want you to see yourself."

And there I was, or someone resembling me, now bathed in a gorgeous light; my skin seemed to glow, velvety shadows hugging my curves. Then I saw my dark nipples pressed against the sheer fabric. I covered the viewfinder with my hand, my pulse racing.

"Wow," I said. "You realize because of my job, you'll have to destroy these."

He smiled.

"I wanted you to see what I see when I look at you. Let's do some more," he said, springing off the seat next to me.

There was that familiar tug, that ache behind my belly

button. I was becoming aroused. Having the courage to reveal this side of me to someone was turning me on.

"Feeling a bit bolder?"

I nodded.

"Do you want to try something else on? Or take something else off?"

What a choice!

"I'll . . . check out that rack again," I said, unsure if I wanted to delay, or draw this out. What did it matter? I was getting into this.

I practically trotted to the bedroom and flicked through the rack feeling a little more daring. I pulled out a pale pink bra laced with gray ribbons and matching bottoms. The bra gave me the kind of cleavage I normally never flaunted. I threw on a matching gray gauzy wrap over the ensemble, deciding to go barefoot with this outfit. That's why he didn't hear me approach the partition, behind which he was now tinkering with filters, adding some kind of scrim over the lightbox.

He looked up. I let my hands drop to my sides, allowing the wrap to gape open so he could take me in.

Courage.

"Beautiful," he whispered, nodding to indicate that I should take my position on the sectional again.

His eyes never left me as I folded down into the pillows. When he approached the sectional, I rolled onto my back, locking my gaze on his. He stood over me, his camera clicking away.

"Open the robe," he said, his voice guttural, urgent. "Good. Now move your hands down your body."

My eyes closed, I let my hands drift over my breasts and down my sides.

"Like that . . . yes."

My hands moved across my stomach then stopped at my panties. I opened my eyes and met his gaze again. He was kneeling before me. Reaching out with his free hand, he clasped my fingers and pressed them under my elastic band, urging me to touch myself. I slid my fingers down, astonished at how wet I was.

"Tell me what you feel like," he said, now nearly straddling me, snapping pictures.

I stretched back, embarrassed, pressing my face into a pillow next to me, and all the while my fingers were moving around under my silk panties.

"I'm . . . wet," I mumbled, finally. "Very."

"Yeah? Show me," he said, his eyes on my hand.

I hesitated.

"Those pictures. You can't ever . . ." I warned.

"They're yours. Don't worry. When we're done, you get every frame. I promise. Remember, *courage*, my love."

I eased my panties off, pushing them down my thighs, kicking them to the floor. My knees together, I placed my hands inside my thighs and turned my head away again. I just . . . couldn't believe I was *doing* this! Marsha would be shocked! Let alone Julius!

Erik positioned himself at the foot of the sectional. As

I spread my legs, he began to click his camera, transfixed. My hands drifted back up. I shrugged off the gray wrap. Then I arched and undid the bra, tossing it over my shoulder. My hands replaced my bra and I found myself squeezing my breasts and writhing, his reaction to this surprisingly turning me on.

"That's it, Solange. That's it," he murmured, inching closer.

I sat up feeling emboldened.

"What about you, Erik?"

He stopped and placed the camera back on the tripod next to us, adjusting the lens to face us, clicking on a button.

"We're rolling video on this, okay?"

I took a deep breath. Could I do this? Yes. I could. I nodded and he drew his hands away from the camera. He pulled his T-shirt over his head, showing off a smooth, rippled torso.

"Take everything off," I said, in *my* voice, with words coming from *my* mouth. Courage indeed.

He gave me a wry smile as he undid his jeans, stopping momentarily to fish a condom out of the front pocket, tossing it next to me. For such a large man, his body was lean, compact, smooth. He had a smattering of scars, a dramatic one on a pectoral, just below his rib cage. He noticed me noticing it.

"I was a fencer," he said.

I raised an eyebrow.

"A shitty one," he added.

I laughed. Naked, he began a slow crawl up my body. Now he was on all fours above me, his hair falling forward, and I pressed my whole self deep into the cushion below, shrinking, my nerves now on fire. *Could I go through with this?*

"Touch my scar," he whispered, taking my hand and bringing it to his warm stomach, now rising and falling with his own quickening breath.

My fingers traced his soft line of hair, following the scar's jagged ridge of flesh, then trailing it down to his erection, stiff and insistent.

"Oh yeah," he murmured, closing his eyes.

I gathered him in my hands. The way he winced, his lip curling back, that's what got me going. He stood up and tugged my ankles down, parting my legs around his knees. His kissed me, his body undulating over mine, both my hands now cupping his erection, caressing more urgently. He took my breasts into his hot, wet mouth and devoured them; this man was hungry for me. Looking down at my body through his disheveled hair, I knew where he was heading and what he wanted to do to me.

He took me by the waist with both hands. He made the moment linger, before sliding them under my ass cheeks, lifting them lightly, reverently, his fingers going from soft to firm as he spread me open to begin his feast. His tongue found my groove, gathering my lips in his, slicking me down. It was shocking and incredible. What is it about a stranger that lets you abandon all your rules and regulations? Or maybe it was *this* particular stranger, all appetite and want.

I moaned, my face pressed sideways into the pillows. The heat radiated through my body, made my skin prickly with desire. I peeked over my breasts as he stopped and felt around with one hand for the condom packet, the other hand still beneath me, then brought it to his mouth. He ripped it open and slid it on. I squeezed my eyes shut and could feel the head of his erect cock prodding into me, inching in, all the way in, his hands now gripping my hips hard as he began his slow, gorgeous assault on me. I saw nothing else against the black backdrop of my eyelids, but I felt everything . . . So *this is what it's like to be fucked hard and well by a beautiful man . . .*

⁓

And this is what it looks like . . .

Later, in the safe confines of my bedroom, popcorn resting in a bowl next to me, the volume on my laptop low, I skipped fast through the stills Erik had taken of me, past the ones of me posing in the lingerie—some that I liked, some that made me wince and slap the screen shut. Then I came upon the naked shots, the ones with my legs spread, my whole body willing, eyes hungry. *Oh my god, look at me!*

I screamed into my pillow from joyful mortification.

And then I queued up the video, fast-forwarding to the part where Erik opened my thighs wide, hovering over me for a second to take it all in, his back muscles flinching, the close-up as he dipped to lick and suck my clit, my fingers pushing through his hair, my eyes closed. *Holy Christ, the look on my face!* Pure sexual ecstasy. Here it was: the reason men like to watch.

I *did* look delicious, didn't I. His head between my thighs, and oh, when he turned me over onto my knees (a not unflattering angle, if I may say), how he fucked me furiously, and how I clenched and stiffened before I came. I was peering at all of this over the top of my sheets, my face lit by the blue screen, my eyes big like saucers.

I made a sex tape! A fucking sex tape! Then came the part where Erik pumped into me, harder and faster, mercilessly, the shaft of his thick penis inching in and out while his fingers dug shadows into my hips. I could tell exactly when I was coming on the video, and I was coming again, now, my own fingers retracing his path as I watched myself being watched by him, his eyes on my back, while he drove into me again and again, calling my name, "Solange,"and saying, "Yes, oh yeah, oh god, baby, I'm gonna come, I'm gonna come now" . . . and he did. And so did I—again—falling back into the pillows of my bed in my own home, my eyes rolling back again in utter bliss. I froze the shot on Erik collapsing across my back, his arms wrapped around my waist, because there it was, evidence of my courage to do something I had never thought I'd do.

And it was all kind of beautiful.

In the morning, before I headed to work, I watched that video one more time, while the dishwasher hummed and the coffee brewed. Then I smashed that lovely USB stick into a thousand pieces in the backyard, burying the shards under an old pine.

CASSIE

W hen Matilda finally called and explained the dilemma, I just couldn't say no.

"Cassie, I wouldn't ask if it wasn't an emergency," she said. "We need someone who wasn't at the induction."

She explained how Bernice was facilitating a very elaborate fantasy involving a photo shoot for S.E.C.R.E.T.'s new participant but she fell ill. They desperately needed a volunteer to be there, someone whom the new candidate didn't know and wouldn't recognize. And just like that, I was back in S.E.C.R.E.T., this time not as a guide but as a fantasy facilitator. I didn't have time to be a full-on Committee member, not yet. Maybe once the restaurant was up and running, and I had more time on my hands. It was the least I could do after all that S.E.C.R.E.T. had done for me.

My instructions for my first fantasy were to go to the Warehouse District that following Sunday. Matilda suggested

I wear a blond wig and heavy makeup just to make sure I wouldn't be recognized. The task: act as a photographer's assistant. I was excited, thrilled for the distraction, though I had to admit, when Matilda told me the new S.E.C.R.E.T. participant was *the* Solange Faraday from Action News Nightly, I was gob-smacked. She was someone you'd never think would need an organization like S.E.C.R.E.T., but I had to remind myself that she was a woman just like the rest of us—like me, like Dauphine, like Kit and Angela once, too, a woman who needed a little sexual boost.

This fantasy indeed had been an elaborate undertaking. First, S.E.C.R.E.T. had to convince the network to hire a new photographer named Erik Bando to shoot its billboards, without giving away the ruse. Angela recruited and trained him. Erik charged the network nothing, S.E.C.R.E.T. covered Erik's costs, and the network photos, in the end, were stunning. Plus, Matilda was right. Helping with Solange's fantasy was a total trip and it (mostly) took my mind off Will. There was just one problem. I had to do her makeup! What a mess I made of that! I was grateful Solange took charge and slapped my hands away.

In fact, she impressed the hell out of me. And playing the part of a bossy blond, becoming this other person, someone more daring, sexier and more confident than I really was, was not just thrilling; it inspired an idea, one I desperately needed to run by Will before the opening night of Cassie's.

We had decided to open on New Year's Eve. And the weeks leading up to the big night were a blur of menu planning, food testing, equipment buying, plus hiring and training new floor and kitchen staff. And somehow, through it all, Will and I were mostly able to avoid each other, communicating almost entirely by text. Many of the tasks we did separately: Will purchased the steamers and fryers, I interviewed chefs, hired the sous chef and the bartender. Will negotiated discount parking at the lot up the street; I made batches and batches of homemade praline ice cream, trying to perfect a unique house recipe, until Dell thankfully stepped in to help. All the while I worked a few shifts at the Café training Maureen, Claire filling in here and there.

I was so busy I forgot to make plans for Christmas. I would have been happy spending it with Dixie, batting her away from the recipes and supplier lists strewn about my kitchen table. But Matilda convinced me to spend it with her and Jesse, who was at his own loose ends because his son would be at his ex's.

It was a cozy affair, if a little awkward. We gathered in the eat-in kitchen at the Mansion. Matilda thought it would be fun to use the house for purposes other than sex. After all, it was a stunning location, and the kitchen featured top-of-the-line appliances. She answered the side door in jeans, slippers and a sweater, looking radiant and eerily young without any makeup, her red, shiny hair down around her shoulders. I was overdressed in my sparkly top and heels.

"Cassie, you look lovely," she said, taking my coat.

"Suddenly I feel like a walking Christmas tree."

"I should have told you pajamas would be appropriate."

I handed Matilda a bottle of mid-price champagne and marveled at the smells wafting out of the kitchen.

"Claudette made a beautiful turkey," Matilda said. Claudette was the live-in help at the Mansion. She was not only discreet but clearly a talented cook. As I followed Matilda to the kitchen, I took in the enormous appliances working overtime and the pine table already set with a basket of biscuits, a tureen of soup and a big bowl of salad.

"Last time I was in this room . . ." I said, not able to finish my sentence because just then Jesse walked out of the powder room, where my fourth fantasy had played out, the one with the famous hip hop star, the one that involved oral sex while a big pot of gumbo simmered on the stove.

Jesse wiped his wet hands on his sweatshirt. "Last time you were here, what?" he said, kissing the side of my head. "Nah, don't tell me. I prefer to imagine it. Hope you brought your appetite."

It had been more than two months since Latrobe's, and I hadn't seen much of Jesse. We'd texted now and again, and made vague plans to see a movie, but nothing solidi-fied. We were both ridiculously busy, but mostly I didn't want to know too much about his involvement in S.E.C.R.E.T. Problem was, though helping with Solange's fantasy had taken my mind off Will, it sent my thoughts right back to . . . sex.

Now, with Jesse on my right looking all kinds of hot in

his red plaid shirt, sleeves rolled up to reveal his tattoos, hair slicked back, face cleanly shaved, it was hard not to sneak glances at him. I squirmed in my seat, watching the muscles in his jaw clench as he chewed on a breadstick. God, he was sexy. I forgot how much I loved watching him eat. He worked with food, so he had a passion for it, and he was nothing if not a man of appetites.

After dinner, he reached over and poured more wine for Matilda, then for me, before refreshing his own glass.

"To Christmas misfits," Matilda said, raising a glass for toasts. "May we always find comfort in one another's company."

"And to ex-lovers. May they be ever in our hearts," Jesse said, "even if they're not in our beds."

I felt my face redden. "Jesse Turnbull, you are drunk," Matilda scolded. "That's not proper dinner talk. Apologize to Cassie immediately."

"To whom?" he said, a weary smile on his face. Without waiting for her reply, he turned to me and placed his hand over my forearm. "Cassie, forgive me, I am a little drunk and that was rude. I didn't mean to offend you."

"I will make us some coffee," Matilda said, rising from the table.

I turned to Jesse, who suddenly seemed agitated. "Are you okay?" I whispered. He couldn't possibly still be upset about our breakup, if you could even call it that—could he?

"I'm fine, but I think it's time for me to fly," he said. "Matilda, tell Claudette dinner was amazing."

I expected her to insist he stay, at the very least for a coffee. But without replying she buzzed for the limousine.

"I got my truck."

"And I have your keys," she said. "You'll get your truck tomorrow. Good night, Jesse."

Jesse rose, stretched, kissed both our hands good night and left without saying another word.

"Something's got him all knotted up," I said.

"Well, wine doesn't mix well with resentment," she said, placing the pot of coffee on the table.

"I didn't realize he was still so . . . vexed."

Matilda gave me a warm smile. "You know I don't like gossip, Cassie. And chatting about a newly departed guest is the worst kind."

I knew better. She was right. I changed the subject.

"Matilda, there's something I want to run by you. It's about Will. And the new restaurant."

I told her Will had insisted on calling the restaurant Cassie's. "So. I've made a decision. I want to invest in it. I want some skin in the game. I have that insurance money from Scott. It's tied up in other stuff, but it wouldn't be hard to extricate. You're a businesswoman. What do you think? Is it stupid?"

Matilda carefully weighed her response.

"I thought that was your retirement money, Cassie. That's all you have. It's difficult for restaurants to turn a profit, even at the best of times. There are less risky places to put your money."

"I know, but——"

"And what would happen if the place went under? How would you take care of yourself then?"

"It won't. If I invest, I'll bust my ass to make that place work."

She laughed. "I say this with great reluctance, but knowing you, you'll make it work. But please, do this for yourself, not for Will. He'd be a fool not to partner with you."

I threw my arms around her and thanked her. Now I just had to convince Will.

On Boxing Day, as Claire and I were polishing the new restaurant's silverware, my mind was occupied with practicing my pitch to Will. I was growing closer to Claire, who was in the middle of clarifying some romantic drama at her new school, the kind teenage girls of every generation seem to create.

"No. Olivia likes Ben, but she thinks *I* like him just because we had sex, like, once? Well, twice. But I don't like him. Well, I like him as a friend. And if he likes Olivia, why does he hang around me more? And why should I stop hanging around him just because he *might* like her? It's *so* stupid. And all the girls are mad at me. If they have to be mad at anyone, why aren't they mad at Ben for having sex with me if he likes Olivia?"

"It all sounds very confusing, sweetie" was my only answer. I still thought of her as a kid, with the kind of problems that just blow over. And, frankly, I was distracted.

I checked the clock. It was almost four. I had agreed to see Jesse that afternoon, after his sheepish morning apology for the drunken outburst at the Mansion the night before. I wondered if Matilda had put him up to it.

"Confusing? Know what's confusing? You and Uncle Will," she said, jumping up on the metal kitchen table, the one that never failed to remind me of my fantasy with Jesse. "So, like, why aren't you guys together anymore?"

Claire had received no effective answer from Will beyond "It's none of your business, kiddo," so I kept my answer equally vague.

"We decided we're better off just being friends." I wanted to add, *And hopefully, business partners*. He was supposed to close up that night, but there was still no sign of him.

"Yeah. Right. Whatever," Claire said, snapping her gum.

Just then Will walked into the kitchen, holding a box of plastic sleeves that would house our new menu cards. Though I still loved the sight of his face, I hated that even now he managed to take the air right out of my lungs.

"Sorry I'm late. Hot off the presses," he said, pulling out a menu sleeve and handing it to me. I plucked the sleeve from his hand. It was still warm.

"They're perfect," I said, aware that our fingers had touched as he passed me the card. While I had to make an effort not to register a reaction to this casual connection, Will seemed utterly nonplussed.

"So is the new dishwasher still leaving spots?" Will asked Claire, pulling away from me.

"Yup," Claire said.

"Damn. Between that and the new wiring, we'll be in the red before we even open."

This was it; this was my "in." *Now. Ask now.*

"Will, I want to run something by you before I go."

"And you," he said to Claire, ignoring me. "Did you find out who left that shitty Facebook comment?"

Claire's shoulders slumped.

"Ben told me it was Olivia," she said. "But I talked to her and she said she didn't."

Will's face reddened. He lifted a finger to her face. "I'm telling you, Claire, if anyone ever writes something like that again on your wall, I'm not going to be able to stay out of it, okay? I have to talk to their parents."

"Yeah, Uncle Will, because every teenager wants angry adults to handle their problems, 'cause that fixes everything." She rolled her eyes, jumped off the table and shuffled back into the dining room.

"What comment? What's going on?"

Will exhaled long and loud. "Apparently, someone— she won't tell me who—has been calling Claire names on her Facebook page. They're getting posted through her friends' accounts. Her friends say they've been hacked, or something. I don't know how all that shit works. All I know is it's upsetting her and it's affecting her at school. She stayed home two times last week."

"What are they calling her?"

"A slut, a whore, shit like that."

I felt guilty suddenly for not pressing her when she brought it up. "That's awful."

"I know. Girls can be so horrible to each other," he said, shaking his head in bafflement.

"Oh, well, you know. Men can suck too." *Zing.* It was out of my mouth before I could stop myself.

A flash of hurt crossed Will's face, but I changed the subject before that can of worms was reopened. This wasn't the time.

"So, Will. I'm glad you're here. Because . . . thing is . . . I want to discuss something with you. I have a proposition of sorts."

"O-*kay*," he said, crossing his arms, all business.

"Yeah. It's about the restaurant's name. I was wondering if—"

"We've been over this, Cassie. The name stays."

"I know, Will. I'm aware of that. And you're aware of my ambivalence about it."

"I am, but you'll get used to it."

"Maybe. But it's just that if it's going to be named after me, then I want to . . . have it mean something. I want to *invest* in it as well."

He blinked several times, his face placid. "I told you, your sweat equity is enough."

"It's not enough for me. I told you when Scott died he left me with some insurance money. And I've only drawn on a little of it. The rest—about sixty-five grand—I want to put into this place. I want to be your . . . partner. Business partner, I mean."

He took no time to think about it.

"No. No way. That's your retirement fund, Cassie. That's all you have."

"No. *This* is my retirement fund. This place. And you need the money and you know it. Investing will make me feel, I don't know, more worthy of its name. Don't say no. I need you to say yes. I want to do this. Or else."

"Or else what?"

If you say it, you have to mean it. No more empty threats. But in that moment, it didn't feel like a threat. It felt entirely necessary.

"Then I really can't stay."

"Don't do that, Cassie. Don't drop ultimatums."

"It's not an ultimatum. It's a fact. I need to do this because I feel lousy. What'll make me feel better is if I get a piece of this restaurant. A piece of the risk. And, hopefully, if I have anything to do with it, a piece of its success too."

He scratched his head. I couldn't decide from his expression if he was a little angry or kind of pleased.

"Well, we could use some money for the unforeseen expenses, like fixing the *fucking dishwasher* that we just installed! And I'd love to run some print and radio ads . . ."

"Then it's all set," I said, not waiting for a full yes or a firm no. Will imagining an easier opening night was enough for me, plus I was running late now. "I'll cut a certified check. We'll deal with paperwork later. And by the way, we have the wine testing tomorrow. We have to pick the house red and white. I know you like those Texas Hill Country vintages, but they're not cheap."

"Right," he said, looking dizzied.

"And I left the insurance forms upstairs for you to sign."

"Great. Yeah. You off?"

"I am."

I grabbed my coat off the hook in the kitchen. *Leave. Leave now before he changes his mind.*

"Okay, then. Have a nice night," I said, bounding out of the kitchen.

I waved bye to Claire, who barely looked up at me over her phone, no doubt her latest drama already morphing into something new. I headed to a certain truck idling a half block from Café Rose. Will and I weren't going to be partners in life, but we'd be business partners, a relationship that I hoped I would one day find almost as satisfying. Sex I would have to get elsewhere.

I opened the truck door, startling Jesse.

"Hey babe," he said, shoving his newspaper aside. "You're late."

"I'm sorry. I was in . . . a meeting."

He was wearing mirrored sunglasses and working a toothpick. He looked like an ad for his truck. I slid into the seat next to him, took his sunglasses off his face and put them on mine. I was flooded with adrenaline.

"What's the plan?" I asked.

I'm not sure what my grin said, but we were both instantly aware that we weren't going out for a coffee or dinner or a movie. We weren't going for a chat. There didn't seem to be a whole lot left to discuss.

"Your place or mine?" he asked.

"Yours."

He peeled away from the curb, and when he steadied the truck on Frenchmen, he reached his right hand behind my head and gave me a warm caress.

"I'm thinking it's time I get you naked, Cassie Robichaud."

Despite my lingering feelings for Will, it was goddamn instant wetness with this man.

"I'm thinking the same thing."

I had waited more than two months. Long enough for Will to change his mind. Long enough for a thaw or a shift, something that would tell me it wasn't over between us. But that moment wasn't coming. And frankly, Matilda was right: having sex made you want to have sex. It was a muscle; exercising it created an appetite. And I was hungry. Sitting next to Jesse, something deep in me released, the way your bra can sometimes come undone and you don't feel it at first. You just start to breathe a little easier.

We were quiet on the short drive. He parked in front of his place in Tremé, and I let him walk around to the passenger side of the truck to open my door. I got out and followed him closely, wordlessly, on the walkway leading to his front door. I needed sex; I needed this man inside me.

In the foyer, I let him take my purse from my shoulder and drop it in the pile of kids' unwrapped toys stuffed under a Christmas tree that would probably be up for another month. He turned my body to face him and kissed me hard, pressing me backwards into his darkened bed-room, a teak-filled room with heavy brown drapes. There, he stood me in front of his wall-mounted, full-length mirror, undressing me slowly, stopping me anytime I did anything to help.

"Don't move. Just stand there," he said, bending to pull off my boots and socks.

I rested a hand on his shoulder. He undid my jeans, wrestling them down, unsheathing my legs. As he slid my panties down I was conscious of how wet I was. My T-shirt and bra were next, tossed on the pile of my clothes on the nearby chair. The strangest sensation came over me, one that went beyond arousal. I realized that for the first time in my life I was just a body. My heart wasn't in the room with me. It was all sensation, movement, touch, feel.

From behind he placed his hands on my breasts. He knew my body well. I pressed back into him, feeling his erection through his clothes against my back, my whole body leaning into it, softly rubbing it, surrendering all over again. I was doing another Step One. *I need hands on me. What is wrong with that?*

I closed my eyes and my head tipped back against his chest.

"You want this?" he whispered, his tongue in my ear.

Eyes closed, I nodded.

"You want me to fuck you?"

I nodded again.

He slid his hand down between my legs, over my pelvis, pulling my hips back. I wrapped my arms up and back around his neck. He slipped a finger, then another one in me. Oh god was I wet.

"There have to be rules."

I looked at myself in the mirror, my body stretching back against his. My pulse quickened. *Uh-oh. Heart, stay out of this!*

"We're both in S.E.C.R.E.T. That could get tricky. Emotionally."

"How?"

"My Step's coming up."

I was looking at his face buried now in my neck.

"I know that," I said.

He moved me closer to the mirror and placed my hands on it. Our eyes locked in the reflection.

"So it doesn't bother you at all that I'm going to have sex with the new woman, the new candidate?" he asked, kissing my shoulder but never taking his eyes off mine in the mirror.

Steel yourself, Cassie. You know what it is to be with this man. This isn't about love.

"I don't have any expectations."

"And I don't either," he said, moving my hair to one side and kissing my neck. "I really like you. No. I *adore* you, Cassie, but we're different. You crave love. I just . . . I crave."

"But you said . . . you said you might have been waiting for a girl like me."

Why did I have to bring that up? And now?

My hands were still pressed on the mirror. His fingers reached around my face and under my chin. He glided them across my lips and slid one into my mouth; I closed my lips firmly around it, tasting soap. I watched myself sucking his finger. I could feel him stiffen even more behind me. His breathing sped up. Matilda once told me that what a man tells you about himself is true. If he says he's a shallow jerk, that's usually true. If he says he's not good at relationships or has trouble committing, ignore this information to your peril.

"I meant it when I said it. At the time."

His finger was still in my mouth, his tongue traveling to my ear. My knees went weak.

"Then you went back to Will first chance you got," he whispered. "I learned my lesson."

He removed his finger from my mouth with a tiny pop. "I told you I was sorry about that, the way I treated you, I—" I thought I detected a hint of anger in his voice.

"I'm not looking for an apology. But it made me realize that I am suited to this. And to fantasies. Not necessarily to real love. Or real commitment. I worry that the opposite might be true of you."

He stepped back and whipped off his T-shirt. This man was elbow-deep in icing and butter all day. How was it possible that his body was so sculpted?

"How so?"

"You want love."

"Doesn't everybody?"

He turned me around to face him.

"No, everybody does not. Some of us just want to fuck."

He gave me a little push that sent me backwards onto his bed. He was no longer smiling. The face of the sweet, supportive friend who had driven me home from Latrobe's was replaced by that of an intense young man, his tattoos lending him a menacing patina, one that I found a little scary and incredibly sexy. I inched backwards on the duvet, centering my body on the bed, as he stripped the rest of his clothes off. He was magnificent naked, his cock erect and insistent. He stood there, casually stroking himself as his eyes took me in.

"Open your legs, Cassie," he instructed, leaning over to his nightstand to remove a condom.

I hesitated. I wasn't sure I liked the tone in his voice.

"Do it," he added, sounding hoarse.

"Ask nicely," I replied, my knees clenched.

He slid the condom on, ignoring me, then climbed onto the bed and kneeled before me, placing his hands on my knees.

"Do you want me to make you? We can play like that too, Cassie. Just say the word."

This was making me wet *and* freaking me out. Did I want that? Did I want him to *make* me?

"Does this turn you on?" I whispered. "Ordering me around like this?"

"Sometimes."

"I thought men in S.E.C.R.E.T. needed clear signals."

"I'm not your fantasy man anymore, Cassie. I'm just a man, who wants to fuck you."

He tugged my knees apart and collapsed over me, his hands on either side. His cock graced the nook between my thigh and pelvis, lying heavy against my skin. The dark bedroom cast shadows across his cheeks and chin. He was breathing heavily, his eyes traveling over my body. I reached up and moved the tips of my fingers across the light hair on his chest, his sternum, the back of my finger tracing up his neck, his chin, across his cheekbones. For some reason I wanted gentleness to contrast with his sudden aggression, but he took my wandering hand and placed it over my head the way you'd move a lever back into its place. There was a moment where I asked myself, *Should I let him fuck me like this? Should I let him restrain me and use me? Should I use him?* I said *yes* in my head, while using my knee to press him away from me in a complicated *no*.

"Too rough for you?" he asked, sounding almost . . . triumphant.

A surge of something (indignation?) rushed through me. "I actually don't mind rough sometimes, Jesse." I remembered Will's spanking, the fun we'd had pushing each other's buttons and limits. "It's that you're angry. That part I don't like."

He blinked a couple of times as though coming to consciousness. Then he rolled off me and collapsed on his back, an arm slung over his eyes.

"Sorry, Cass. I'll take you home," he muttered. "I gotta be somewhere anyway."

I hoisted myself off the bed and began to gather my clothes. "Don't bother. I'll walk."

"Cassie." He reached to grab my arm. "Let me take you home. I'm being a fucking dick. I'm sorry. Really. We don't have to—"

I jerked free of his grasp and began plucking my clothes from the floor and dressing with my back to him. I felt a strange power surge through me—a new sense of agency.

"You're right, Jesse, we don't have to fuck, because *I* decide whether we fuck or not. And *I* get to have the kind of sex *I* want. And what I *don't* want is to just lie there and let someone fuck me the way I did with my ex-fucking-husband, waiting for it to be over!"

I was breathless. I turned to face Jesse and saw his expression registering shock but also awe.

"That's what you feel this was?"

"*No!*" I screamed. They were different men, Scott and Jesse, but this feeling was familiar. "No, it's not the same. But you *are* being a dick."

"I know. I'm sorry."

Jesse looked up at me. "This might be inappropriate," he whispered, "but you are very sexy when you're like this, Cassie."

Jesse reached for me like I was a cornered animal that might bite. He tugged loose the T-shirt I was holding, dropping it to the floor. Then he pulled me by my jeans, securing his hands on the top button, popping each one open, a warm smile spreading across his mouth. His cock was so hard it was like it had heard nothing of what was just said.

"I think you need to make amends to me," I whispered.

"How about I start by kissing your pussy. Would that make it better?"

"Maybe," I said, my hands going to my breasts. This *man!* One minute I wanted to slap him hard, the next I wanted to fuck him harder.

"Tell me what *you* want me to do. Use your words, Cassie, the ones I taught you," he said, placing my foot on the bed next to his thigh, splaying me before him. He wet his lips.

"I want you to lick me, Jesse," I said, my fingers in his hair.

"You want me to suck your clit?"

His eyes were dancing with mischief. He liked me like this, bratty and transgressive.

"Tell me what else you want me to do, Cassie."

"I want you to fuck me," I said, climbing towards him. "I want your cock in my *cunt.*"

"Yesss, that's it," he said, collapsing back, taking me with him.

I remembered the way Angela had wielded her power over Mark that time in the Mansion, when I was behind mirrored glass watching them. I channeled her now, mimicking her movements, the fierce way she tore into him. I shoved Jesse down on the bed, ignoring his erection, to take my own pleasure from his mouth, his darting tongue finding my grooves, his smooth fingers exploring my body, every curve and crevice, his tongue lashing back and forth over my clit, my whole body now over him, writhing with desire. He knew me so well, knew how fast to go, how slow. He knew how close to bring me to orgasm before spinning me around and throwing me down on the bed so he could enter me quickly, his hips grinding me.

"You're so fucking sexy, Cassie," he murmured, his arms ropy and ridged, his stomach muscles tensing with every feverish thrust.

As he fucked me, arousal flooded my core, until I had no choice but to come, on command, on *his* command.

"That's right, Cassie, I got you . . . come for me, baby, come now . . ."

He was scorching, his eyes burning into me. I flung my arms up in surrender. Eyes open, I came so hard, so searingly, I felt something akin to disbelief—disbelief that he could do this to me, to my body, that he could make me come like this, my spasms gripping his cock so hard he nearly emptied into me. At the last second he tugged out with a moan and spilled onto my heaving stomach, in hot, helpless spurts.

"Holy shit," he said, collapsing atop me.

I held his sweaty head between my breasts. After a few seconds of gasping, still in a state of astonishment, Jesse fell off me, sliding comically to the floor in a weak pile, both of us laughing at the mess we had made of each other.

"Holy shit," he said.

I was about to reply, *I know, that was amazing*, but he was already up and sprinting to the bathroom to shower.

"Sorry, Cass. I almost fucking forgot! I have a thing at nine."

"Oh," I said, getting up to gather my belongings. "What do you have to do at nine? Another girl? Haha."

"I'm helping out tonight. With S.E.C.R.E.T."

"Oh," I said. "I was kidding."

My entire center dropped out as I took in what this meant. Solange. He was "helping out" with the new candidate. He was going to have sex with Solange. Oh, this did not feel good at all. Fuck, fuck, *fuck*.

"Relax," Jesse yelled from the washroom, reading my mind. He shut off the taps. "I'm not the main attraction."

What did that mean? A few seconds later, he brought his naked, dripping body back to the bedroom. He hurriedly plucked his jeans off the floor and threw them on commando-style.

"Can you drive me to the French Quarter, Cass? That's where it's happening. You can take my truck home. I'll cab it after."

"I'm not going to *drive* you to your fantasy! We just fucked!"

And there it was, my Jealous Girlfriend Voice.

"Whoa! Calm down, Cassie. I would *not* have sex with you *and* a S.E.C.R.E.T. candidate on the same day. I'm not that much of a tacky fucking asshole. Tonight's just a quick walk-on role. I'm just facilitating. Like I said, I'm not the main attraction."

I was afraid to open my mouth.

"I knew this was too complicated," he said. "Maybe we need to stick to being buddies."

"No. It's okay. I'm cool," I said, shrugging on my T-shirt. My stomach grumbled so loudly we both noticed.

"You need food. That's why you're cranky," he said. "If I dress in the truck we'll have time for a quick bite. Come. Please?"

He was offering a truce and I wanted to prove I could handle this, both of us being in S.E.C.R.E.T., both of us

enjoying each other sexually without having to get all pos-
sessive about it. I shook off my own doubts and negativity
and took the keys he dangled in front of me.

I drove into the French Quarter while he slapped on
what looked like some kind of security guard costume.

"Well, I guess I know what your role is going to be," I said.

"Ha," he said, adjusting the belt. "Even if I were the
main fantasy man, I doubt she'd accept the Step. I look like
a fucking dork."

After I parked near Jackson Square, we walked over to a
loud line of food trucks and each ordered a couple of creole-
style rotis. We found seats in front of Stanley's. I told
myself we would be okay. We had just had an off night.

"The fantasy's going to happen here? It's pretty crowded,"
I said, prompting him.

"That's part of it. Being in public. Crowds," he said,
thoughtfully looking around and chomping his food.

He wasn't giving me much. "Huh. I had one of those. A
public sex fantasy."

"How did it go?"

"It happened at Halo. At the bar. While the band was
playing."

"Oooh. Details please."

I felt a surge of pride. I would have spilled the story
then and there, but *shit-fuck* I spotted none other than
Solange Faraday making her hurried way through the
crowds towards the old military museum at the end of
the square.

"Jesse," I hissed, using my body to block Solange's view of him. "We have to go. *Now*."

I grabbed his sleeve and pulled him low, his face in front of mine.

"What's going on?"

"It's her. *Solange*." I pointed over my shoulder. "She shouldn't see you."

He lowered his chin, shrinking lower. My back to her, I lifted Jesse to his feet and we sidestepped from St. Ann to Chartres, where we opened our gait and walked briskly to where the truck was parked on Royal.

"That was close," he said, leaning against his door to catch his breath.

"Far too close."

"So *that's* her? That's Solange? Well, well . . ." he said.

"You've never seen her on the news?"

He gave me a look that reminded me he wasn't much for current events.

I had to admit my heart hurt at his enthusiasm. Even in just a coat and boots, she looked spectacular. Women like her were always more beautiful because of their lack of awareness of their looks. Add to that the knowledge that the man sitting next to me would have mind-blowing sex with her, if not tonight, then soon, and I felt woozy. What had I gotten myself into? If it was just sex with Jesse, why was I feeling so unsettled? And if that's all that Jesse and I had, what was the big deal?

"Okay, baby. I gotta go. It's showtime."

"What's the scenario?" I asked.

"You know the rules, Cass. There's no fuck-and-tell in S.E.C.R.E.T. *If it's not your fantasy, it's none of your business.* At least the guys honor that. You could probably wait, if you want. I could meet you at Coop's. This won't take long."

"Oh really? Poor Solange," I said, with no small amount of snark. "I'll just walk home. I'm not in the mood for waiting."

"Hey," he said, pressing me back against his truck. "You know what S.E.C.R.E.T. is, right?" He bracketed me with his arms. "You might have stuff coming up, too, that I don't get to know about or have a say in."

This was true—if I were actually training recruits. Right now I was just helping facilitate fantasies, but Jesse didn't need to know that. Part of me wanted him to think my involvement was more sexual than it actually was.

I smiled, pulling myself together. "I can't stay. I'll call you later," I said, handing him his keys.

He gave me one last probing look and walked away in an exaggerated Charlie Chan wobble because he knew I'd have my eyes on him until he rounded the corner and was out of sight.

If sharing him with S.E.C.R.E.T. was the price of dating him, I had to seriously consider whether I could afford to pay it.

SOLANGE

I followed the instructions on my Step Three card exactly: *Only wear what's in this box and nothing else. Head to Jackson Square just before 9 p.m. Walk in a clockwise direction around the perimeter of the fence. Then, at 9, enter the museum by the south door. It will be open.*

In the box was a beautiful trench coat, a gray tweed hat with a shallow brim, black stiletto boots . . . and garters and stockings. Nothing else.

This is what I'm supposed to wear? In the middle of winter?

I was not really the obedient type. But this Step was all about trust, so I followed instructions. I wore the clothing as I was told, showed up at the square when I was supposed to, a little early even, walking the perimeter, fists shoved deep in the pockets. *Calm down. No one can tell you're naked underneath this coat.*

Between my nerves, the drone of the idling food trucks and the smells emanating from them, my stomach began to rebel. I pulled the belt of the trench coat tighter, my senses on high alert. The French Quarter was packed, the night balmy for Boxing Day. I suspected the fantasy in store for me was going to be a real challenge. I knew when I wrote *to transgress* in my fantasy folder, the Committee would understand I meant doing something naughty in public—*but not getting caught*, I wrote, an important clarification. This Step was about going to that edge, about trusting I'd be taken care of, that I'd get away with it without any repercussions on the rest of my life.

I checked my watch. It was time. I slid through the gap in the steel gate surrounding the museum grounds. No lights were on in the old Spanish fortress, which had once been a courthouse, then a prison, and was now a military museum. I had yet to bring Gus here, despite his obsession with soldiers and history, mostly because I generally avoided the French Quarter. Too many tourists, and frankly, parking was a bitch.

I tested the first door but it was locked. So was the next one. The last one finally yielded. I stepped into the dark, expansive marble lobby. The only things I could see through the windows were shadows of the pedestrians still moving around the square outside.

"Solange."

I leapt out of my skin.

"Jesus!"

I turned towards a very tall man standing in a dark corner, his shoulders wide, his eyes and nose shadowed by the brim of his fedora. I could see the firm line of his full mouth offering a cocked smile.

"My apologies," he said, a little too loudly for my liking. "But before you come any closer, tell me, do you accept the Step?"

Holy hell. A British accent. Plus he sounded altogether too relaxed. I looked around the dim lobby nervously. *What if we're caught in here?*

Trust. Doitdoitdoit.

"Are we alone?" I whispered, my heart sounding louder to me than my own voice.

"I think so," he said, his tone bemused. He put his hands in his pockets and stepped out of the shadows towards me, confirming that he was, indeed, a very fine black man, one from across the pond.

"You *think* so? You don't sound very convinced."

"Do you accept the Step, my darling?" he asked again, with not an iota of concern. And that *accent.*

I looked around the lobby again. Even if someone saw, what could they say? That Solange Faraday entered the museum in the French Quarter after hours? So what? That a handsome man encircled my small wrist with his expansive grip? Who cares? He could easily be my boyfriend. Maybe he worked here and had forgotten something in his office?

But once inside, there were no witnesses. No one could see him pull me towards an old-fashion elevator, coaxing me in and smashing the cage shut behind him. They couldn't hear my heart pounding as he turned to face me, taking off his fedora and throwing it to the floor to reveal his sculpted face, his amused eyes, black and intense, his closely shaved, rather magnificent head.

"Solange, one last time, do you accept the Step?"

"Yes!" It came out fast and loud. This man was so devastatingly attractive, there was no way I could turn him down, despite my fears about the privacy of our encounter. I wanted him to talk more in that liquid velvet accent.

I swallowed as he came closer and loomed over me, his deep voice now a rasp. He grabbed the wall of the elevator cage behind me.

"Well, my dear, how shall we play?"

Except for two guys in college and a brief setup last year, I'd dated mostly black men, including the one I married. Not that I wasn't attracted to other races—clearly I was—but *this* man standing before me summed up everything right about how God made a man. Without waiting for my reply, he hit a button and the old-fashioned elevator shuddered to life, lifting us perilously above the ground. He took off my hat and threw it to the floor too.

"Look at you," he whispered. "Here for me. Is that right, my love?"

I could feel the cage vibrate against my back as I watched the marble floor of the museum's lobby shrink away from us. His hands reached for the knot of my coat belt.

"Yes," I said, averting my eyes. I did not want to come across as a breathless schoolgirl, but I was utterly speechless.

I watched as he easily undid the knot. He hit the button again and the elevator stopped with a jerk, suspending us in the cage over the lobby. We could see everything below, including the parade of pedestrians out for a night on the brightly lit square, but no one outside could see us.

Or so I assumed. Hoped. Prayed.

"We're high up," I said, swallowing.

"I like heights," he said. "Do you?"

"Not really." Truth be told, I was feeling a little faint.

"You're in good hands. I fly planes." And I *was* in good hands. *Firm, experienced, pilot hands.*

He slid one of those good hands into the slit of my coat opening. When his palm hit the skin on my stomach, I quivered. I actually *quivered*. When was the last time I had done that? Had I *ever* quivered with Julius? With his other hand, he clutched my chin and tilted my head up, the light of the elevator casting his chiseled face in shadows.

"Now, there's a rule. We have to be very, very quiet, darling. Can you do that for me?" he asked, slipping my coat off my shoulders, revealing my bare torso.

I forgot I was naked under the coat! He looked down at my breasts, his hands tracing my curves, his expression one of deep concentration, as though I were a valuable piece of art no one was allowed to touch. There was a plan hatching in this man's brain, I could see that, and before I could open my mouth to speak, he opened my arms and lifted them over my head, instructing me in the barest of whispers, "Hold on to the cage behind you and don't let go."

I did so. "What if someone down there sees us? What if we're caught? I'd lose my job, my credibility—"

"I want you to listen to me." His voice was as warm and reassuring as a cashmere throw. "Remain silent no matter what I do to you, and all will be well. Relax. I've got you."

Now his mouth was on me, kissing my neck and my breasts, caressing me into a state of arousal. I moaned quietly and let my head fall back against the mesh, felt the cool air on my skin where he kissed and bit his way down to my stomach, making my legs shake. To steady myself, I put my hands on his head. Not that he needed guiding. This man knew what he was doing. This man knew *where* he was going. His palms flattened against the soft brush of my hair, prying me open like a treasure. Impatient, he slung one of my thighs over his shelf of a shoulder and pressed me back against the cold, metal rail lining the elevator car. At first, all I felt was his warm breath against my clit, his arms wrapped under me. I let out an involuntary whimper, a plea really, as his broad shoulders leaned in, spreading me farther open to him.

"Want me to make you come right here, right now, love?" he crooned.

"I do," I said. "Yes."

"Say please, Solange."

"Please."

The ache was becoming unbearable. I had to watch, I needed to see this. Our eyes met, his looking up at me with wicked mischief. Then the tip of his tongue met my clit, and in my head I said *yes*—until I heard something . . .

Clack.

What?

Then more.

Clack-clack, clack-clack.

Faraway footsteps! I let out a gasp, and my man reached up and covered my mouth with his hand. The footsteps drew closer and closer, until the intruder came to rest directly under our elevator cage. My stranger released his hand and, oh god, went back to licking me, *with even greater urgency! Quiet. We have to be quiet!*

The air in my lungs thickened. *Shit, shit.* I froze, my hand on his head. I stared down in horror, but he seemed calm, focused, his mouth continuing its delicious task, his licks becoming more insistent. Soon they were joined by his fingers thrusting into me. I squeezed my eyes shut and tried to still his beautiful mouth on me, to stop him—momentarily—until the intruder left. But *we* were the intruders! And the risk of getting caught seemed only to inflame him more. He continued teasing me, his cheeks hollow, two fingers insistent, hungry, driving into me. He was enjoying my silent agony, and at one point took his finger from my dripping wetness and placed it against his shiny lips.

Shh, he mimed.

Out of the corner of my eye I saw the arc of a flashlight appear. I pressed my hips forward into my man's face, taking on the full assault of his licks, grabbing the cage to brace myself.

"Who's there?" came the intruder's voice from below.

Fuck. No! Terror coiled around my arousal as I squeezed

my eyes shut. My mistake was looking down; this man was delirious in his need to pleasure me, his head moving back and forth. Silent, white-hot pleasure crashed over my body. I threw my head back, barely missing the cage, as the rush of blood flooded my ears, drowning out everything else, even, very briefly, my fear of getting caught.

I was coming hard, despite myself, because of him.

And I was coming harder than I ever have, completely against my own will, a thing that had never happened before and likely never would again. He was *making* me come. And so I tried both to shake it out of my body and to savor it, while the footsteps moved farther from us, down a different hall. This man kept his mouth on me even as I subsided.

After waiting a few more safe beats, I rested my hand on his beautiful head.

"Holy shit, that was close!" I whispered, barely able to catch my breath. "You could have gotten me in big trouble."

He pulled away and delicately wiped his mouth with two fingers.

"Trust, Solange," he said.

I could feel the energy leaving my limbs. He rose, eclipsing the light in the elevator. My arms went limp around his shoulders and he lifted me like I weighed nothing, perching me on the wooden rail lining the box.

God. We're not done?

"I would never put you in jeopardy," he said, smoothing my hair off my face with his big hands. "Unless that is what you wanted."

He suddenly released his belt and undid his pants, letting them fall down. It took him a masterful second to secure a condom, and then, pausing for a moment to listen for any more sounds from below, he rubbed the firm head of his exquisite cock into my wet cleft, then eased into me. This man fucked me with a punishing desire, his muscled arms laced beneath my thighs, pinioning me just so. With every thrust, the outside world of mute pedestrians, dumb tourists and oblivious security guards drifted farther from my thoughts. He fucked me so hard, yet so silently, against that elevator wall that I sensed parts of my body I hadn't felt before. And no matter how hard I tried to delay the tide of bliss, the pure joy of being fucked like this, here and now, before I knew it I was coming hard again. My lungs filled with dense air and his hands clutched my body as he thrust into me, over and over again.

"Yeah," he said, his eyes on me. Seconds later, he came, his mouth encircling my ear, his tongue making me dizzy, his words, "Yes, yes, oh yeah," following us down, down, down, as he pressed a button for the elevator to carry us back to earth.

I felt warm heading towards the waterfront parking lot to my car clutching my Step Three charm in my palm. Maybe because my skin was still overheated. But I knew the full effect of this public sex act wouldn't hit me until I was safe at home, chin-deep in a tub of hot water.

"Solange!"

What the fuck! I jumped and dropped my charm on the pavement, where it bounced with a *plink, plink, plink*. It wasn't the beautiful stranger from the elevator but my *ex-husband, Julius*, standing right in front of me, a triumphant look on his face.

With his shoe, he had stopped my charm from rolling under a nearby food truck. What the hell was he doing here? On Boxing Day? And where was Gus? My hands automatically went to my waist to tie my trench coat tighter. *He can't tell I'm naked. He can't possibly know where I came from or what I was just doing. Calm. Down.*

He bent to pick up the charm. "You dropped this," he said, handing *Trust* to me without so much as a glance.

Ohgodohgodogod!

"Thanks! Hi! Julius! Wow!" I slid the charm into my pocket.

He looked at me curiously. We hadn't stood this close to each other in a while. Waving from cars and after-school handoffs had become the norm as Gus got older. I almost didn't recognize him. He looked . . . good. Happy.

"What are you doing down here?"

Quick. Think. "Well . . . I should ask you the same thing. Where's Gus?"

"He's still at Janet's. I just came out here for an hour to see how my new business was doing on a holiday."

Janet was his younger sister. We still kept in touch because Gus and her sons were close in age. I glanced over his shoulder at the idling food truck behind him. It didn't look like the other food trucks. It was painted glossy black, *Julius's Bayou Bites* scrolled on the side in red cursive letters. It had a wraparound standup bar that looked to be collapsible and made of cedar planking.

"This yours?"

"Yeah, it's mine."

"How come you never told me?"

"I don't know. Just got the permit a week ago. I didn't want to say anything until we launched. It's been crazy, the reception—really great so far."

Through the truck window, a young employee handed a customer what looked like a small, brown burrito in a nest of waxed paper, surrounded by hush puppies. I shivered, feeling a winter breeze up my coat, and clenched my thighs.

"That looks *good*," I said.

"It's like a roti, but creole-style. You remember my mom's sauce? I use that as a simmering base—reduce it, put in some chicken, shrimp or pork, or just veggies, and cheese to hold it together. Bake it in a pocket. Done. It's all organic, meat's farm-raised, not fried. Try one?"

"Sure!"

Julius disappeared into the truck. Seconds later, he brought out a warm pocket of food and handed it to me. The crowd of artists and buskers lining up against the wrought-iron fence, waiting their turn, all gave me the evil eye for being served before them. I took a ravenous bite.

"Iss *'ood*," I said, mouth full. Damn I was hungry, and this was delicious.

Julius watched me eat with glowing pride.

"So, I thought you hated the French Quarter. I could never get you to come down here. Especially on a chilly night."

"I don't hate it," I said. "I just hate finding parking here."

He was smiling that smile, the one he used to wear when I caught him watching me sing in those clubs all those years ago.

"This all looks great, Jules. I mean it. A classy food truck. Traditional food done up a little different. Healthy. Good idea. *Great* idea."

"Thanks. That means a lot coming from you," he said, sounding a little sheepish, his shoulders back, chest all puffed out.

How many times had I told this man to stand up straighter, not just physically but in every way? Nagging him all those years, I had turned myself into his mother. Instead of growing, the man had shrunk.

"You know, if it takes off, I'm going to franchise this."

"I hope it works," I said. "Sure looks like it will . . . Well, Merry Christmas, Jules. I gotta get up early, so . . . I'll pick up Gus tomorrow? Noon, your place, right?"

"Yes."

As I reached for an awkward hug, Julius leaned in and kissed me on the cheek and we smashed into each other. Could he smell sex on me?

"We should do a catch-up dinner soon," he said. "Make sure we're on the same page with Gus for the new year."

"Yeah, for sure," I said, adjusting my hat, which had been knocked askew during our awkward clutch. "I'll set something up."

"No, *I* will. I'll figure something out in the next couple weeks."

"O*kay*," I said, almost as a question. Julius initiating a parenting meeting? Wow.

"It's good to see you outside of your usual comfort zone, Solange."

You have no idea, Jules, I wanted to reply. *No idea.*

CASSIE

S taff had been hired, invitations sent, and most people were responding with a resounding "yes." It had been a while since a brand-new restaurant opened on Frenchmen Street. Establishments often changed names, but Cassie's was a whole new space and place. People were curious.

I no longer choked on the name, now that I was an equal partner. Also, as an equal partner I had fifty percent say in whom we hired, and when it came to hiring a chef, I felt there really was no other choice but Dell.

Will balked.

"She doesn't have the training."

"*Pfft*, training. She tested every recipe. She practically designed the menu."

"We'd be fools to lose her at the Café."

"Her waitressing skills are replaceable. Her cooking isn't. In fact, her cooking brings people in. It's her waitressing that chases them away."

"Good point."

It took a day for Will to relent, on the condition we hire an assistant chef to help with the more delicate dishes.

"No problem," I said. "You know how amenable Dell is to advice in the kitchen. Especially when it comes from young know-it-alls right out of cooking school."

Dell nearly broke down in tears when I offered her the chef hat and more than doubled her pay, but she didn't thank me. One of the things I admired the most about Dell was her knowledge that she was doing us a bigger favor by saying yes than we were by offering her the job.

"I have so many ideas!" she said, placing the hat on her head and admiring herself in the mirror. "So many."

My investment also meant Cassie's was opening with zero debt, a rarity for a restaurant. And I had some money left over for a splurge at Saks, because, like a lot of women, I still believe that deep superstition that the right dress can make or break a night. In my case, a lot of pressure was placed on a short little crimson cocktail number with long sheer sleeves.

Fifteen minutes before we opened the doors, I stood in front of the full-length mirror in the staff washroom taking in my transformation. Almost two years ago I was a shy, depressed waitress, resigned to a life of routine smallness. Today I was a confident entrepreneur, a vivacious single woman who had a lover and a business partner, who was wearing a sexy little red dress on New Year's Eve for the opening of a restaurant named after her. And yet, despite my accomplishments, I had to admit the heels, the makeup, the matching lipstick, my hair a tumble of dark curls—all of it still felt like a layer on top of me, not quite a part of me.

Passing through the kitchen on my way up the service stairs to the new restaurant, I heard a long, slow whistle that stopped me in my tracks.

"Look at you, boss lady," said Dell, beaming—*at me*. It almost brought me to tears. "What happened to that little mousy waitress?"

S.E.C.R.E.T. did this, I wanted to say, my hand clutching my noisy charm bracelet. I rarely wore it to work, not wanting to answer questions about it, but tonight the gold shimmer set off the outfit perfectly.

"Thanks," I said, tugging at the dress. "You don't think it's too much?"

"Too much what?"

"I don't know. I feel like the dress is wearing me."

Dell blinked in sheer incomprehension. Even if she understood my insecurity, she was refusing to address it, a policy I would do well to mirror.

"I said a prayer for good business," she said, turning back around to stir something that smelled incredible.

I could have kissed her. She may not consider me a friend, but I hoped she'd come to respect me.

Just then Claire and Maureen came bounding into the kitchen from the Café, dropping dirty dishes on the conveyor belt.

"Frick and Frack. I told you to leave the bins on the floor!" Dell yelled. They had yet to earn anything but her approbation. "We have a dishwasher coming in at night who'll do the unloading!"

"Sorry, um, but we have to clean up the Café, and I have a party to go to," Claire said, reaching into her pouch to check her smart phone.

She did it so absently, so automatically, I wasn't even sure she was aware of her own actions. I winced: the wired generation.

Claire had offered to help upstairs for opening night, but when she was invited to a party, Will insisted she be a normal teenager and go. A party meant she might still have some friends out there.

"Is Will here?" I asked, as nonchalantly as possible, to no one in particular.

"Upstairs," Dell said. "Ice machine's not working. He just took a big tray up."

"Like we don't need ice down here," said Maureen.

I scrammed, leaving Dell to deal with the tensions that sharing a kitchen between two restaurants with overlapping shifts was already causing.

The new service staircase that led to Cassie's upstairs still smelled like freshly oiled wood. Tonight signaled another new beginning, I thought: the start of a career rather than a job. Since making the investment, I had been given a crash course in entrepreneurship, and I deemed myself a natural. About money and business, I could make decisions. Sex, too, possibly. Love, not so much. I hadn't seen Jesse since Boxing Day, when he left me in Jackson Square to help facilitate a fantasy. My focus since then had been work, opening the restaurant, making this place a success. And truthfully, when Jesse had told me he had his son tonight and couldn't make the opening, I was relieved. I wasn't looking forward to seeing how Jesse and Will interacted, and I didn't need any drama or distractions.

The dining area was empty except for Will, his back to me as he adjusted the sparkling place settings. I'd never seen this suit on him: dark blue, expensive-looking, made from the kind of material you wanted to put your hands on. He appeared leaner from behind, too, more spry. The last time I saw him in a suit we were heading to Latrobe's that fateful night. Had he *ever* looked sexier than that night?

Maybe tonight, maybe right now.

"There you are," I said.

Will whipped around, and my heart caught at the sight of his face—happy, open, yet registering nothing about how I looked in this dress.

"Hey, Cassie. Can you believe it? Opening night," he said, blithely going back to his place-setting adjustments. "Oh, and happy new year."

"Yeah. Right back at you."

Is that all you're going to say? I wanted to scream, my heels digging into the distressed barn-board floors.

"You look really nice, Will."

"Thanks. Claire picked out the suit. Turns out she has very expensive taste," he said, turning towards me again and smoothing down the lapels.

I tried conjuring some of the powers from my charms: *Bravery. Exuberance. Confidence.* I needed all of them tonight.

"Well . . . here we go!" I said, placing my hands on my hips. Enticing smells wafted up the stairs from the kitchen: Dell's buttery chicken and creole sauce, her mini chicken pies, cushaw casserole tasting spoons, spicy shrimp skewers, cornbread stuffing with pecans and roux, her Cajun sticky-rice balls.

"Smell that?" he asked.

"Heavenly."

I took a step towards him. I could have sworn he flinched when I stuck out my hand and said, "Congratulations on tonight. On the opening."

His eyes darted to my bracelet before he took my hand, shaking it once, twice. *Pull him in for a kiss. End this standoff, this nonsense.* Before I could muster the courage, a burly sound-man walked in carrying a giant boom mike and recording equipment.

"This Cassie's?" he asked, breathless.

"Yes," Will and I said in unison.

"I'm from Action News Nightly."

"Excellent," Will said, impressed.

Matilda had told me she was going to ask Solange to send a producer and a crew for some visuals of our opening night, and here they were!

"I just need to know where I can plug in my lights," the crew guy said, impatient with us, probably pissed he was working New Years' Eve.

Will pointed to an outlet by the bar.

I looked at my watch. "Holy shit! It's time! I'll go unlock the front doors."

"It's time. Wow," Will said. "Oh, and Cassie?"

At the top of the stairs, I turned to face Will.

"You look . . . spec*ta*cular," he said, placing a hand over his heart, feigning weak knees.

My smile was involuntary, and probably so goofily big it undid everything sexy about my outfit. But there you go. I'd wanted and needed to hear that, and he'd come through.

I headed downstairs with renewed vigor and propped open the main door. Within a minute, the first guests arrived, mostly local restaurateurs here to check out the competition, try Dell's food. Between bites and small talk, I kept an eye on Will, who was never very good at the meet-and-greet. But tonight, there was something new about him, a swagger, a determined pride. We both had it, I think, and we worked the room separately, coming together after the first hour of schmoozing to give a brief report.

"I think it's going well," he said, nodding.

"Yes. And the food? The shrimp skewers are flying off the platters."

"I knew they'd be a hit."

"Dell's a genius."

"No, you are for insisting we make her lead chef."

I smiled at him again, instinctively wanting to reach out for his hand, when his face went from looking at me adoringly to slack at the sight of something over my left shoulder. I turned around to see Tracina enter, holding baby Neko, followed by her fiancé, the one and only Carruthers Johnstone.

Here we go.

"Go. Say hi, Will. Get it over with."

"Gimme a second," he said, turning away from them.

He hadn't seen either Carruthers or Tracina since the night their daughter, Neko, was born. Inviting her hadn't been a new idea. I'd brought it up months ago, back when we were in the throes of our own reunion, while in bed one night, our legs and arms entwined.

Will was unequivocal. *"No.* Can't we just have our own fresh start without the past coming in to haunt us? Why does our future have to involve forgiving Tracina?"

"You don't have to forgive her, but you do have to be okay with her coming to the Café. We all want to see the baby. After all, she's named after the place!"

The baby's name was Rose Nicaud, like the Café, which itself was named after the first African-American female entrepreneur in New Orleans, a slave who sold coffee from a cart she pushed up and down Frenchmen Street. She saved enough money eventually to buy her freedom. The story of her feat was on the back of every menu.

"The Café matters to Tracina. Her friends work here, Will. It's time to make amends. Then we can all move forward."

"Since when do you care about Tracina? When did she become your friend?"

It was a good question, and one I had a hard time answering. "I don't know. It just happened."

It was true. We *were* friends. It started with checking in on her right after the baby was born. Babies are magnets; they pull people to them, and this little girl had a particularly strong pull. Tracina and I had gone for walks in Audubon Park, chatting like girlfriends do, and no one was happier than Tracina when I told her Will and I were finally together, in no small part because it assuaged some of her guilt about leaving him for the man she really loved, the father of her child.

But when I told her a short while later that Will and I had broken up, she was angry. Angrier still when I told her why.

"What double-standard man bullshit is that? That you can't have a bunch of sex without making him feel all threatened? If he didn't hate my guts, I'd march over there and hit him over the head with my grandma's cast-iron fry pan."

Tracina had long guessed at my involvement in this "sexy little group" to which her best friends Kit and Angela belonged.

"Why else would Kit and Ange hang out with y'all?" she said with no malice, just pure Tracina-style bluntness. Tracina also admitted that after Kit and Angela told her about their participation in S.E.C.R.E.T., she begged to be included, at least in the fantasy parts.

They told her she didn't qualify.

"When it comes to sex, apparently my shit is *too* together. Is that a bad thing?"

I told her it wasn't; she was the kind of woman we all wanted to be like, at least when it came to her relationship with sex and her own body, which looked incredible tonight with a new lush layer of baby weight softening her edges. Watching her hoist and pat Neko, while teetering in heels and wearing a short, sparkly dress, I marveled at how sexy motherhood looked on her.

"Go," I said now, gently prodding Will to greet her, the baby and her beau.

After pulling in a deep breath, Will crossed the room and gamely stuck out his hand to Carruthers, not like they were old friends or would ever become new ones, but with a kind of familiarity, like they'd fought on opposite sides of a fierce skirmish, neither truly coming out a victor. Will then turned to Tracina and gave her a quick kiss on the cheek, his eyes glued to the bundle she carried. When Tracina opened the little flap on baby Neko, Will smiled for the first time in weeks, a genuine Will smile, one that stretched from ear to ear.

In that moment, my heart broke for him. Again.

Tracina poured the baby into his arms, and he cooed and rocked her, smiling and smiling, my cue to go over and tug a now baby-free Tracina to a quiet corner.

"You look insanely great, by the way!" she said, grabbing my hands and holding them out to take in my red dress.

"You think? I feel like a fraud."

"Stop it, it's fucking great. Is Will still being a dickhead?" she asked, snatching a glass of wine off a passing tray. "I pumped her milk so I'm getting my drink on tonight."

"Will's being . . . well, you know, Will."

"You want my advice? Give him a nice, wide berth. Let him remember what he's missing."

"We are strictly business partners, Tracina. Our chance came and went."

She ignored me. "What I mean is, don't be emotionally available to him, if you want him back."

"I told you we're just—"

"Be mysterious. Be busy. Get dating again. Who was that guy you were seeing last year?"

"Which one? The musician or the pastry chef?"

She gave me the side-eye. "I did not know you were *that* busy." We laughed.

"I know you, Cassie. Everything you're telling yourself about Will, I said it to myself about my Carr. So like I said, you really want a guy? Behave like you really don't."

We both looked over at Will. If you could watch a man fall instantly in love, his face would look like Will's, the world around him melting away, the object of his affection receiving his full attention. The baby took obvious glee in his rapture, her giggle audible from where we were standing. Her hands sweetly punched at his nose and chin, until, unprompted, she started wailing and Tracina's whole body went on high alert. On cue, Will made his way back over to us, followed by a doting Carruthers.

"Oh sure, she starts crying and it's time to give her back to Mommy," said Tracina.

"If I could help, I would," Will said, reluctantly exchanging the baby for Tracina's empty glass.

"Nah. It's cool. She wants her mommy. And a clean diaper." Tracina took the now-bawling Neko downstairs to the staff room, leaving the three of us standing around awkwardly for a few seconds.

"Thank you for coming," I said to Carruthers, patting his arm.

His smile was tight. "I am always happy to support local businesses."

Matilda arrived just then, blessedly, and I excused myself from this painful company to greet her, despite Will's *help, don't leave* expression. As I walked towards Matilda, my phone vibrated in my pocket—a text. From Jesse.

Come over after party? Finn's asleep.

Finn? Oh right, his son. I kicked myself for not asking his name ages ago. Before I could reply, Matilda pulled me in for an embrace.

"Cassie! You look stunning."

"Thank you. Though I'm beginning to worry that maybe opening on New Year's wasn't the best idea."

Just then more guests crowded the top of the stairs. Before I had a chance to break from Matilda to greet them, Will was upon then, instructing some guests where to hang their coats, showing others to the bar.

"Well, judging from the turnout, it was the best idea ever."

Matilda paused for a moment to marvel over the mint juleps placed before us on a tray. I grabbed one, sucking it back so fast I gave myself an instant headache.

"You drank that like a thirsty trucker," she said, carefully lifting a glass off the tray.

"I'm a nervous wreck," I said.

"Well, you don't look rattled."

"Tracina's here too," I said. "She's downstairs. With the *baby*."

"Wonderful. I just love to start a new year with a bit of forgiveness for old transgressions. It's very good for the skin. Speaking of flesh, there is an interesting opportunity coming up in S.E.C.R.E.T. I thought I'd offer it to you first."

I lifted an eyebrow. "We can talk about it tomorrow," she said. "But I think it will be great fun."

Angela bounded up to us, wearing a chic pantsuit, her hair scalloped and pinned like a flapper's.

"Were you just talking about fun?" she asked, plucking the olive out of her drink. "Because it is *here*."

After a few minutes, I left Matilda chatting with Angela and went to poke around downstairs. I found Tracina in the kitchen marveling over Dell's delicious dishes, and Dell and Maureen marveling over the delicious baby. I smiled at the scene. Everything felt so right, so good, so full of love and promise after all those secrets and lies. I had a sudden desperate urge to be at Will's side, and when I left them to go back upstairs, I was kind of shocked to find a party in full, pre-midnight countdown. Couples began to pair off in the dark. I looked around and finally spotted Will, who was wildly gesturing to me.

Had he been looking for me?

I took a deep breath and made that long, anxious walk across the room, cursing the crowds, remembering back when it was just us, that first time on the old ratty mattress after the burlesque show, and again, not so long ago on a different mattress in this same room . . .

" . . . TEN, NINE . . ."

To say that brief walk towards him was an out-of-body experience would not be an exaggeration.

". . . FIVE, FOUR . . ."

His face looked so expectant, his smile so open to me.

". . . THREE, TWO . . ."

". . . ONE!"

I landed next to Will just as a flood of lights hit us, so bright and intense I had to use my hand as a visor to protect my eyes. What the hell? Oh! Right! The camera's spotlight. This was the interview. Will had been calling me over not for a new year's kiss but for an interview with an impossibly young, impossibly cute female TV producer.

"Cassie, happy new year! So nice to meet you!" the producer said, pushing back her thick, hipster grandpa glasses.

Will and I stood next to each other with the stiffness of the couple in *American Gothic* as the camera panned over the dark crowd to us.

"Get close!" the producer yelled over the jubilation in the background.

Will threw an awkward arm around me. I looked up at his face, but his eyes remained firmly fixed on the producer. I pulled my lips into a tense smile.

"So . . . we're rolling. Tell us where we are tonight, Will!" she yelled.

"We're at the opening of our new restaurant, Cassie's, an upscale comfort food experience on Frenchmen!"

"I hear you named the restaurant after this lovely woman standing next to you. She must be very special."

"Cassie's my business partner!" he said, giving me a jocular jolt, like you would a sister or a classmate. "She owns half the place, so it's not like I had a choice!"

Hahaha. *What?*

"Cassie, how are *you* feeling tonight?" the producer asked, putting the microphone in front of me.

I looked at it for a second, clearing my throat. "Nervous. Excited . . ." I was seized by sudden inarticulateness. Doom crept up my body. I wrapped my hands around the microphone and pulled it in closer.

"We're confident Cassie's is exactly what Frenchmen Street needs right now. This place is warm, sexy, a place that combines the best of Southern home-cooking with a bit of grown-up glamour. Our menu puts a fresh nouveau spin on Southern hospitality. And our wine list is incredible. Half American, half French, just like the city itself."

"And we'll have live music from time to time," Will added, his arm still draped around me.

After the producer thanked us and lowered her mike, the camera light flicked off and Will swiftly dropped his arm.

"Perfect! Cassie, you gave me the clip I needed," said the producer. "Thank you both so much. I'm going to rush back to get this on the 1 a.m. roundup," she said.

"No. Stay for one drink," Will insisted. "Surely your crew can bring the tape back so you can stay for a toast."

"Yeah!" I said, trying to muster the same enthusiasm as Will. "Stay for a drink!"

"Well, I suppose it *is* New Year's Eve," she said, taking off her glasses. She turned to her cameraman to instruct him to head back to the station without her.

"Great! Let me get you some champagne," Will said. "And Cassie, I also insist on closing up. You don't need to stay to the bitter end. You've been here since the morning."

My heart sank even further. He could barely touch me during the interview and now he was trying to get rid of me so he could flirt with some sweet young producer girl.

"You sure you don't mind?" I asked evenly.

"Absolutely not," he said.

"Cool. Thanks," I replied, backing away.

"You should be with your boyfriend on New Year's Eve. The party's winding down anyway."

Was that hurt, anger or, worse, antipathy I noted in his voice? I didn't stick around to find out. I left him with the cute producer and did one last painful circle of the room. Then I took out my phone and texted Jesse.

Leave your door open. I'm on my way.

Matilda once said the hallmark of adulthood is knowing when it's time to leave. Suddenly, I felt all grown-up.

⌒

Jesse's door was unlocked when I arrived. I eased it open, carefully removing my sparkly heels in the darkened foyer, throwing my coat across the back of an armchair. I quietly padded to Jesse's bedroom, clutching my S.E.C.R.E.T. bracelet to my wrist to stop the tiny tinkling sound from traveling down the hall. I thought the light under his bedroom door meant he was still up. But alas, when I cracked it open, there Jesse was, fast asleep, his son Finn's surprisingly long legs splayed across his thigh, both of them gently snoozing. I didn't know kids, so I had nothing to measure him against, but he looked big for a six- or seven-year-old. It was a touching tableau, too touching to disturb, so I shut the door and tiptoed back to the foyer, grabbed my coat and threw it back on. Outside on the porch, I dug around for my cell and called back the taxi that had just dropped me off. I shivered on the steps waiting. That's when I noticed another text, this one from Will.

Didn't see you leave. It was a great night, Cassie. Thanks for being by my side on this. See you tomorrow. X W

My heart skipped at that stupid little X. I felt like an idiot teen, grabbing at any sign a boy liked me. What was I doing huddled on a dark porch in the middle of a cold night pining over an *X*? Because hard times are harder alone, but worse is having good things happen and no one with whom to celebrate. How nice it would have been to toast Will on New Year's Eve, in *our* restaurant, after everyone had left: a couple of snifters of brandy, a kiss in silhouette—

"Hey."

I jumped. It was Jesse, shirtless, loose pajama bottoms slung around his lean torso, his arms crossed tight around him.

"Sorry, babe. I fell asleep. Finn must have crawled in. Been trying to get him to break that habit."

"It's okay. Go inside, it's cold. Cab's turning around."

"I'll put him back in his bed," he whispered, crouching to put his arms around me. His nose nuzzled my hair.

He gave a full-body shiver and I rubbed his forearms vigorously.

"He might wake up again," I said. "I don't want this to be how we meet. I didn't even know his name until today. Finn. It's cute. I like it."

"You sure you don't want to wait inside?"

"No. It's okay."

"I'll call you in a few days," he said, kissing the back of my head and ducking back into the house.

I had to laugh.

Minutes later, my head pressed against the cold taxi window, I made another resolution: I was not going to make my life about the guy, about *any* guy. I was going to devote myself to Cassie's, which was not just my business but my investment, my calling, my future, my life. I was also going to say yes to the thing Matilda had talked about, no matter what it was. After tonight, I was to be a woman about my work. I would look after my own passions. I was not going to be about a man.

At home, I threw my little red dress on the back of a kitchen chair, too tired to hang it, and I collapsed into bed. I was soon joined by Dixie, who wasn't looking for love or affection either, just a warm body, and there was absolutely nothing wrong with that.

SOLANGE

January was a blur of work and carpools. Julius's food truck business was taking off and now *his* schedule was the moving target. But early February meant the ramp up to Mardi Gras, and more than once, poor Gus found himself coloring on the glass coffee table in my office, killing time after school until his dad could pick him up. I had to swallow my complaints because there had been years and years of Julius picking up the parenting slack while I was chasing stories or on a stakeout that went longer than planned.

"Why's Dad taking so long? I'm bored," he said, playing a game on my phone in my office, the coloring books no longer capturing his attention.

"I'm sorry you're bored, baby," I said, peering over the half-dozen vases stuffed with flowers on my desk. "You have two busy parents doing their best."

Were we doing our best? His dad was busy trying to get a business venture off the ground and his mom was trying to reclaim her sex life. I felt mother's guilt spread through me in a cold wave.

I checked my watch. Matilda and I were to celebrate that night. My port lands story, the one I broke last year that landed a bunch of politicians in jail, had been nominated for a local Emmy that morning. Or rather, *I* had been nominated, hence the flowers.

Just then Julius rounded the corner of my office carrying a fistful of yellow roses.

"Hey! Sorry I'm late! Heard about the nomination on the radio. Way to go, Solange," he said, grinning. When I hugged him, he lifted me right off my feet with an intimacy that turned the heads of a few people in the newsroom.

"Yes, well, thanks," I said as he set me down again. I tucked my blouse back into my skirt.

"You're gonna wiii-iiin," Gus singsonged.

"What makes you so sure of that, buddy?" I asked, as Julius gathered up his son's jacket, backpack and several toys strewn about my office floor, and I plucked my phone from the kid's hands.

"'Cause you're the Formidable Solange Faraday," Gus said.

Julius cocked an eyebrow at me.

"Uh, I see," I said, uncertain whether Gus meant it as a compliment. It's true that when I wanted something I went after it at all costs; I'd taught my son that was how you achieved success. Was it wrong to be formidable?

"Okay, let's go, bud," Julius said, not wanting to linger on the topic of ambition a second longer. "See you in a few days, Solange. And try to have some fun tonight. Let loose. Celebrate!"

"I will, thanks," I said, and kissed Gus good-bye. I wanted to add, *I'm not all work, Jules. I play too. In fact, after my celebratory dinner, which will, admittedly, involve a bit of work, fun does await me. More fun than you could ever imagine me having.*

But getting nominated for that story made me hungry for another notch in my journalistic belt, one I hoped Matilda could help me carve.

⌒

By now, we had a regular table at Tracey's, a tippy two-top near the server area in front of the kitchen. Matilda was already waiting for me, with yet another clutch of flowers— four oversize peonies, my favorites—and two glasses of champagne. As much as I was enjoying the fantasies and looking forward to more, I was also relishing newfound female companionship. Before S.E.C.R.E.T., I had no idea how much I missed that. And because she was so smart, challenging and honest, Matilda's company was particularly welcome. She had a lot in common with Marsha Lang, minus all the worries about staying on top and looking good while doing it.

"Congratulations, my dear," she said, clinking her glass to mine. "Here's to uncovering more great stories in this great city."

More great stories. Yes! This was my in.

"Since we're on the topic of great stories, do you know who'd be my dream 'get'—the person I'd really like to interview?"

"Michelle Obama?"

"No, I mean locally."

"Who?"

"Pierre Castille, the Bayou Billionaire. Don't you think he'd be fascinating?"

"I imagine he's a busy man."

She had an amazing poker face. Ever since I saw Pierre Castille drunkenly escorted from the S.E.C.R.E.T. charity event, I had been convinced that there was a link between him and S.E.C.R.E.T. But Matilda was giving nothing away. Realizing the roundabout method wasn't working, I set down my utensils and clasped my hands together on the table. After more than twenty years as a journalist, I had learned there are times when you have to lay your cards on the table.

"Matilda, I know you know Pierre Castille. I know you're associated with him in some way. Further, I think you know how to reach him."

She studied my face placidly. "What's your particular fascination with Mr. Castille?"

"I told you. He's a local big shot, a power player in a city where a lot of powerless people live. And he's elusive. No other news network has interviewed him, so that would be a feather in my cap. And I'd like to ask him some questions about his plans for some land he owns and how his fortune could be better used to—"

Matilda exhaled. "He was a recruit, Solange. In S.E.C.R.E.T. As I'm sure you've suspected."

I *had* suspected, but still, I tried to mask my astonishment.

"Really? And what happened?"

"Without going into great detail, he pulled some stunts that left our organization in a potentially compromised situation, both economically and in terms of our anonymity. Last year he behaved fraudulently, almost criminally, towards a candidate. So yes, we were associated with Mr. Castille. But we did not escape that association unscathed, my dear. No one does. Not even, I suspect, the Formidable Solange Faraday."

Twice in one day people close to me had called me formidable. This time, though, I saw it wasn't a compliment. This time, it was a warning, but one I tried to ignore.

"I'm not sure I quite follow. If S.E.C.R.E.T. was in financial trouble, why did your organization give away fifteen million dollars last year?"

"That was Pierre's money," Matilda said, and she went on to explain how Pierre had fraudulently purchased a painting meant to finance S.E.C.R.E.T. for several years to come. "If we'd kept that money, he'd have effectively become our benefactor. And that's exactly what he wanted—for us to be under his control. We couldn't have that."

What a shocking story this would make, filled with intrigue, sex and a tainted fifteen-million-dollar deal.

"Well, I should warn you that I *am* going to put in a request for a feature interview with him," I said. "But I'll steer clear of topics that might . . . inflame him." If there was a way to expose Pierre without inadvertently exposing anyone in S.E.C.R.E.T., especially myself, I wanted to find it.

"Putting in the request and having it granted are two different things," she said. "He's a tough man to coax into the sunlight."

Matilda downed the rest of her champagne and then shook her head as though to clear it of bad memories. Tonight's prying session was officially over.

"That's as much attention as I'd like to pay to that man. Because you, my dear, have a lot more to celebrate. Your night is just beginning, after all," she said, signaling for the bill.

Of course! I had momentarily forgotten the other purpose of our dinner—my Step Four fantasy was meant to begin from here.

"Ready?"

I glanced around the crowded sports bar. "As I'll ever be!"

Matilda dug into her purse and pulled out a set of car keys. I looked at the logo on the chain and burst out laughing.

"Are you kidding me? A *Rolls*?"

She dropped the keys into my palm.

"Rolls-Royce *Phantom*. You have the car for twenty-four hours. The GPS has been pre-programmed. Just hit 'Go' on the main menu and follow the directions."

"It's so much car! It's *too* much car!"

"It is a lot of car. We're nothing if not generous. But you'll . . . need the room."

Right. "And what am I looking for exactly?"

Matilda glanced around the restaurant and leaned a little closer to me. "You'll know," she whispered.

I thanked her and said good-bye, spinning the key chain around my index finger as I made my way to the door.

The Rolls was parked boldly right in front of Tracey's on Magazine. A few stray smokers, all men, heard me beep it open with my key chain. A long, slow whistle accompanied me as I strutted around to the driver's side to slink in, just in time to avoid the rain. I'd never be sure if that whistle was for me or the car, but it didn't matter.

Inside, the buttery leather seats and that dense smell of new-car luxury gave me a momentary high. I felt around for the windshield wiper controls and cued up the GPS system. A smooth female voice instructed me to *Please drive to the highlighted route.* I buckled up, threw the Rolls into gear and started off, my bracelet and three charms jangling with my every rotation of the upholstered wheel.

The GPS voice was relaxing, sexy. The directions took me out of the downtown core, out of the city, past the park and down towards the 90. With every rainy mile, I was putting work concerns behind me. I'd figure out some way to get at the Pierre story some other time. Tonight was for me. I wanted to say, *See, Julius? I'm not all work, no pleasure. You can have both. You can.*

I let my mind wander. Maybe I was heading to some out-of-the-way bed-and-breakfast. Or some secluded mansion near Slidell where a handsome stranger was already pouring drinks. All I knew was that the day's events, the nomination especially, had made me, well, horny, and this was a fantasy I was going to let myself enjoy. After all, wasn't this one all about *Generosity*?

The highway morphed into Pontchartrain Drive some-where over the Bayou Sauvage. If not for the driving rain, I would have enjoyed my slow build of arousal. But the weather was so bad that on a particularly steep bend I had to cut my speed in half, my visuals now down to a few yards in front of me. I started to get that "mom panic," that sense that I shouldn't be putting myself in jeopardy because there was more at stake than my life—no matter how much I wanted to accept this Step. I imagined the reports: . . . *and no one knows why local news anchor, Solange Faraday, was driving a rented Rolls-Royce on the outskirts of the city on this cold, wet night . . .*

I was on the cusp of turning around when my tires hit a bump on the road, instantly sinking the car on the front right side. I clenched the wheel and eased off the accelerator so I could steer down a gravel side road. I came to a tricky stop on the shoulder. The rain was torrential by now, but I left the headlights on and threw my trench coat over my head to check the damage. Sure enough, the front right tire was flat.

Shit, shit, sonofabitch. There goes my Step Four, I thought, collapsing back into the front seat and fishing out my phone. I punched auto-dial on my AAA number.

Nothing.

"You have *got* to be kidding!" I muttered. No cell service. I was in a dead zone.

Seconds later, things went from bad to scary when a set of headlights approached me from behind, inching closer and closer, until I could make out the front of an old, white pickup truck.

Outside my windshield it was pitch black. Behind me, the only light came from the reflection of the truck's headlights on the wet road. I heard the engine shutting off. I watched the driver's silhouette exit the truck and slam the door. It was a man. He ran in the rain towards my car. *Shit.*

I hit the button to lock my doors.

Tap tap tap.

"You okay in there?" the driver yelled through the streaming wet glass.

I couldn't make out his face, but his forearms and wrists were covered in vivid, black tattoos. The sight of them against his pale skin sent a chill up my spine.

"I'm okay!" I yelled. "Just a flat. Someone's on the way! Thank you! Bye!"

He hesitated, his torso—the only part of him I could see—turning left, right, taking in the blackness that now surrounded both of us. His head was over the top of the car. His white T-shirt was soaked through, clinging to his muscles, more tattoos apparent through the increasingly translucent material.

"Okay then, just checking!" he yelled through the window. "I just don't want to leave you out here alone. I'll go wait in my truck 'til someone gets here! No worries!"

Oh god. Will he follow me when I peel away? How far is Mandeville?

Through the rearview mirror, I watched him trot back to his truck, so wet his jeans hung low on his narrow waist. I started up my engine and blasted the heat, and was getting ready to drag the Rolls in its current state to the nearest *anything*, when I saw him struggle with his door. After a few seconds, I could see him run around to the other side, making the same full-body effort with the passenger door.

This isn't happening. Why is this happening?

He seemed to stop and think, for maybe three seconds, before running back to my car, defeated, his arms wrapped around him.

Drive away, drive away, Solange. This is how people get killed. They're stupid. They don't react fast enough.

Tap, tap, tap.

"I'm so sorry to bother you again!" he yelled. "I locked myself out of my truck!"

"Sorry to hear that!" I yelled, moving the gearstick into drive.

"Wait! Stop! Don't be scared! I'm harmless—a lover not a fighter! In fact . . . shit, *okay!* If you accept the Step, I might not catch pneumonia!"

Relief flooded my body and I fell back into my seat, the engine still running.

"I'm supposed to ask you later," he yelled, "but I think I'm freaking you out. I'm not a threat, I swear! So can I—?"

"Of course! Yes! Come in!" I yelled, unlocking the doors.

He hopped around the front of the car to the passenger side, opened the door and plopped down next to me, sending a spray of water in my direction.

"I'm such an idiot," he said, grinning. "I can't believe I locked my keys in my truck! With my coat inside. And no cell service. And it's *fucking* cold out." He placed his open palms directly on the dashboard heat vents. "Every fantasy, I fuck something up."

The rain was finally letting up a bit.

"Well?" he said, rubbing his hands furiously.

"Well what?"

"The Step . . . do you accept it? I know I probably don't look too savory, so if you're reconsidering, I'd totally understand."

He was wrong about that. I was not reconsidering. I had noticed the way his jeans draped around his lean hips, and how his wet shirt clung to a well-formed torso covered in tattoos. Not my type, normally, but there was something so damn sweet about this guy. And he was funny. Whoever really loved him was in a lot of trouble.

I could hear his teeth chattering. "You're really cold."

"Yes, ma'am."

"Okay. I accept the Step, at the very least to help you get warm."

"Thank fucking god. Whooo. Okay. Crank that heat higher. I need to get my circulation going before I lay my hands on you."

Alrighty then.

"This was supposed to be a lot sexier. There was this whole gas station seduction thing that was supposed to happen. GPS lady was about to warn you that you were on empty, right——?"

I looked at the gas gauge and sure enough it was on empty.

"And when you pulled up to the gas station up near Mandeville and noticed that your *wallet* was missing, I was going to offer to pay and . . ."

"My wallet?"

"Don't worry. Matilda has your wallet. She took it at the restaurant. And you're not on empty. I messed around with the gauge. But then the fucking tire blew. And that wasn't in the plans! Speaking of which——pop the trunk," he said, suddenly turning efficient. "You have a coat?"

He opened the glove compartment while I fished in the back seat for my trench.

"*Yesss!*" he exclaimed. "In the history of the fucking world, this might be the first time a pair of gloves is actually found *in* the glove compartment. Sit here, sweetheart. When I'm done with that tire, I'm gonna start in on you. Trust me. This fantasy ain't over."

He was *adorable*. It took him less than ten minutes to change the tire, and he insisted I stay warm in the car. When he finished, he found Handi Wipes under the front seat and scrubbed his fingers before rubbing his hands vigorously in front of the vents again.

"Done. Drive. I'm your GPS now, darlin'. Just go slow. I need to warm up more."

I threw the car into drive and peeled away from the shoulder. He leaned towards me again, his hand heading straight for my knee. I shuddered, not from repulsion, but from the chill. Poor guy! He began firmly rubbing his hand up and down my inner thighs, stealing heat for himself and creating it for me.

"You are hot in many, many ways," he murmured.

Next, his fingers found the edge of my underwear, and I gasped. He stopped, waiting for a sign from me, his mouth at my ear. I squirmed, wordlessly shifting so he could inch his fingers under the elastic.

Yes.

"Ever wonder what it would be like to have an orgasm while going sixty-five miles per hour?" he whispered.

"Is that even possible?"

"Anything's possible in this car. With me."

He reached down between my legs and pushed my seat back a few more inches, though I could still reach the gas, the brakes. My back pressed against the warm seat, I felt his fingers trace my grooves, already damp from anticipation. I let out an involuntary sigh, wanting to close my eyes, but I had to keep them on the road.

"Now kick off that pump," he whispered, "and bend your left knee against the door."

I released my left foot from my shoe and raised my knee, my skirt rolling up my thigh towards my waist. He bent his head down until it was practically resting in my lap. He kissed my inner left thigh as his fingers tugged my panties aside. His head dropped lower, and I laid one hand on his damp hair. For a brief second, I felt his breath on my clit as his tongue teased it. The rain, which had been pelting sideways on the blackened road, had subsided. My whole body throbbed as the tip of his tongue did a little dance, and his fingers gently prodded, sliding in and out *while I was driving!* I concentrated on the road ahead, cracking my window to stay alert. He lapped at me and finger fucked me at the same time. I had never felt such a delicious rush: the adrenaline from the speed, and this man's face in my lap, his tongue lashing me as the dark night whipped past us.

On a wide bend, he stopped and tilted his face up. "Turn down the next side road and go faster," he said, his fingers pressing deep into me as he brought his mouth down to dazzle me some more. The reflection from the dashboard played across his hair; I wanted this delicious man inside of me, and I wanted him now. The headlights illuminated a crossroads, and I signaled to no one my turn down a darkened, tree-lined road, gravel spattering against the bottom of the car. I momentarily panicked about divots and scratches, but shook away those thoughts as I turned up the volume on a sexy jazz station.

"I want more of you," he whispered.

He yanked himself away from me, then wrestled, arched and bent as he began the difficult and near-comical task of removing wet jeans from his cold legs and pulling on a condom. He sounded like a man fighting another man in a phone booth. And yet, the more clothes he removed, the more aroused I became, such a revelation for me. Maybe I was more prone to being visually aroused than I thought.

He felt around for my right hand and placed it on his cool chest.

"Pull over. Kill the dash lights, Solange. I'm going to need you to warm my whole fucking body up," he said, adjusting his seat back.

I slammed on the brakes and skidded to the shoulder of the empty road. Throwing the car into park, I cut the dash lights but left the engine running for the heat. My hand traveled over his stomach, his erection meeting my palm. This man was blessed. Or I was.

He perched a condom on the head and I unraveled it down his thick shaft, warming it as I went. He thrust up and into my touch, groaning in pleasure. I looked out the front window. The road was dark and empty, not a light for miles. His hands were behind his head and he was taking this in.

"Get your panties off," he ordered. "I'm so fucking hard for you."

As I frantically yanked them down and pulled my skirt up around my waist, all I could think was: *What is happening to me? This bratty stranger gets in my car and goes down on me while I'm driving, and now I can't get him inside me fast enough?*

I was incredibly wet by the time I rolled over the middle console, my chest pressed against his, my head gracing the ceiling despite the fact that he'd pushed his seat back almost ninety degrees. He cupped me, letting one finger release more slickness. I looked down and watched him part me, the tip of his cock kissing, dipping up into me as my knees dug into the sides of the seats. I sunk onto him and *oh how exquisite he felt*, his fists at my hips. I gripped and tightened around him as he filled me up.

His hand at the back of my head, he took my hair in a fist and pulled my mouth down to his. He kissed me roundly, beautifully, as he thrust up into me, gently at first, his muscles undulating beneath me. But then he turned into a machine, hips gyrating, abs flexing and pumping, my knees now up alongside this torso, fucking up into me, my hands traveling to the car's roof to stop my head from hitting it.

With both hands he unbuttoned my blouse and released my bra, so my breasts were loose under the lacy cups. He gathered them in his hands, a tangle now of fingers and breasts and lace and such beautiful fucking, shallow then deep, then deeper still. His mouth found a nipple and he sucked, locking his eyes on mine. Slick pleasure shot through me. He pressed a hand between my breasts, up my throat, encircling my neck. His other forearm gripped my lower back, pulling me to him. His thrusts grew more urgent; the groans came quicker. He was close and I was going to surpass him, my orgasm now a tight ball, my throbbing clit its very center; I could feel it nearing. I pressed the roof of the Rolls with my hands, fucking him back down onto the leather seat, taking my pleasure from his cock until I couldn't stop it anymore. I came loudly into the dark night, the windows steamed and dripping with the sweat of our combined heat.

"Oh god," I screamed.

"Fuck yeah," he said, his hips moving faster. He came, too, his fingertips marking my flesh with every pulse of his cock as it emptied into me, sliding in and out, and in, and then out, as he subsided.

"Holy Mother of Mary," he said, breathless, his voice an octave lower.

"You could say that," I murmured, easing up and off him. I rolled back onto my seat, tugging my skirt down half-heartedly. I lay there splayed, reveling in that feeling of being utterly disheveled by an excellent fuck. I didn't care that my flesh was exposed, my breasts peeking out of my loosened bra and unbuttoned blouse. I needed to catch my breath.

"Well, that was . . . I'm very . . ." I couldn't finish my sentence.

Minutes later, bra clasped, blouse buttoned, skirt smoothed out, I patted down my hair and cleaned up a bit of the eyeliner that had drifted in our sweaty tussle. I started up the Rolls and threw it into drive, turning back down the highway where we'd left his truck.

"Should we call a tow truck to unlock your door?" I asked. "Happy to wait with you until it gets here."

"That's very generous of you," he said, pulling on his jeans and reaching into his pocket for a set of keys. "But I'm good."

"So that was all . . ."

"Yeah, it was a sympathy play."

I smacked his arm.

"I was desperate! Oh—this is for you," he said, pulling out my Step Four charm from the same pocket. He held it in front of me, pinched between his thumb and forefinger: *Generosity.*

"Thank you," I said, feeling a little undeserving. "I sure didn't start out feeling all that generous towards you. You really scared the shit out of me."

"Yeah, but you eventually came around."

"I have a feeling most women do. You have that thing."

"And what *thing* is that?" he asked, turning to face me.

"That thing that makes women want to give . . . and give."

"Oh, if only that were true. But right now *I'm* still doing the giving."

He took my right wrist in his hands and in the dark of the car, while the gold glinted in the glow of passing headlights, he secured my new charm to my bracelet.

CASSIE

was true to my resolution. I became a woman about my work, throwing myself into the task of owning and operating a restaurant with the same delight and fervor I saw Tracina throw into being a new mom and Dell throw into running the kitchen. I didn't have much time for Jesse, and I had nothing beyond professional chatter for Will.

But resolutions are made to be broken. And when I stopped by the Coach House just before Mardi Gras to talk to Matilda about a possible S.E.C.R.E.T. assignment that I'd been putting off, a peek at the fantasy board confirmed that Jesse had played more than just a passing part in Solange's most recent adventure. There it was, a Step Four *Generosity* card with Jesse's name on it, "Completed" stamped across it in vivid red.

I had to steady myself against the table.

"Cassie?" Matilda's eyes darted from me to the board and back to me. "Why don't we go to my office for a chat, shall we?"

Sulkily, I followed her. As we passed Danica, Matilda asked her to bring us coffee—and just like that, I was all about a guy again.

I wanted to know everything: what they did, where they went. But one look at Matilda's face and I knew she wasn't about to divulge details. Committee members weren't kept informed of fantasies they weren't working on directly. This ensured anonymity and greater privacy. And Matilda had a zero-tolerance policy on gossip. I shook my head. *You are a woman about your work. S.E.C.R.E.T. is part of that. Get over it. Fast.*

"You saw the board?"

"Yes," I said. *Here it comes. A lecture about not getting emotionally involved with Jesse, about dating in S.E.C.R.E.T. and sparking complicated feelings of jealousy and possession and blah, blah, blah . . .*

Danica popped in with our coffees.

"Thank you, my dear," Matilda said, easing mine in front of me. "So you saw that we're planning Solange's Step Seven fantasy already. We decided we'd try Ewan, Dominic's friend. The one you recruited last year?"

Ewan was the sexy redhead I'd seen playing pickup soccer with one of Matilda's recruits. I couldn't resist his bratty smile, so when I asked for Dominic's number, I was thrilled when Ewan threw his in too. Okay, so she either wasn't going to bring up Jesse's Step with Solange, or she didn't think I had seen it.

"But wasn't Ewan rejected?"

"He was rejected by last year's Committee. But his sole naysayer has retired, and with you on board this year we'd have unanimity. Now, Step Seven, as you know, involves something a candidate's curious about. Turns out Solange is curious about trying something that I think might also intrigue you."

"Oh?"

When Matilda said the word, I nearly spat my coffee across her desk.

"A *threesome?*" I sputtered. "Why *me?*"

"You brought Ewan in."

"But I've never done . . . *that* before."

"Precisely why you're perfect for this. Neither has Solange. And Ewan has to learn not only how to participate in a threesome but how to make a sexual neophyte—in this case, you—comfortable with a new situation. Remember: all your fears will be Solange's fears, your reluctance much like hers. You'd be Solange's sexual stand-in for Ewan's training. Now you and Pauline don't necessarily have to do anything together, or to each other, unless you want to. The focus is on what the man does to and for both of you."

"Pauline would be the third?" Okay, this was getting freakier!

"Yes. This is her specialty. Sorry. I probably should have told you that first."

"Does Pauline know you're asking me?"

"She suggested you. But you should sleep on this decision. It's a few fantasies away still. So don't feel any pressure, Cassie. It's all in fun."

"Right. Of course. Fun."

I slept on it. Next to Jesse. At his place.

In the morning, after a quick tussle, my head in the crook of his arm, I began to prod. It could not be helped. It was like my brain and mouth had been hijacked by the old pre-S.E.C.R.E.T. Cassie.

"So you did it!" I said, acting all celebratory.

"Did what?" he asked groggily.

"Solange. Her fantasy. I saw your name scratched out on the board."

He didn't speak.

"I guess that was it, then, your last kick at the can," I continued. "After all, Solange is the last S.E.C.R.E.T. candidate for a while, anyhow."

"Huh. I suppose you're right," he said, stretching dramatically.

"Hope you went out with a bang, so to speak."

I immediately regretted my stupid joke. Without responding, Jesse hoisted himself off his bed.

"Come on, Cass, I'll drive you to work. I gotta be in early. We have a four-tiered wedding cake to build for tonight."

I didn't budge. Fists on hips, Jesse just looked at me tangled in his sheets.

"Don't, Cassie. I don't ask *you* for details."

"If you did, I'd tell you."

"I don't want to know."

"Why? Because you'd be jealous, or because you don't really care?"

What is wrong with me?

He waited a beat and then he said something that stung me to the core. "You're regressing."

While he shuffled off to shower, I got up and padded around for my phone. Still wincing from his comment, I texted Matilda.

Happy to take part with Pauline. Am curious too.

After he'd showered, Jesse dropped me off at work with a tender kiss that I had a hard time returning. When he said he'd call me later, I muttered something about being busy and that I'd call him.

"Cool beans," he said.

"What does that even mean?"

"I am not going to get into it with you. Go."

~~~~~

Dell was already in the kitchen, her recipe folders out. This was our routine every Tuesday morning. We sat side by side on benches next to the pastry table to tweak and assess which plates from the week before were hits and which were met with tepid approval. Then we adjusted the special menu and coming inventory accordingly. Why bother buying thirty Cornish hens if no one ate them?

"People loved the Bordelaise shrimp spaghetti last night," she said, as I pulled up a stool next to her. She didn't even bother with "hello."

Now this was a woman who was all about her work.

"Eggplant fritters were good too," she added.

"Yeah, more of those," I replied, making dramatic checkmarks. I had to shake this mood. "Let's not press the frogs' legs."

"Let me try them with my gran's jerk rub."

"Okay, yeah. But not this week. And maybe bones out next time."

We went through the salads carefully, since produce was expensive in February and Mardi Gras week demanded crowd-friendly fare.

We were concentrating so hard I barely noticed Claire crossing the kitchen to head out back for a cigarette, alarming for two reasons: I thought she had quit smoking, and she seemed to be in a zombie trance.

"She's a moody little thing," Dell said.

"She's a teenager. They're all moody little things. You still are," I said.

Since the restaurant opened, I'd been spending less time with Claire, which might be why I hadn't noticed her gradual drop in energy, or that dark cloud that now followed her everywhere. I grabbed a cardigan hanging on a hook and threw it around my shoulders to follow Claire out back. I found her blowing smoke through the fence.

"Brrr, it better warm up before the parades or I'm skipping them."

"I know, I know. I'll wash my hands after my cigarette," she said, not looking at me.

"I know you will. What's going on? You seem down." I sounded like the guidance counselor in an after-school special.

She turned to face me. It's funny how you can look at someone without really seeing them. This time I saw her face pulled gaunt and made shadowy from bad sleep. She looked older, haunted. She could have passed for a preoccupied thirty-year-old mom. Maybe she was pregnant!

"Can I leave a little early today, Cass? Maureen can close the Café on her own," she said, her voice quavering.

I noticed orange and yellow stains on her fingers, the chain-smoker's affliction. It wasn't just sadness in her eyes; there was something else too. Something like terror.

"What is going on, Claire? Spit it out."

"Forget it," she said, tossing the cigarette and storming past me.

I grabbed her upper arm, which was thin and startlingly cold to the touch. I wouldn't let go.

"Stop. Okay? I need you to tell me what's going on. Is it school? Olivia? What?"

"Just some kids at school. It's nothing."

"What are they doing now?"

She looked around the vacant back alley as if half expecting her tormentors to be hiding here.

"They're making my life a living *hell*," she said, bursting into tears.

She was a toughie, a dreadlocked, tattooed teen swaggerer who beneath it all was just a deeply sad little girl. I threw an arm around her and let her cry. I knew what it was to be bullied and to feel small. When I was her age, if my sister Lila wasn't picking on me at home, there were a pack of mean girls whose sole job on the planet seemed to be to find my most tender spot and push against it until it bruised.

"Hey, hey, hey," I said as her sobs subsided. "Is this about that whole Ben thing?"

"Yeah," she said, looking astonished that I remembered the name of a guy she'd been spending time with. "I thought it was over. But they're fucking harassing me."

"Who is?"

"All of them. The girls. Olivia . . . the others. Her friends, who used to be my friends. Ben showed them a picture. It was meant . . . just for him. God! I was the nothing girl, then I was the new girl. Now I'm the dirty fucking whore."

I winced as she recounted how the girls had posted this picture online. It involved, I assumed, some nudity. That was followed by taunting posts labeling Claire a filthy slut and whore, asking her to move back to Slidell where she belonged. I would have thought a creative arts school would be populated by more progressive, open-minded kids, but it seemed the cruelty of youth knew no bounds.

"Have you told your uncle?"

"Right, so he can go talk to their parents and embarrass the shit out of me and make things even worse? If he knew how bad it was, he'd tell my dad and my dad would make me move back to Slidell, and I don't want to. I love it here. I love living with Uncle Will and working here with you guys. I don't want to go back to the boonies. I wanna stay here. Dell's teaching me stuff." Her body vibrated like a little bird's.

"What can I do? How can I help you?"

She started sobbing anew, her head bowed forward, the weight of her dreads pulling it low. Dell poked her head out back, ignoring the sadness coming off our little scene.

"Meat delivery's here. They want a check," Dell said, eyeing Claire with concern.

"Okay. Be right there."

I turned back to Claire and placed both my hands on her arms, centering her in front of me so she would listen clearly.

"Go home, Claire. We'll figure this out. But you have to tell your uncle Will."

"I can't."

"Then let me talk to him tomorrow when he comes in. What's being done and said about you, we have to find a way to let these girls know they can't do that. It's the only way."

She nodded, her mouth and nose now covered by her apron. I wanted to fold her up and put her in my pocket forever. I wanted to protect her from the world's cruelty. Instead, I kissed her on the temple and went back inside, leaving her alone to smoke another cigarette and pull herself together. I had never wanted kids of my own, yet mothering this one seemed to come to me so easily and felt so good.

Later that night, mid-shift, after carting up plates for busy waiters who were in the weeds and stirring sauces while Dell plated some beautiful langoustines, I had a moment of clarity. I used to let people bully me, too, for years. I never believed that I had a say or a voice. I thought bullying was something to be tolerated, first from my sad, repressed family, then from my drunk of a husband. But I got over that kind of thinking and Claire would too. I had found a purpose and a meaning in my life, and I could help her find that too. She would come to see that life was bigger and brighter than the shit she was going through in high school. If I couldn't stop the bullying she was being subjected to, at least I would help her see that things could get better later. She had to believe a better world was waiting for her.

At the end of our busiest, craziest shift yet, Dell and I perched on bar stools, brandy snifters in hand, panting a little at what we'd accomplished.

"I think that was the best night we've had," I said, clinking her glass. "And it's not even Mardi Gras."

"When you dropped that beautiful langoustine—I know you were thinking about wiping it on your apron and putting it back on that plate."

"I was *not!* I would *never* do that, Dell!"

She gave me a sidelong look and we both burst out laughing.

"I did almost do that. I panicked!"

"You did great tonight, Cassie. A real *restaurateur*," she said, exaggerating the Frenchness of the word.

I almost cried.

My phone vibrated in my pocket. When I saw it was a text from Will, my heart leapt from my rib cage. I wished

L . MARIE ADELINE

he had been there that night, had seen me handling everything so calmly and competently.

He wrote: *You still at work?*

Oh dear. What was this? A booty call?

I am. We had a great night tonight! Best yet. What's up?

I stared at the screen, heart racing, waiting for a reply. The phone rang instead. It was him.

"Cassie," Will said, not sounding like Will. "I'm at the hospital. Can you come? It's Claire. Something happened."

SOLANGE

I was always happy when Mardi Gras was over, though one never said that out loud in New Orleans. There were a few of us closeted haters, Marsha being the only one in the newsroom who was out and proud of her disdain.

"Mardi Gras gives me a month-long ice cream headache of the soul," she said, checking her teeth for parsley. We often ate lunch in her corner office, mostly to avoid listening to Bill Rink bleat on and on about his post-divorce sex life.

Mardi Gras meant more stories to report on, most of them nasty, most happening after midnight, at the tail end of our twelve-hour days. That's why, for the first time, Matilda sent my Step Five card to work instead of home. The courier found me in Marsha's office. As I signed for the thick envelope, I felt my face redden.

"Did you win the Publishers Clearing House sweepstakes?" Marsha asked.

"With my luck it's probably a subpoena," I said, ducking out to avoid giving a straight answer.

Behind the closed door of my office, I opened the envelope. Inside was a sturdy card inviting me to the "Mansion after Dark." There was also a heavy glove box wrapped in silver paper with a black bow. It wasn't a pair of gloves inside, but rather a set of brushed silver *handcuffs*. *Holy shit.* Looking through the glass at the bustling newsroom, I discreetly shoved the box onto my lap. Keeping my head down, I poked through the tissue to better examine the cuffs. My assistant, Denise, stuck her head through my door and I dropped the cuffs on the carpet beneath me like they were on fire. Luckily my desk hid whatever it was that made that metallic thud.

"Hey, Solange. I'm taking the FedEx packages downstairs. Do you have anything that has to go out today?" she asked, her curious eyes following the clanking noise under my desk.

I had hired her because I thought she seemed like a younger version of me—a driven workaholic. Turned out, she only looked the part. She was all about "work–life balance," something I hadn't even heard of when I was her age.

"No thanks," I said.

She eyed the silver wrapping paper on my desk. "Did someone send you a gift?" she asked.

Yes, in fact, it's a gift of silver handcuffs, Denise, what every girl wants!

I blinked at her, giving her a tight smile. "I have a lot of work to do. Can you close my door on your way out?"

Denise got the message, backing out of my office and shutting the door quietly behind her.

Two thoughts came to me in the limousine on the way to the Mansion later that night. One, other divorced women with children never told me that there was a plus side to heartbreak and divorce—free time! It was almost like they didn't want to admit that splitting custody was an opportunity to regain a little bit of long-lost autonomy. I almost didn't want to admit it myself. Of course there was that pang tonight, when Gus trotted over to his dad's idling Jeep, his backpack bigger than his torso. But once I waved and shut the door, there was also that sense of space and possibility. *I can do anything I want tonight.* For years, I rarely took advantage of that. I loved Gus's company, I really did. Especially after he turned eight and his personality began to reveal itself. He was such a nice kid, and smart to boot; fun to hang out with. But when he wasn't with me, I spent a lot of my free time worrying about him and what he was doing without me, afraid to turn off my phone, or to really relax and enjoy myself.

But these last few months with S.E.C.R.E.T., I had begun to allow myself the gift of autonomy, to savor and enjoy this strange and lovely experience. I leaned back into the warm leather of the limo's seat, heading to the "Mansion after Dark" and thinking of all the alluring adventures that awaited me there. New Orleans at night sped past the tinted windows, giving the shops along Magazine Street a sexy glow. The limo rounded left on

Third. My stomach rolled at every stop sign until we pulled into the gates of the Mansion, its windows aglow with a pale orange light.

A uniformed woman stood at the base of the stairs holding what looked like a white shawl over one arm. She greeted me when I stepped out of the car.

"You must be our Solange. I'm Claudette." She shook my hand, then motioned to take my coat and purse. "Right this way, my dear."

It occurred to me: my phone! It was in my purse and I'd just given it away. My phone connected me to my child, and to my job.

"Can I keep my purse? It's just . . . my phone's in it. Also the . . . *handcuffs*," I added, lowering my voice.

"Leave your phone on. If there is any reason to interrupt you, we will not hesitate. You won't need anything else in that purse. I'll take good care of it."

"The handcuffs?"

"Purely symbolic."

I followed her into the spectacular foyer. The whole house was lit by dim sconces that trailed along a hallway to the left and up the wall of the ornate spiral staircase. The place was gorgeous, the black and white tiles forming a spiral on the foyer floor that swirled around a trio of Botticelli-like female forms standing under a willow tree— one was white, one brown, one black, and all were naked. The whole place seemed coated in a layer of French design that felt both historical and right up to date.

"Follow me," Claudette said, turning to climb the impressive staircase.

I gripped the gold banister tighter than I'd held anything in my life. She brought me to the second door on the right and handed me what she'd been holding, which wasn't a shawl at all but a pretty white cotton shift dress.

"Here you go. Please remove all your clothes and put this on. Wait on the bed and you'll be summoned."

Summoned? Ew. I did not like that word. I was not going to be very good at this, I decided, as I stepped into the small, plain bedroom painted the palest of blues and minimally decorated. It had the feel of a high-end hospital room. I took off my jeans, carefully unbuttoned and removed my blouse, and folded both on the bed. Socks, undies, bra were also folded and stowed. The cotton shift was simple, flimsy, with a small lace fringe along the hem. But I . . . *obeyed* (ew), letting it cascade over my body, until it ended just at the tops of my thighs.

Sitting on the edge of the oversize twin bed, my legs swinging over the side, I could hear a loud clock ticking but I couldn't see one on the walls. The room was furnished with a tall, plain dresser between two white doors, blue damask curtains and a round, multicolored rope rug on a wooden floor painted white. Bored, I leapt to my feet and walked over to the dresser. Should I? I was an inveterate snoop. *That makes me a good journalist,* I justified, wrapping my fingers around the handle of the top drawer and gently tugging it open.

"Don't open that drawer, Solange."

I gasped. It was a calm male voice, deep and soothing, coming from some corner of the room.

"Who is that?"

There didn't seem to be a place for a person to hide except maybe under the bed or behind one of the two white doors.

"Never mind that," the voice said. "There's only one question to be concerned with."

He sounded like a late-night radio DJ who played only slow R and B, a voice that was commanding yet a bit bemused.

"The question is: Do you accept the Step, Solange?"

"How can I accept if I can't see you?"

My expert eyes scanned the room looking for the camera or the speaker system. Nothing. Just silence.

"Are you still there?" I asked. Whenever I was nervous or afraid, my default setting was defiance. But this time was a little different. I decided to be . . . deferential, for a change.

"I'm sorry. Can you ask me that question again?"

Silence.

"Please?" I added.

The voice crackled to life. "Solange, will you accept the Step?"

Relent. Relent. Relent. I was here to experience new things. Hadn't I enjoyed every Step so far? Why dig my heels in now?

"I do."

"Excellent. Will it be pain or pleasure, Solange?"

Oh dear. Second thoughts crept in.

"What do you mean?"

"Which do you prefer? Pain or pleasure?"

My eyes didn't know where to look: the walls, the doors, the bed, the dresser, the floor, the ceiling.

"I . . . pleasure, I guess," I said, fear shoving me to the safe zone again.

"Then I want you to step through the white door."

I looked at both doors carefully. "They're both white."

There was no answer.

"Tell me which door!"

Still no reply.

"Are you there?"

Nothing. The clock ticked louder, or maybe my heart's rapid beat enhanced the sound. I looked back and forth between the two white doors. What if I picked the wrong door? I wanted to hear his voice again. *Fuck it. Just pick a door. This isn't Trivial Pursuit. There can't be a wrong choice.*

I chose the door to my left, the one nearest the windows. I turned the knob and pushed it open. The room inside was inky black, the air dead still. The light from the room I was standing in only illuminated the edge of an oriental rug covering a beautifully scuffed wood floor. I felt around for a wall switch, and that's when a gloved hand encircled my wrist and yanked me inside, shutting the door behind me.

The darkness engulfed me. I screamed. Another gloved hand gently went over my mouth. I was pulled back against a fully clothed man, taller than me by a head.

"Shh. Solange. You'll wake the neighbors."

It was *him*, the bearer of the same mellow voice I had heard over the intercom, his mouth now inches from my ear.

"You fucking *scared* me!" I shouted through his fingers.

"Shh. It's okay. You're safe. You're very safe," he said, keeping my mouth covered. He kept saying it as he walked me deeper into that room, my upper body restrained by his strong arms, my legs prompted by each of his legs.

"If I let you go, do you promise not to scream?"

I nodded, intrigue beginning to replace fear. His hand fell away from my mouth and he released me.

I took a deep breath. "Where am I?" I asked, my hands drifting up and feeling around.

"You're in the Den."

I could hear him circling me. I tried to follow his footsteps but I couldn't make out a thing.

"I can't see anything."

"You don't need to. You need only to feel. Can you trust me? Can you let me be your eyes?"

"I'll try."

"Good."

I wrapped my arms around myself.

"Are you cold?"

Could he see me? How? "No. I'm nervous."

"I'll take care of that."

After a few seconds, he was behind me again.

"I'm going to place my hands around your waist, Solange, and I'm going to guide you over to the wall. Will you let me?"

"Okay."

It was the strangest, warmest sensation, being surrounded by pitch-darkness, his lean body folding around
mine; it was like being spooned while standing. I quickly
absorbed his body heat as he guided me across what seemed
from the echo to be a large room.

Then he stopped. "Put your hands out in front of you.
What do you feel?"

At first I thought it was just a wall, but padding around
I felt a sort of diagonal beam, which crossed another shoot-
ing up in the opposite direction. Along the beams I felt an
apparatus of some kind—hoops—soft but firmly formed.

"Can you find the center?" he asked. "Here. Let me
help you."

He took me by the waist again, spinning me around to
face him, positioning me against the cross of the two
beams. By now I was comfortable with his hands on my
waist. I liked the firm and confident way he handled me,
even though I hated the term itself: *Handled. Man-handled.*
The term was demeaning, and yet what this man was doing
wasn't demeaning at all. It was . . . relaxing. He took one of
my wrists and with a swift *click*, locked it in place above my
shoulder along the beam.

"Hey, what is this——?"

But before I could get the whole sentence out, he
secured my other wrist. I felt his hair gracing my thigh as
he bent to do the same to my right ankle. Then the left
one was immobilized. The final restraint was an arm-like

lever covered in a soft rubber sheath that clicked into place around my waist.

"Are you comfortable, Solange?"

I was completely restrained on a diagonal cross with padded limbs.

"I guess. But I can't move."

"Good."

"What are you going to do to me?"

"Everything you want, nothing you don't."

I squirmed, arousal spiraling up my limbs.

"Are the restraints too tight?"

I tested and pulled, still astonished to be in this situation, restrained in a contraption wearing what amounted to a lacy nightie, while a total stranger with a soothingly sexy voice was clearly in charge.

"I think they're okay. What is this thing I'm on?"

"It's called a Saint Andrew's Cross. It allows . . . access. We can stop anytime you want. Just say the word. I suggest simply 'Stop.' Say it."

"Stop."

"Say it louder."

I yelled it out.

"Good."

I felt his hand under my chin and then his fist blossom open as his thumb trailed along my bottom lip. I opened my mouth slightly, loosening, releasing. His other hand traveled over my breasts, caressing my nipples through the thin fabric. Both hands traveled down my sides, over the restraint. Instinctively, I brought my legs together as his hands drifted closer and closer to my most vulnerable parts. But I couldn't budge. This was both very frustrating and very, very arousing. I tried to use my arms, to no avail. This feeling of being completely restrained yet totally free, and blind to what was happening or what was going to happen, was crazy. My body didn't know what to do with the sensations, except bit by bit to give in to them, to all of them.

As he lifted the hem of the nightie, I writhed against the restraints. My breathing quickened. I felt his hair tickle my shoulder, his lips barely touching me as he made his way softly, achingly, lower and lower, his thumbs pressing my skin. I felt his tongue now circling my belly button, the tip dipping in, traveling lower still, his mouth following his firm fingers, which were now pressing back my folds, testing my wetness, at first tentatively, and then driving into me. He began the delicious task of firmly thrusting into me with his thick finger, while kissing along my inner thigh seam, blowing cool air against the incredible wetness he was creating. My knees bowed in, pushing against the restraints, my full weight on the one around my waist, my wrists pulling in.

This was *crazy*. I couldn't help him, I couldn't guide him, I couldn't press against him or wriggle away. I could only take it in, accept it, the sensation of his mouth on my clitoris. It was all I could do not to explode on contact. But I wanted to hold something back. His mouth was humming and moaning, while his fingers continued their exploration of my tender insides, finding the perfect friction, the perfect rhythm, the perfect combination of pain and pleasure, all the action focused on that one damn spot, while the rest of my body was pinned and spread.

"Oh!" I felt a shot of pleasure. Arching, I pressed against the restraints, seeking more, and he gave it, his tongue dipping into me, while his fingers worked their magic.

"Solange," he murmured, purring my name, his finger fucking me, his tongue working me into a frenzy, and I couldn't hold back anymore. With every thrust and lash of his tongue, he brought me closer and closer. He pulled the orgasm out of my very core, my cries beginning as whimpers, building to moans, until I was pressing against all the restraints yelling, "Oh yes, yesss!" And I came with full explosive release—so fast I felt like a teenager.

I came so intensely into the dark, black room that pleasure seemed to pour out of my very bones. He had turned me into a wall of wet ecstasy, taking away all my knowledge of where he began and I ended. While I was barely coming down off that blind precipice, a small motor whirred alive and I had the lovely sensation of falling gently backwards.

"Relax, Solange, I'm reclining you."

Inch by inch, the blood flooded back into my fists as the momentum of the cross brought me from standing to lying back. I was not fully prone but it relieved my wrists nonetheless.

"Are your hands okay?"

I whispered, "Yes."

"Good, because I'm going to fuck you now—is that all right with you?"

I muttered another "yes," my head lolling against my upper arm for support. He split my legs open wider and maneuvered his body between them. He released my ankles, bending my knees and spreading them wide. I felt the restraints weighing them open, this time secured around my bent knees, as though I was now trussed open for his pleasure. I heard a belt, a buckle, the thud of shoes, the swish of discarded pants, the crinkle of foil, the sweet prodding and then the luscious fullness as he entered me, tentatively at first, until he sensed how wet I was, how well he had prepared me for this. His thrusts were agonizing at first, long and slow, in and out, and then he set about fucking me faster, hard and steady, his fingers clutching the restraints. This was intense, the angle of the table, the way he pulled my thighs wide, how he thrust so deep he was hitting me in places that I had thought unreachable. I was all sensation, from the center of myself out. I felt another orgasm spiraling, coming from god knows where, but it felt deep and visceral and I cried out again, scream-ing, "Oh, oh, it's happening, oh god, yes . . ." and I came again, feeling him shudder too, his fingers digging into the flesh of my thighs as he released into me, the intensity of his thrusts softening as his own orgasm ebbed.

Then, with a few deft clicks he released my wrists, my thighs and me, leaving me panting in the dark, my arms and legs still starfished out, barely able to believe the sensations cascading through my limbs. That rush of relief when the restraints were loosened—it made me laugh, *laugh*, the way you laugh when you see mountains or the ocean for the first time. The way you can laugh at something you were once afraid of when you realize it can't hurt you, when you realize it never could.

The first thing I did, after securing my Step Five charm—*Fearlessness*—to my increasingly crowded little bracelet, was to take a bottle of water from the little fridge in the limo. I was parched, sore, spent and glowing. Checking my phone was the *second* thing I did.

That was progress.

A text from Julius popped up on the screen, and during the seconds before I read it, a cascade of awful scenarios crossed my mind. This time I stopped them and just read the damn text. And guess what? Nothing horrible had happened! Nobody was at the hospital. Nobody was hurt. Quite the opposite! Julius had actually scheduled Gus's yearly checkup with the pediatrician, something I usually did. The appointment was for the following Thursday afternoon. Julius wanted to know if I could make it.

For sure. And thanks for organizing that, I replied.

The second text was from Denise at the news desk.

Pierre Castille's office called. He declined the request for an interview. Sry.

Damn.

Thanks for letting me know, Denise, I wrote back.

I wanted to add: *Would it kill you to type out* sorry *instead of* sry? Seriously. Or as Denise would write: *srsly.* Then I laughed out loud. No sooner had the restraints come off than I reverted to my strident self. Damn.

Seconds later, my phone dinged.

No worries, the text read.

I thought it was from Denise, but it was Julius. *Julius?* I noted the time: 12:30 a.m. Uh-oh. My heart skipped.

What are you still doing up? Everything ok with Gus?

All good. Doing payroll. What are YOU still doing up?

I'm in the back of a limo, with sore wrists and ankles from the restraints used to tie me up against a wall, where an unseen stranger fucked me silly . . . Ha!

I typed, *Can't sleep.*

Me neither.

The joys of parenthood.

Truth.

Try counting sheep.

That doesn't work.

Read a book? Maybe one of Gus's?

One with sheep in it?

Exactly.

Stop! I shoved the phone into my purse. Too weird— texting my ex-husband after a sex fantasy. Especially *that* sex fantasy. I had submitted to an unseen stranger simply because he was confident and persistent.

I thought of Pierre Castille. The word *no* was anathema to me; I hated being rejected. It suddenly felt paramount to get that man to submit to me. And there was only one other person who could help. I took my phone back out and texted Matilda, requesting a coffee and a catch-up. Soon.

CASSIE

W ill had forgotten he even had the sleeping pills. In fact, they'd expired, but they were nonetheless potent enough to put Claire into a brief coma. And though she didn't take all of them and admitted later it was just a cry for help, it was a cry we all heard loud and clear.

After she left the hospital, Claire was away from school and work for the rest of the month of February. The first week she spent with her folks back in Slidell, during which she permitted Will and me to log in to her social media accounts to see what she'd been dealing with, and to gather evidence, for what, we didn't know yet.

"Holy shit," Will muttered, scrolling down her pages, the light from the computer illuminating both our faces.

The comments came from several young women who flung words like "ho," "hoebag," "whore," "bitch," "cunt" (even "cum rag," which I thought was "scumbag" spelled wrong, until I really read it). Up and down her wall, the abuse poured, under her pictures, and in reply to every post.

"Look at all this hate," I said. "Poor kid."

Some of the posts listed ways in which the people posting were going to hurt and dismember her if she didn't "leave Ben alone," as though Ben had had no say in their relationship. They described how they would also run her out of the school if she didn't "fucking off yerself." Claire the joiner, the artist, the hard worker, the friend and niece, that girl was lost amid all these ugly, vile insults and threats. But the label that seemed most prominent, the one hurled most often, the one that seemed to stick, was the word "slut," usually pasted beneath a certain photograph posted over and over again, of Claire holding up her shirt to bare a breast, just one. If that was the notorious photo, I thought, it wasn't even a sexy one. It looked insouciant, more like the product of a dare between her and the photographer, presumably Ben. But posted over and over again with horrible slogans and tags attached, it took on darker tones.

Claire missed New Orleans and when she begged her folks to let her come back to her uncle Will's, they were too afraid to say no, worried they'd set off more self-destructive behavior. When she returned to Will's, a home with disconnected Wi-Fi, we all spelled one another off to spend time with her, Dell filling in for the both of us when necessary. Of all of us, Dell was the most perplexed, her face dropping when I told her how Claire had coped with this abuse.

"Well, once she's all better, please don't mind me if after I hug her, I slap her a little," she said, fighting back tears.

The staff at Cassie's was incredible, picking up shifts at the Café Rose so Maureen wouldn't be overwhelmed or on her own, especially during Mardi Gras.

Will demanded the addresses of her tormentors. Over the course of that month, he made personal visits to each kid's home, requesting meetings with parents, asking the girls to delete the posts, to write apologies and to give assurances that they understood the scope of their damage.

"I only wanted them to consider what it would feel like to be Claire," he told me, while we shopped for new floor runners and plastic cutting boards for the restaurant. He looked as lost as I'd ever seen him, wandering the aisles of Home Depot. "Why did this happen? What did she do to deserve all this shit?"

"Nothing. She did nothing."

Later, in the checkout line, I said, "I admire her."

"Why?" Will asked.

"Because even after all of this, she never apologized for having sex with a boy she wanted to have sex with. I could learn a thing or two from a seventeen-year-old girl."

That was a sincere comment; I wasn't trying to make a point about Will's behavior at Latrobe's, but it was out of my mouth before I realized the implications.

Will averted his eyes when he said, "We could all learn from her."

Eventually, Olivia, the main bully in Claire's group, was booted out of the school, but Will wanted a more serious charge against her, something akin to criminal harassment.

But the school stuck to its "girls will be girls" policy, hoping Olivia's expulsion would be enough to start the healing. I stopped Will more than once from going over to Olivia's house to yell through a locked door, which would only have come across as a different kind of bullying.

Meanwhile, Claire gradually got better and returned to work after March Break as if from a war, shell-shocked and tender. On her first day back, she took Dell aside.

"I swear I'm okay now. I won't do anything stupid like that again," she said.

"Hard going through something like that all alone," Dell said, patting her dreads. "Next time, open your mouth. Tell somebody. Tell me."

It was surprising to see Dell act so caring, until I remembered that she'd launched four kids, including a set of twins, and two grandkids into the world, quite successfully, and mostly alone.

The kitchen was a crazy hive of activity when Will breathlessly barreled in, tossing a small paper bag on the prep table in front of me.

"Cassie, I tried to reach you but there was no answer. No black truffles, only white. That okay?"

"You asked for black, right, Dell?" I hunted around for my phone, realizing I'd probably left it in Jesse's truck when he dropped me off that morning.

"I did."

"Does the color of the damn truffle even matter?" Will asked her.

"It always matters," Dell said, pressing that point home in the form of a lesson to Claire.

Will exhaled and dropped his chin to his chest. "Fuck. I can't do anything right."

"Come on," Dell said, drying her hands on a tea towel and grabbing Claire by the sleeve. "I'll show you where to hunt and gather."

Dell and Claire left us standing in the kitchen. I immediately rose to leave, the way I always did when it looked like I was going to be alone with Will.

"Wait," he said. "I want to talk to you."

My stomach clenched. I turned to face him.

"I wanted to say thanks," he said. "I already thanked Dell, and now I want to thank you."

"For what?"

"For being such a support for Claire. And such a good example."

"A good example?"

"Of a grown woman who has her shit together." He continued without waiting for my reply. "Every time you show up here without hurling something at my head, you're setting a good example. Every time you pick her up and take her to a movie, and come in here early and deal with Dell because you're better at it than I am, you set a good example. Every time you make a smart decision about the menu, or handle an irate customer with more grace than one person should possess, you set a good example for her. And I just want to say thank you. And I owe you."

I was getting that deep, warm feeling you get when you look for longer than usual at a face you love. I let myself enjoy that moment, the two of us standing there being kind to each other in a quiet kitchen. Months of resentment slid away. And then, without my permission, my hand lifted to touch that face I once had loved so much. And he let me. He let me touch him without flinching, without stepping back and away. Somehow I had expected the feel of his skin to be familiar, but it was new to me.

"You don't owe me anything, Will. I care about her."

He reached up to touch the back of my hand. "Well, I owe you something, Cassie. At least an explanation."

"For what?"

"For what I said to you, that night. At Latrobe's. For the way I treated you."

"No. Don't—"

"No. You need to hear it. You've made all the difference in her life. In both our lives."

Who knows how long we would have stood there marveling at each other's faces, our hands touching. We never had a chance to find out, because Jesse walked in at that moment, shattering everything.

"Okay. Yeah. I'm sorry," he said, immediately spinning away from us as though he'd walked in on his parents having sex. Before bolting, he carefully placed my phone on the nearest counter. "You left it in my truck."

Will gave me a tacit *go after him* nod. Strange how the tables had turned; now it was Will urging me to fix things with Jesse. Guilt, that constant, awful companion, followed me out the door.

Steps behind Jesse on the sidewalk, I called his name, one, two, three times. He finally froze in his tracks, his back to me, probably giving his face a second or two to arrange itself into an *I don't really give a shit* expression before turning around.

"I didn't mean to intrude," he said. "Your phone kept ringing and ringing and I thought—"

"You didn't intrude. We were just having some kind words over Claire. That's all."

"How is she?"

"Good. Better. Yeah. Don't leave like this, okay? Come back. Come in for a beer."

I clasped the hem of his T-shirt, giving it a gentle tug. Jesse wouldn't move.

"I can't right now."

"You're mad."

"No, baby, I'm not mad. Just realistic."

And with that, he got into his truck and drove away from me, at first slowly, until he turned the corner at the Praline Connection and sped up, leaving dust in his wake.

SOLANGE

At least twice a year a big movie opened in New Orleans, generally one also shot here. The state provided lucrative tax breaks to drum up film and TV business. But even when I was younger and greener, when it should have been fun to cover red carpet events and to meet famous people, I balked. It was so easy to get pigeonholed as a "female" reporter, instead of a serious reporter, to be given frivolous stories and to be seen as shallow or, worse, glamorous. So when I was assigned to interview a certain Major Movie Star (a.k.a. MMS) in town for his film opening, I didn't just *say* no, I barked it and left the assignment meeting.

Denise followed me out, pushing me into my office and shutting the door. She was hyperventilating.

"Solange, you don't get it. He . . . *requested* you. He followed your port lands story while he was here filming the movie. It's an exclusive interview. Either you get it, or no one from this station does."

"Oh, *wow*. He picked *me?* How, like, *amazing!*" I faux-squealed.

"I know, right?" she said, my tone having completely eluded her.

"My answer is no," I said, turning to some papers on my desk.

"Solange Faraday, you know I am a great admirer of yours. You're my mentor, in fact. But if you think one interview with a hot, *smart* actor is going to undermine your entire career, then you don't have much confidence in your body of work."

"Out of the mouths of babes," I muttered. I stopped moving papers around. Gus *was* with his dad that night. I *could* do it. But . . .

"There will be conditions," I said. I told her I wasn't going to focus all my questions on the movie or his love interest in the movie. Nor did I care about which Italian or British starlet the MMS was currently dating, let alone why he had never married. My plan was to ignore his personal life and talk to him about politics, about his well-known international philanthropy and his opinion on voter apathy. If the network wanted a feature interview, I'd give it to them, on my terms.

"And you're coming with me to deal with his publicist," I said to Denise, who didn't even bother to hide her glee. "I don't talk to publicists."

When the day came, reluctantly, sternly, I put on some coral lipstick and my nerdiest glasses and buttoned up my blouse to the top, hoping this outfit would convey, "I am not the starstruck type. I am here for a story, not for a star."

Jazz Fest wasn't for a couple more weeks, but the Ritz was a madhouse. Denise was a pro, ushering the crew and me through the glut of other cameras and ensuring that we were going last, always the best spot to have if you want extra time with your subject.

When it was our turn, the publicist poked her head out of the suite and called my name like it was my turn at the free medical clinic, pronouncing my name "*Soh-LANG*."

"See what I mean?" I said to Denise. "Demoralizing."

Before we had a chance to do a sound check and color balance, the MMS sauntered into the suite looking all kinds of dapper, his trademark salt-and-pepper hair combed back, his bemused grin firmly in place, his dimpled chin a kind of taunt, his gravelly voice beautifully calibrated. It looked so easy to be him.

"Ms. Faraday, it's an honor," he said, his eyes smiling. "Thank you for agreeing to do the interview. I know this isn't your usual beat."

What happened next was embarrassing; I blushed. And my reaction was so sudden and difficult to mask, I had to avoid eye contact with Denise lest I appear a total hypocrite.

The thing about charisma is you can't fake it. Phony charisma falls flat. I had interviewed enough politicians, including Bill Clinton when he was the governor of our neighboring state, to know the difference between fake and real charisma. So let it be said that despite his considerable charms, Bill Clinton had nothing on this MMS. He had a gravitational pull, this man. You wanted to get right up into those dark eyes and run your fingers through that thicket of hair. I shook the MMS's hand warmly, and then he introduced himself to my crew as if they didn't know who he was.

We sat in our seats opposite each other, and the DOP gave me the thumbs-up sign for *We're rolling.*

After the requisite chat about the movie at hand, and how great it was to shoot in New Orleans, *blah blah blah,* we launched into a discussion on his favorite topic: how to get the right people to run for office.

"That's something you've said you're firmly not interested in, right? Running for office yourself?"

"Too much dirt on me," he said, uncrossing and recrossing his legs. "I wouldn't survive the scrutiny and I hate to waste people's time."

"Surely there's no more dirt on you than there was on Clinton. And he served two terms."

"True. He came out of that relatively unscathed. Can't say the same for the women in his life."

He gave me his infamous smirk, while undoing the cuffs on his shirt. I, too, had to uncross and recross my legs, squeezing my thighs together. *Shake it off. Don't go gaga.*

"Are you saying a vivid sex life disqualifies you from holding public office?"

"No. But having one you're completely unapologetic about does tend to make it hard for America to love you.

That is what I'm saying. You are free to do what you want, as long as you exhibit a bit of shame now and again. I'm just not willing to do that."

"You could help lift that stigma. Take the shame out of sex."

"That's not my job. I'm just a guy who dresses up and pretends to be other people for a living."

I rubbed the back of my neck, thinking about what would happen to my career and my credibility if my membership in S.E.C.R.E.T. were discovered. It would be over for me. There might even be questions about my fitness as a mother, though I doubted they'd come from Julius. He might not be impressed, but he wasn't the kind of man who thought having a bunch of sex disqualified you from anything, let alone motherhood. Still, I shuddered at the thought of being exposed.

The MMS changed the subject. He began discussing some of the humanitarian work he'd done overseas, particularly in Sudan. I challenged him on his follow-through and on why people don't take the political and social endeavors of Hollywood stars seriously.

"I don't expect anyone to take me seriously," he said, leaning forward, hands clasped between his knees. "I expect people to take the *issues* seriously though. People are crazy if they think wars overseas have no effect on their local economy, let alone on national security. There's a reason you have to take off your shoes to fly from Petaluma to Peoria and it has everything to do with what's going on in places like Syria and Darfur."

As planned, we wrapped up a little late. Once our mics were off, he stood to shake my hand, holding it between both of his for a few lingering seconds. Or maybe I imagined that.

"This was an enlightening conversation. It'll be a great segment. Thanks," I said, reluctantly prying my hand loose.

"Other way around. Thank you, Solange Faraday, for asking real questions."

First and last name? And a grin? *Wow. Okay.*

We watched him disappear to an adjoining suite followed by his publicist and a dozen other people in his entourage. My guys silently rolled the cables. Denise folded up the tripods. I changed into my flats. Just as I was about to duck out with my crew, the MMS reentered the suite, this time wearing a sweatshirt and jeans, his face freshly washed.

"They keep the booze in *this* part of the suite," he explained. "Have a drink with me, Solange."

My crew suddenly turned sheepish. Denise shot me a look that screamed: *Holy shit! Do not turn him down!* But I was thinking this: *What if everyone in the newsroom knew I flirted with the subject of an interview? What would they think?*

The answer that came to me was delivered in Marsha Lang's inimitable voice: *Who fucking cares, Solange?* Our male network on-air talent had bedded plenty of women who were attracted to their minor celebrity. And Bill Rink, weather jackass, was a renowned cocksmith due to . . . what? His ability to wield a dry-erase marker over a plastic map of Louisiana?

I am forty-one years old.
I am a grown woman.
I am a good mother.
I am single.
I work hard.
I can do what I want.

"Sure. I'd love a drink. Scotch, please. Neat," I said, turning to face Denise, to whom I mouthed, *Oh my god!*

And just like that, he and I were alone.

"Now it's my turn to ask *you* a question," the MMS purred.

I turned to face him. "Sure."

I suddenly regretted putting on my flats and my nerd outfit.

"My question to you, Ms. Faraday, is: Will you accept the Step?"

For reasons I'll never be able to fully explain, I thought he was teasing me, having secured some insider knowledge of S.E.C.R.E.T. by virtue of his supreme powers as an MMS. Which is why instead of saying *Hell, yes!* I blurted out, "How the fuck do you know about *that?*"

He looked taken aback as he placed the crystal cap back on the decanter he was holding.

"Is that a yes or a no?"

Is this actually happening?

"Are you saying you . . . that *you're* a recruit? For S.E.C.R.E.T.?"

There was that sly smile again. "I am."

"But how? Why? Why would *you* be a recruit?"

He came out from behind the bar and placed our drinks on the glass coffee table.

"Well, I can ask the same of you. Why would *you* be a participant? A beautiful, accomplished woman like yourself. What do you need S.E.C.R.E.T. for?"

I stalled, a storm gathering in my stomach. Part nerves, part joy, part shock. Before I could answer, he continued.

"Because it makes total sense for *me* to do something like this. No-strings-attached sex with beautiful women any way I want, any way *they* want. And I get to leave without a trace. No obligation to follow through, guaranteed discretion, no money exchanging hands to cheapen the experience. Kind of perfect for a guy like me. Because I don't do . . . intimacy. The emotional part. I don't do that. On the screen, yes. In life, no. But I don't expect that's going to be a detriment tonight because I just want to have sex with you. In fact, I'd very much like to fuck you. What do you say to that, Ms. Faraday?"

My mind raced to Step Six. *Confidence.* I had it in spades when I was "on," while I was interviewing a subject, playing my role as a journalist. And certainly this man exuded confidence. Enough for the both of us. But now, as a woman who'd thrown on some comfortable shoes and was wearing thick glasses and, Christ, *coral* lipstick, I suddenly felt inferior, old and dowdy, unworthy of this kind of star attention from this man—famous, handsome, smart, powerful—this man relaxing in an armchair looking exactly like a king overseeing his domain.

"Don't be shocked, Solange. I'm just a guy in a pair of jeans, having a Scotch after work, who'd like to get a beautiful woman naked and in my bed. If she'll have me."

I approached the coffee table, picked up my drink, took a long haul and choked on the vapors. I wiped my mouth and placed the drink back down on the table.

"I accept."

He smiled, seemingly relieved. *As though there'd been any doubt about my answer.*

"Good," he said, placing his empty glass on the table. "Now come here."

Jesus. It was on.

I stepped closer to his chair, coming to a stop in front of his knees. *This is happening, this is actually happening.*

"Please take your clothes off."

"Right here?" I looked around the room. "Can we at least . . . dim the lights?"

He opened the drawer in the table and took out a remote, hitting one button to bring down the lights, another to play a slow, liquid song, the kind your hips involuntarily sway to.

"There," he said. "Proceed."

I closed my eyes for a second and drew in a long breath, feeling the Scotch burn my tongue and throat.

"You want me to . . . strip. For you. Right now."

He smiled, leaning back. "Yes. I'd love that."

Doitdoitdoit.

I untucked my shirt, my shaky fingers finding the buttons, and at the same time I kicked off my flats. *I am going to strip. For this MMS.* His eyes followed my fingers as they opened my silk shirt. I looked down. Fuck. The lacy beige bra wasn't the worst one to be caught wearing, thank god, but I was not only in mismatched black underwear, *I had control-top nylons on under my pencil skirt! Christ, no!*

"Um, so, about my lingerie . . . I didn't know that I'd be . . . I would have worn—"

He laughed. "My favorite thing about this whole scenario? Your lack of lingerie. Do you have any idea how sexy it is to have a real encounter like this with a real woman wearing real . . . underwear? May I?"

He sat up and placed his hands on my hips, turning me around so my back was to him. *Now what?* He unzipped my skirt, letting it drop to the ground. Then I felt his firm fingers slide under the elastic of the pantyhose, peeling it down over my ass, my thighs.

"Impressive," he said, plying the spandex. "I'm not just referring to your spectacular ass, but you could kill a man with these."

Before the mortification could fully set in, he planted a long kiss on one cheek, then the other, his hands squeezing my ass together. His fingers gathered the back of my blouse and tugged it down off my arms. He flung it over the chair in front of me. Now he got busy with the clasp of my bra.

"You're gorgeous, you know that? Your skin, your ass . . ." he said, turning me to face him again, my breasts hovering over his face, and me so drenched by then, it was all I could do to restrain myself from climbing on him. And yet I was seized with something like . . . the giggles.

"What's funny?" he asked, his brown eyes looking up at me, his scratchy chin against my stomach.

"You. *This*," I said, now laughing openly, my hands in his hair, *that hair*.

"You're laughing at me?" he asked, collapsing back into the chair to lift his hips to strip off his jeans.

"Oh, I don't mean funny haha."

He smiled, pulling off his sweatshirt. For a fifty-something man, he was lean, not too muscular, just fit. I noticed white tufts of hair amid the black fur across his chest, beneath which his skin was burnished and tawny. His cock was among the nicest I'd seen, cut and fierce. He wrapped a hand around his erection, his eyes dancing across my body.

"Touch yourself, Solange," he said.

You can do this. My hand traveled slowly down over my stomach, which I was tensing, sucking in. I tried not to think of the dozens of supermodels this man would have seen writhing naked beneath him. How many were mothers? How many had stretch marks? Were over forty? Had that awful red mark around their tummies from wearing *control-top panties*?

Yet nothing in the MMS's demeanor suggested he was anything less than pleased with what he was seeing. My fingers slid inside me. I closed my eyes; his attention too intense by now.

You can do this. I opened my eyes again and followed his

lead, becoming the assertive, sexy woman he assumed I was. As my frenzied fingers worked their magic, he took a condom out of that same little drawer and quickly slipped it on his thick cock. He slid down a little more on the chair, motioning me closer with his hand.

"I want you to fuck me, Solange," he said, as I straddled his firm thighs, my fingers getting lazy. I don't think I have ever wanted something more; every ounce of me, from my hardened nipples to my weakened knees, wanted to fuck this man, to get him inside of me. I hovered over him for a few seconds, my fingers centering his tip beneath the opening of my wet slit. His fingers pressing the flesh on my thighs, he guided me down, and I sank around him, throbbing with every inch I took in. His mouth formed an O of utter astonishment, his brow knitted with the concentration of a man taking in every ounce of pleasure and committing it to memory, like he was filming this with his eyes, filing it away. I began to rise and fall, feeling his shaft press against my front wall where my g-spot, so often elusive, seemed to swell and awaken.

"Look at you . . . fucking me," he said, his hand giving me a light slap on my left cheek while his hips thrust up into me.

I lost myself in the tide of hard and soft sensations, his cock pressing against that deep part of me, over and over, until he began to bring me to the brink of release. His hands traveled down to my hips, his fingertips raking my flesh as he fucked me harder, or maybe I was fucking him. All I know is the harder he gripped my hips, rocking my clit over his groin, the more difficult it became to fight back the tide that was washing over my body and mind.

"Christ, you're fucking gorgeous," he growled, reaching up to cup my breast with one hand, while his other thumb stroked my fat clit just so. And then I felt the first spasm coming fast after that, my skin burning, my head rolling back, as another wave, a bigger, wider one, took me higher, to a new place of pleasure, where all I could do was laugh as he thrust into me, his hard cock cutting into the very core of me, his expression almost triumphant.

What else can I call it but cuddling? That's what we did after we fucked one more time on the hotel rug, pulling a coverlet beneath us, followed by more sex in the shower, where he explored my sore pussy with that famous mouth of his. Sated, we cuddled in the tufted king-sized bed in the other room of that luxurious suite, interrupted only when Room Service called back to confirm what kind of cake he had ordered a few minutes earlier.

"I don't know, *all* the cake," the MMS said, rolling his eyes at me.

Later, after he fed me a bite of chocolate layer cake, a nibble of strawberry pie, and a sliver of passion fruit cheesecake, he got up and fished around in the pockets of his discarded clothes. He returned to my side, theatrically placing a small purple box in the center of my naked belly.

"And the winner is . . ." he whispered, lifting the gold foil lid. "You."

While he made the sound of a crowd going wild, I gently plucked out my Step Six charm, clutching it to my chest in an exaggerated display of gratefulness.

"*For me?* Oh thank you, thank you *so* much," I crooned. "And I'd like to thank the Academy, and of course my agent, and all the lawyers you generally have to thank in these situations, and the little people, of course . . ."

"What about your co-star?"

"*Who?* Nah, I'm going to take all the credit for this one," I said, playfully shoving him away from my imaginary spotlight, blowing kisses to my imaginary fans.

"As well you should, Solange Faraday," he said, pulling me back into a giggly embrace. "As well you should."

CASSIE

There were three reasons I agreed to help train Ewan for a threesome: 1) Matilda was right. I didn't have the nerve to put "threesome" on my own fantasy list, despite the fact that it was something I'd always kind of wanted to try; 2) I was attracted to both Ewan, the redhead we'd be training, and Pauline, the S.E.C.R.E.T. member who would be the second woman in our triangle. She was gamine, lean and boyish. In fact, it was her flirty, sexy behavior with her husband at the Café that initially lured me into S.E.C.R.E.T., made me curious, made me want the sexual confidence she had; 3) I wanted to even things out with Jesse after his Step with Solange.

This was the biggest reason.

Juvenile, I know, and then Jesse one-upped me again by magnanimously offering to drive me to the Mansion the night of my training session, like it was no big deal to him, like a guy you're sleeping with should be so generous as to drive you to a place where you're probably going to have sex with someone else, maybe even with more than one person. He said he had to be at a "thing" in the Garden District anyway, so it was on his way. Ever since he walked in on Will and me sharing that intimate moment a few weeks earlier, Jesse had maintained his policy of waiting for me in his truck. The day of my threesome, I found him a half block over, in front of the bike shop.

"Hey," I said, hopping into the cab.

We said very little on the way to the Mansion. I hadn't given him much information about what was going on that night. I took S.E.C.R.E.T's policies on gossip as seriously as he did. But when we pulled up, he asked if I knew whose Audi was in the driveway. I said that it could be my recruit's.

"When did you recruit someone?" he asked, throwing the truck into park.

"Last year, at Audubon Park with Matilda. She had her eye on one guy, and I liked his friend."

That's when I saw it: a subtle hint of jealousy flashed across his face; his nostrils flared, his eyes darted to the ground.

"Well. You better get a move on," he said. "Don't leave Audi guy waiting."

I leaned over to give him a kiss just as he turned his head to adjust his side mirror. In another life, my earlier one, I would never have left a guy pouting in a truck. I would have pressed and prodded and found something to apologize for.

This time I simply said, "Thanks for the ride," before getting out, shutting the door of his truck and heading into the Mansion.

~~

For fun, Pauline and I chose the Harem Room, with its arches and columns, dim golden lighting, oceans of throws and pillows, and mattresses the size of area rugs. Pauline was already in the dressing room off the Jacuzzi area when I arrived, a glass of champagne in her hand. The room was small but opulent; dozens of toiletries and perfumes lined the mirrored counter, and there were plush chairs and benches along the walls.

"You don't mind if I sip?" she said. "I don't like being tipsy, just a bit loose."

"Fuck no. Good idea," I said, pouring half a glass from the bottle chilling in a bucket by the sink.

"You nervous?"

"Not at all," I said. I waited a beat. "Yes, I'm nervous. You sure we shouldn't go with Kit? Or Angela? I mean, we're supposed to be training him, and I've never . . ."

She laughed and stepped towards me, the bathrobe gaping open to show her black garters. Her nipples were so pale they were almost invisible over the black lace demi-cups of the corset.

"Cassie, trust me. You can't really fuck this up."

I took a big gulp of champagne. Then another one. Pauline pried the glass from my hand.

"That should just about do it, Cass," she said, handing me the white lace copy of her outfit. "Put these on. I'll go in there and warm him up. Give me ten, then I'll call for you."

"Shouldn't we both go together?"

"It's his first threesome. If we both start in on him, it'll be a bit overwhelming."

"Right."

She disappeared through the small door leading to the Harem Room. I rolled up my pale silk stockings and dabbed a bit of jasmine oil behind my ears. The champagne helped my body to melt a little, to go liquid with possibility. I dragged my hand across my nerve-racked stomach and let it travel down, watching it in the mirror. I slid a finger along my panty line, then under. I had been thinking about this day for a while, so no wonder I was wet.

I heard Pauline call my name. I moistened my lips with my tongue, letting my robe fall to the floor.

If the light in the dressing room was dim, it was practically nonexistent in the Harem Room, save for the dozen or so red candles flickering along the fireplace mantel. I walked in just as Pauline, straddling Ewan, was kissing a gentle path down his neck to his chest, circling a nipple with her tiny, pointed tongue. She looked up and her eyes met mine.

"Look who's here," she whispered to Ewan.

Eyes glazed, mouth slack, he turned to face me, his expression that of a man scarcely able to believe his continued good fortune.

"You're from the park," he said.

Pauline continued making her way down his torso, her hands sliding under his jeans, tugging them off. I stepped towards them, remembering now what I had found sexy about him, his bratty smile, his light blue eyes that crinkled at the corners, his freckles, his messy red hair, his incredible soccer-player body.

"Why don't you come over here, gorgeous," he purred, smoothing out a space next to him on the red satin sheets. "We've been waiting for you."

"That's good," Pauline cooed, as he adjusted himself so she could more easily remove his boxers.

His beautiful erection landed along his thigh with an audible slap. *Jesus Murphy.* Pauline possessively wrapped her hand around it.

"Hi," I whispered, my hands on my hips, looking for my entrance. We knew each other not at all, and yet, from our meeting in the park last summer, to now—I felt propri-etary towards Ewan. My heart was pounding. I leaned over and placed my hands on the mattress, then crawled towards him like a leopard to prey, letting him take in the way the corset pressed my breasts together. Ignoring Pauline, I caged his chin with my hand, kissing him fully, my tongue darting in and out of his warm mouth, let my hand trail down to meet Pauline's hand, as both our fingers firmly danced up and down his cock, her mouth taking in his tip, my fingers getting caught up in her wet lips.

One of his hands still circled and played with Pauline's short, cute hair, while his other caressed my stomach, down the front of my panties, and he slid a long, muscular finger inside me. I glanced at Pauline, her mouth on his cock, sucking it, licking it, sending vibrating shocks through his body that I could feel. She stopped every once in a while to give him a bit of instruction.

"If you like what I'm doing, tell me, darlin', tell me. Tell me my mouth is magic."

"Fuck. It is. Your mouth is magic," he murmured, looking down at her with astonishment.

"What do you think of Cassie?"

"She's so beautiful," he said, his eyes turning to take me in.

I was beside them, on my knees, reaching back to kick off my heels.

"Do you want to suck her tits? Say it, baby. Tell her to get herself naked like me. You can ask that."

"Okay, yeah, take your clothes off, Cassie," he said.

"She's not wearing *clothes*, babe. She's wearing lingerie. Why don't you tell her to strip for you," Pauline sweetly suggested, her gentle eye-roll perceptible only to me.

I stood up next to the mattress and rolled down my panties. I let them dangle from my finger inches in front of Pauline. She grabbed them, smiling, and pulled me towards her, while Ewan clasped his hands behind his head. I looked at Pauline's perfect little mouth. I had never kissed a girl, but how different could it be? As it turns out, it was entirely different. I soon understood why some men liked women so much. Her lips were fluttery, soft and sweet, but they kept me guessing, licking and flicking, sucking and biting my lips. Ewan whimpered involuntarily as he watched Pauline's kisses make their way down my neck to my breasts. I looked at him, my eyes half closed.

"Oh god, this is hot!" he said, and it *was*.

Pauline stopped what she was doing. "Baby, don't say 'This is hot' like you're watching us on TV. Say, '*You* are hot.' *You*. Use my name, use Cassie's name. Tell me what I'm doing that's making you so fucking hard. Have you seen this dick, Cassie? It's a masterpiece."

Ewan groaned and grinned, his hand reaching up to pull me to him, as he told me how bad he wanted me to fuck him, how Pauline was making him crazy. She turned her attention now fully to his erection, kissing and nibbling the tip, while indicating to me to turn mine to his adorable, bliss-smeared face. He lifted my thigh over so that I was straddling him, my knees on either side of his rib cage. It blocked his view of the masterful blowjob Pauline was administering, but his warm hands circled my thighs as he gazed up at me. He lifted me so that I was suspended over his face, while he arched and moaned as Pauline's oral ministrations brought him close to an orgasm.

"Holy *fuck*," he whispered. He was tortured by this in the best possible way.

He stretched his hand up towards me.

"I want your pussy in my mouth, Cassie," he said. "Let me taste you."

My knees nearly buckled as I lowered onto him, his palm catching me, a thumb sliding over my clit as he centered me over his mouth, his tongue flicking me alive. I wanted to come fast, right then and there, my hands on the wall in front of me.

I threw my head back; this wasn't going to take long. He dragged his tongue from my back to front, thrusting it into me. I arched, my back to Pauline. His hands were now on my buttocks, squeezing them and rocking my pelvis over his mouth, as my knees dug into the pillows on either side of his face.

"Feels *so good*," I purred.

Then I felt hands climb up, handling my breasts, but these hands were small and warm, and that's when I realized Pauline was holding me from behind. As she eased down onto his cock, and he ate my pussy with increasing gratitude, she caressed and pinched my breasts. His deep, pleasurable moans sent waves through my body. She rode him behind me, using my body as leverage. As she fucked him harder and harder, she placed her dizzy, wet fingers on my ass, while Ewan's tongue fucked me ferociously from the front.

The rush built at a feverish pace. Too fast, too much.

"Fuck, yes, *yes, oh*," I screamed, my thighs split over Ewan's face, Pauline's fingers on me, in me, my whole body buzzing, convulsing, taking and taking, and then I came, hard, and loudly, feeling Ewan's tongue as he began to lose it too, moaning directly into my body as Pauline rocked an orgasm out of him, taking one for herself as well. We were like a pleasure machine, feeding off one another from all angles. Hands and mouths and skin on skin, slowing to a rhythm, a beat, then a low pulse.

Pauline collapsed against my back, both of us rolling off him, spent and giggly. For a few breathless moments, I lay next to him, my legs tangled in the red sheets, as Pauline curled behind me, her body smooth and small. Ewan lifted a muscular arm and laid it across both of us, protectively, gratefully, as I nestled into his chest. But I couldn't sleep. I was wide awake.

I pointed to the door to signal to Pauline that I had to go. She blew me a sleepy kiss. As I pulled the robe around me, I listened to her sweetly debrief Ewan on bits he could improve.

". . . talk about how her skin *feels*, and don't just say she's beautiful. You have to be more specific. Tell her you love her ass, how her mouth is sexy, that kind of thing. And focus more on Solange than on me. I won't mind. Also, it's not the time to be astonished. Try to be, like, "Yeah, man, *of course* two beautiful women are fucking me . . ."

I closed the door behind them and bolted for home, anxious for my own bed but buzzing from the top of my head down to my toes. I felt like I had had an expert massage following a vigorous workout. I was glowing, energized and ready for anything.

SOLANGE

When I put a threesome on my fantasy list, I meant it, and I was ready and willing when the day came, right up to the moment my hand reached the knob of that door in the Mansion, the one leading to a room where two people, likely a man and a woman, or it could have been two men, or hell, two women for all I knew, were waiting for me on the other side.

That's when I froze.

In the early, heady days of my courtship with Julius, I had brought up the idea of a threesome while we were inside one of our blissful, post-coital bubbles. I remember it was hotter than hell in our little back bedroom. He had just bought an air conditioner, the window-unit kind. After he had fully installed it, brackets and all, he realized the unit was too far from the nearest plug to actually turn it on. He laughed and fell on the bed, pulling me down with him. What I saw as a sad metaphor for a man who never finished a task properly, he saw as funny, and as a chance to get me naked again.

We lived in a little rental in Bywater way before the neighborhood was cool, before a baby made spontaneous afternoon sex impossible. I was doing my master's in journalism, singing part-time in ratty bars, and coming home to Jules's warm, sleeping body at night. He was trying to transition out of DJing and into band management, but he wasn't signing enough acts. We wanted to be different from our parents, and different from our friends who were rushing to the altar and buying bungalows in Uptown and Carrollton. In fact, when we finally did get married, we did it on a lunch break at City Hall, much to my mother's consternation and my dad's relief. I didn't want him going into debt to pay for a wedding like it was his patriarchal duty, or some reflection on my "value" as a woman. As a couple we were artistic, progressive, expansive, bold, and that included, I thought, loosening our hold on each other so we could explore our sexual limits together. I was reading a lot of new-age relationship stuff at the time; threesomes were no big thing.

Julius was having none of it.

"So, let me get this straight. You would have no problem kissing my mouth right after I go down on another woman, making her scream right in front of you. You'd be cool with that?"

"The trick is to have no emotional attachment to the third party," I said, quoting those books.

"Oh. I see. So I'm not supposed to give a shit about one of the two women I am with—emotionally or personally.

I'm supposed to reserve feelings only for you, and my cock for her. And that makes it okay," he said, laughing.

"Who says it's gotta be another woman? What about if it's me and two men?"

He laughed. Then he laughed some more.

"You have a problem with that?" I asked.

"*Yeah* I got a problem with that. And it's not the problem you think. I just don't like the idea of boiling sex down to a whole lotta limbs and lips and cocks and pussies. Why would I bother digging through a pile of flesh just to get to what I already got, here, now, all to myself?"

I lightly beat his damp chest, my sticky fingers trailing up and down his stomach, turning his laughter into shuddering as soon as my hand found him hard again.

"You talk fancy, Solange," he said, moving his hips to my hand's rhythm, "but you're crazy in love with me. I know you. It would *kill* you to share."

"You're telling me you *never* think about another woman when you're fucking me?"

This made his dick go harder.

"I'll tell you what, maybe I have. Maybe I haven't. But right now, in this moment, I'm thinking only about fucking you," he said, pulling me in closer.

This man was mine, his dick under my command. *Mine.* It was fierce and sudden, that feeling of *mine.* His cock eased into me, while I clasped my hands behind his neck. I loved how his torso went ropy from exertion. I loved how he fucked me. I could feel that surrender, that holy thing that sex can bring to you when it's done right, when it causes the big "yes" at the center of the flesh; the yielding that comes from feeling safe, right, wanted. It was like that with us for a long time.

And then it wasn't.

A threesome had remained on my secret list of things to try even before Matilda provided the opportunity. The day I filled out my fantasy form, the tip of my pencil hovered over that box for a long, long time. Then I checked it. This morning, I had found myself racing around my bedroom while a limo idled in my driveway to take me to the Mansion. Six times I changed outfits! And six times I had to remind myself clothes didn't matter; I'd be naked the whole time, right?

Wrong.

I barely took off my robe.

I wrapped my hand around the knob and froze. I couldn't even open the door. My curiosity had just . . . dissolved.

When I got home, I called Matilda and we met the next day for lunch at Tracey's.

For some reason I felt like I had to apologize.

"Nonsense. Nothing to apologize for," she said. "Was it a matter of attraction? What do you think we got wrong about your scenario?"

I didn't have the heart to tell her I didn't even open the door.

"Truth is, I just . . . It seemed attractive in theory, but when it became real, I realized it wasn't something I actually wanted. It just felt like too much. God, does this make me a coward?"

"Coward? Solange, for you that fantasy had nothing to do with bravery and everything to with curiosity. The curiosity just wasn't there."

True, but the bigger truth was that Julius's words had begun to resonate. And in that moment I started to crave something more with my sex, something deeper, maybe more . . . emotional.

"Don't give it another thought. I promise we'll orchestrate a stellar Step Seven do-over. Think about what else you're most curious about these days and we'll set it up," she said.

"It can be anything?"

"Of course," Matilda said, wiping her mouth with her napkin and setting it down.

The idea came to me so swiftly I didn't have a chance to temper it or to really think about what I was asking her to do for me.

"Well, it's not really a matter of *what* I'm most curious about, but rather whom."

Matilda looked around the crowded restaurant. She leaned forward.

"Please don't ask me—"

"Pierre Castille," I said. "He turned down my last interview request, but something tells me he wouldn't turn yours down. If my next Step is truly about curiosity, then perhaps you can make him my Step Seven do-over. Part of my fantasy could include doing a feature-length interview."

"Solange, Pierre is manipulative, unpredictable, dangerous even. And I cannot vouch for your safety, which is the first and most important prerequisite for any S.E.C.R.E.T. fantasy."

"Who says I'm going to accept the Step?"

She looked at me gravely. Could she tell that even as I said those words, I doubted them? He might be all those things Matilda said, but he was also undeniably sexy. And this wasn't about love, after all. What was curiosity anyway if it wasn't sticking your hand in a lion's mouth? I had based my entire career on those kinds of dares. I had walked away from a step for lack of curiosity before, so who knows what would happen if I were face-to-face with Castille. Maybe I'd walk away again. All I knew was when I contemplated that opportunity, I felt that familiar adrenaline rush flooding my veins. Once that happened, there was no turning back.

Matilda seemed both impressed and angry about my plan. "He's a dangerous man, Solange."

"I'm not afraid of him. In fact, he should be afraid of me." I laughed, trying to turn the tail end of my comment into a joke, but her silence hung heavy in the air.

It was the kind of silence that journalists and salespeople know to leave alone because the next person who speaks loses.

"I'll tell you something," Matilda said, begrudgingly, affectionately, "formidable doesn't even *begin* to describe you."

The next day, sitting in Julius's car en route to a parent–teacher meeting, I fought a weird urge to tell him about the threesome and that it was because of him I'd backed out. Instead, I took in the familiar scent of his Jeep, marveling that the man was on time, a little early even.

"You look nice," he said. "You're wearing your hair different. I love it curly."

"I just haven't blown it out."

"That's pretty," he said, touching my bracelet and the skin beneath.

We still had an easy intimacy, the kind where a hand on a knee or a casual caress while adjusting a tie wasn't out of the ordinary, but it hadn't happened in a while. I debated taking off my S.E.C.R.E.T. bracelet, but with six charms now gracing the chain, I couldn't resist wearing it everywhere I went.

"Are you going to compliment my bag now? How about my shoes?" I said, deflecting attention away from the bracelet.

"I'm not throwing out compliments for nothing. I'm serious. I'm liking it all," he said, eyes on the road now.

"Well, thank you. But I didn't wear this for you. This is my 'I'm a Good Mother Despite my Demanding Job' outfit."

He laughed softly.

After a moment of silence, I changed the subject. "Anyway. So how's the food truck business?"

"You know . . . business is really good," he said, with some hesitation. "We're ordering up another truck. I take delivery in a few weeks. This one's going to the Freret Street Market. We're hoping—"

"Be careful not to expand too fast, Jules. That's happened before and you went bust."

I immediately regretted my words. It was his money, his business, his risk. I had no stake in this. And as long as he continued to pay child support on time, without complaint, I had no right to give unsought financial advice. Or any advice.

But instead of defending himself or shutting down, he simply said, "I understand your concern, Solange. I haven't had the best track record. But I know what I'm doing this time. I'm taking all the right steps. I feel good about this."

I said nothing more about the business, and during the parent–teacher meeting I let him do a lot of the talking while I took in his profile, marveling at the way love can change into something else, something different and yet so very familiar. I listened to Julius ask pertinent questions about Gus's ability to finish his homework. Julius felt he was overloaded with take-home work and asked the teacher to reduce it a little so he'd have more time to relax and just be a kid once school was done for the day.

"His pediatrician doesn't think he has attention-span issues," Julius said in the meeting. "A healthy mental bandwidth can just be stretched too thin sometimes."

"Oh, I concur," the teacher said. "This is a good plan. We'll make it work."

Afterwards, Julius dropped me off at work.

"Thanks. That was good," I said, patting the back of his hand.

"We did well. Listen, I'd like to pick up Gus tomorrow morning a little earlier. Take him golfing."

"I didn't know you golfed," I said, slotting that with a bunch of other new stuff about Julius I seemed to be discovering.

"I don't. But I think Gus should try it. It's harder as you get older to learn new things."

"Yes, but not impossible."

"That's true," he said, leaning over to kiss me good-bye, his goatee tickling my cheek.

I almost turned my face to meet his lips. I almost changed the peck to something else. *What the hell is going on? Is it his smell? Is it all the sex I'm having?* Sometimes, too long in close proximity to this man, his smell would mess with my rational mind, making me take leave of my senses.

As his Jeep drove away, I checked my phone messages: there were two from the office and one from Matilda. I listened to hers first.

Solange. Call me. I have news. Pierre—he's agreed to be . . . recruited this one time. But there are conditions. Call me.

Holy hell. She came through. *Curiosity* indeed! I immediately hit "call back." Matilda picked up on the first ring.

"What are the conditions?" I said, before even uttering "Hello."

"Well, Solange, he doesn't want a camera there for the interview portion of the fantasy," she said, her voice sounding as though this might be a deal-breaker.

"Fine," I said. "I'll just sell it as a cover story for *New Orleans Magazine*. They owe me, after all."

"The other condition is that the fantasy has to happen in Paris, where he's been living ever since our event at Latrobe's."

My heart skipped a beat. I had never been to Paris!

"That shouldn't be a problem."

"How about Gus?"

"He has a terrific father, last I checked, who often takes him for longer stretches when necessary."

"And what about the news station?"

She really didn't want me to go.

"I'm owed a vacation."

Matilda exhaled loudly, clearly sensing there was little she could say to dissuade me.

"Solange, I don't like this."

"When I signed up, you said anything I wanted. *Any* fantasy. I want this one," I said.

When I became like this, when I sank into that trance-like state of single-mindedness, Julius used to cut me a wide berth and let my obsession run its course. After all, this was the kind of tenacity that won me accolades. But it also got me in trouble. I was hoping for more of the former and none of the latter.

"Fine, Solange, but I have my own condition," Matilda said. "We'll make this your eighth Step. I have something else in mind for your Step Seven do-over."

"Remind me what eight is again?"

"*Bravery*, Solange," she said. "Though I've never met a woman in S.E.C.R.E.T. who needed less work on that quality than you."

CASSIE

J esse and I were in a post-sex tangle, an arm and a leg overlapping lazily, each of us lost in our thoughts. I almost fell asleep, completely forgetting the last-minute Committee meeting Matilda had called that afternoon. I soon snapped out of it, launching off Jesse's bed with a groan. I was so tired, I could have slept straight through the afternoon into the night.

For the past five months, it had been nonstop work, work, work. But it was already paying off. There were line-ups at Cassie's every night, and there was a palpable buzz on the street about the place. We wouldn't turn a profit that year, but we'd certainly make money next year, if things continued as they were. And we had scored a featured review in *New Orleans Magazine*: "Don't miss this new eatery on Frenchmen called Cassie's. It has the cozy warmth of your best friend's house, one where you don't have to take off your shoes and you always know that whatever's served will be vivid, surprising, yet somehow deliciously familiar."

I pressed my foot on Jesse's butt, which was cutely peeking out from the sheets and the only spot on his body not covered in tattoos.

"Jess. You sure you still want to drive me?"

He groaned. It used to require all my effort to keep the emotional intimacy between us at bay. But I was happy with what we had at that moment. I was busy and distracted. So was he. I had great sex when I wanted it. And Jesse remained my stray cat, happy to see me, starved for affection, but ultimately wanting nothing more than to be let out to roam at night, which I was happy to oblige.

I bent to pluck my socks from the floor, but Jesse snatched me back onto his naked lap, where I blithely continued to dress myself. His hands slid between my legs, opening my thighs. I bent to retrieve my bra from the chair. This was our game.

"I'm late."

"I don't give a fuck," he whispered into the crook of my shoulder. He began to grind me on his lap, reawakening his barely asleep erection.

"I have to go," I said flatly, closing my eyes and reaching up and back to rake my fingers through his messy hair.

"Then you should go," he whispered, sliding his fingers into the front of my panties, finding me, unsurprisingly, very wet. "You should definitely leave."

With one swift movement, he spun me onto the bed face down, my limbs splayed. He tugged down my panties, leaving them askew across the backs of my thighs. I could feel him hovering over me, taking in the sight of my ass in the air, his knees knocking my thighs apart. Then, without warning, he entered me fiercely, all thrust and muscle, like he was taking something from me, something I was instantly reluctant to hand over. But my resistance didn't last. I couldn't help it. I clutched the sheets and arched my back, giving myself over to him, as he plunged deeper and deeper, his hard fingers bruising my hips, his cock pinioning me onto the bed, my whole body tightening around it. My clitoris was perfectly positioned against the coverlet and he knew it, timing his rhythm and thrusts to make me come. Even if this was all I ever got from him, it was everything I wanted in this moment.

"You like this, don't you?" he murmured, his fingers entwining my hair and tugging my head back a bit. The intensity of his thrusts increased.

I nodded, mute with pleasure, the build accelerating.

"I love fucking you, Cassie."

And with that I exploded around him, my body convulsing as I arched to pull pleasure from his thrusting cock. I could see his veined shaft in my mind's eyes, easing in and out of me as he spurted across my ass and back. Our bodies were moving together, each taking something from the other until we both began to plummet from the heights, back down onto the rumpled bed.

"Holy shit," I said, collapsing across the sheets. He rolled onto his back next to me, breathless, laughing lightly. "I'm going to be late."

"No you're not," he said, suddenly rising and clapping like a sergeant. "Let's go, let's go, let's go! Shower, dress, I'll start the truck."

I leapt to my feet, seeing stars in my peripheral vision. The fastest shower on earth was followed by frantic dressing, and Jesse was on the porch by the time I threw my wet hair into a low ponytail. We were quietly distracted as he made his way across the city to the Garden District, taking a detour down Frenchmen. It felt weird to just pass by the restaurant, my neck craning to catch sight of people, *my* people.

The Café was in its mid-Sunday slump. I saw Maureen's arm sweeping a table clean. Claire had the day off, too, so she'd be at Will's, maybe watching TV, maybe reading, hopefully not sad and hopefully on the mend. She'd made the difficult decision to skip summer school, preferring instead to split her time between working at the Café Rose and Cassie's. She loved helping with the prep, Dell regularly commenting that she was naturally gifted in the kitchen. Will was adamant, though. As long as she wanted to live with him, she had to go back in September to some kind of school. I would never tell Will it was actually Jesse who suggested that Claire enroll at the Culinary School of the Arts. He had even offered to write her a letter of recommendation. When I mentioned it to Claire as an option, her face lit up. She squeezed me breathless, and for a brief moment I could see what she must have looked like as a child— happy, unburdened, her future wide open before her.

By now, I thought, resting my head against the window of Jesse's truck, Will would be upstairs, running through the menu with the wait staff, replacing the plastic liquor decanter tops that would have soaked overnight. That was about the only business disagreement we'd had in five months, Will being baffled as to why you'd take *all* the decanters off at night to reseal *all* the bottles.

"So they don't gum up," I said. "So fruit flies don't get in the booze."

"Every bar I've ever been in my whole life leaves the plastic spouts screwed on."

"Oh? Which ones? So I can remind myself *never* to go there."

He gave in. We gelled at work, Will taking on parts of running a restaurant I didn't love (marketing, operations, scheduling), leaving me the parts I loved (accounting, customer service, menu planning). And because of our split duties, we really hadn't spent much time alone. Our interactions often involved a brief schedule handoff, or a meeting in the hallway to finalize a shopping list or one in the kitchen to give a quick verdict over a simmering pot of something amazing Dell was cooking up.

Then yesterday, something weird happened. Will emerged from the staff dressing room having freshly showered. He was on days. I was on the floor that night. But showering at work was something he had never done, even during the messiest renovation days. Dell and I were in the kitchen, perched on stools, flipping through a spice catalogue for fish rub recipes. Normally clad in dark chinos and a plain blue or white dress shirt, this time Will was in all black: black button-down dress shirt with French cuffs, black flat-front slacks and a new pair of black suede shoes. He smelled so good and looked so damn sexy he took my breath away.

To camouflage my reaction, I gave him a pursed, thin-lipped smile, and with as much flatness as I could muster said, "That's a nicely made shirt."

"Thanks," he said, smoothing it down. "It cost enough. By the way, Dell, that seafood gumbo is outstanding. They're in for a real treat tonight."

"Thank you muchly," Dell answered, waving over her shoulder.

Will headed out the back door without saying good-bye and my heart plummeted. He probably had a date. I hadn't asked. I didn't want to know. But I knew. He had a date. Or a lover already. The promise of sex was all over him.

But what business was it of mine? None. After all, at that moment, my own lover was driving me to a place where people gather to plan sex fantasies with the same commitment and concentration countries put into hosting the Olympics. Jesse took St. Charles Avenue to Third, instead of the usual route along Magazine Street, something I didn't notice until I saw the clanging streetcars rolling over the high grass along the boulevard. I had a postcard of an old streetcar pinned to my fridge. I bought it the day Scott and I moved here, now almost a decade ago. Had I really lived in New Orleans that long? I thought owning a business would make me feel more rooted, but there were times I still felt like a tourist in this city.

We pulled up to the Mansion.

"Have fun today at Sex Club," Jesse said, pulling me in for a kiss. "Call you later."

"Okay."

That feeling of nostalgia followed me up to the Mansion's front portico. How much had changed since I first came through this gate! Back then I had been so scared, shy, completely unsure of myself. Why had I felt discarded? It wasn't only because I didn't have a man in my life. It went deeper than that. I had separated from myself and seemed to be running on a different set of rails than the rest of the world. Today, life wasn't easy or always happy, but it was full and it had purpose.

I pushed the wide doors open just as Angela was exiting the powder room and crossing the checkered-tile foyer, dressed casually in a T-shirt, jeans and pumps.

"Hey, Cassie," she said, kissing me on both cheeks. Sometimes I forgot how tall she was until I was standing right next to her. "Been meaning to come to the restaurant. How's it going?"

"Good. We're having a busy spring. Makes me wish we had a patio."

"They're overrated. You know how hot the city gets in summer. Everyone wants the AC."

"I guess you're right. But we *are* thinking of clearing out the bar area and maybe putting a band there. So . . . ?"

"Yes. I'll do it. And I know a great accompanist who plays on this little portable keyboard, so we wouldn't take up too much room."

I was pleased. Will and I had had Angela on our wish list for possible performers. I hadn't been sure she'd deign to sing at our little joint.

"Everything good with you and Jesse?" she asked.

It was common knowledge that we were an item of sorts without being an item at all. Still, I wasn't sure how to reply.

"Jesse's good. He's fun."

"So I hear," Angela said as she walked ahead of me through the dining room's double doors.

Ouch.

I watched her make her way around the long oak table to greet Bernice, Michelle and Brenda. Matilda was at the side table talking to Kit, both of them nibbling from the impressive array of food laid out—spring rolls, pakoras, wine and cheese. Amani was refreshing the shrimp platter. I began to wonder who else among the Committee had had sex with Jesse during some training session or another. At Tracina's baby shower last year, I found out Pauline had "freshened up Jesse's oral skills." Even Matilda's name had come up as a possible partner, though I found that hard to believe—not because she was almost twenty years older than him but because she was so particular, so elegant, so refined . . . and he was so . . . Jesse. I could imagine Michelle with her blond curls tumbling across his chest, or bisexual Kit, who could easily lure a third into their bed. Damn, I felt it, that old stream of jealousy coursing toxically through my blood. I had been warned about Jesse. It was never a secret. I knew what this thing was. I understood our limitations. Still, I was shaking as I took a seat between Matilda and Maria, doing my best to hide this sudden bout of insecurity. In two minutes, I'd gone from feeling grateful and hopeful to fraudulent and useless.

Shake it off, Cassie. This isn't about you.

I nodded hellos to the assembled gals, including Pauline, whose presence could still make me blush a bit.

"Thank you all so much for coming," Matilda began. "I know this is a last-minute gathering, but we have a couple of things on our agenda. As some of you are aware, Solange's threesome fantasy did not, as we say, pan out."

Damn. I had been meaning to ask, but I figured no news was good news.

Matilda turned to me, reading my mind. "Cassie, don't blame yourself. She changed her mind. It happens."

"I'm sorry it didn't work out," I said.

"Me too," Pauline said, poutily.

"We all are. But remember that this is a process of discovery, and Solange learned something valuable by not following through. Don't cry for Solange. She has a couple of heady adventures lined up for her. In Paris."

"And I'm more than happy to help with any of them," Angela said, raising her hand.

"I'm afraid this one's Bernice's," Matilda said, signaling for Bernice to empty a manila envelope of photos onto the table. *Ooh*s and *ahh*s for Paris became *ooh*s and *ahh*s for the pictures, which showed what looked like the first-draft lineup for a team of the Best-Looking Black Men on the Planet.

"Ladies, before you scramble through that pile, take a look at *this* photo."

Matilda pushed back a screen on the wall to display a blown-up shot of a handsome black man, older, hands on his hips, standing in what looked to be Jackson Square. He had a light salt-and-pepper goatee and was wearing sunglasses pushed up on his closely shaved head. He was smiling to someone off camera to his left, a dimple in his left cheek. The look on his face suggested he wasn't aware that this photo was being taken.

"See this man?"

"Indeed we do," someone muttered, causing a fit of giggles.

"This man is Julius Faraday, Solange's ex-husband."

There were more *ooh*s and *ahh*s and *Did you say "ex"?* and *Go, Solange.*

"All right, now listen," Matilda said, trying to scold, but she, too, was having a hard time hiding her grin. "For reasons that might be obvious, we need to find among these headshots the man who *best* resembles Julius, but Julius as a younger man, the way Solange would have known him when they first met."

I got up to join the cluster in front of the board and take a closer look at Julius. He was shockingly well assembled in his turtleneck and leather jacket. His front teeth had the barest hint of a gap. Were it not for his connection to Solange, I would have suggested him as a recruit. I also would have offered to train him. But he was her ex, and exes were off-limits. Or so I thought.

"Him," Michelle said, pinning one of the headshots next to the photo of Julius.

"Nuh-uh," said Angela. "*This* dude."

The man in the photo she indicated had a smile similar to Julius's, but his hair was longer. After some debate about a smile being more important than eyes, Angela's pick won in a landslide vote, after which Bernice disappeared with the headshot to "make overseas calls." The rest of us got up to leave because we thought we'd completed the task of the evening.

"Hold on, ladies. We have one more order of business," Matilda said, reaching under the table for another manila envelope. "We're selecting one more recruit this evening. And in an unusual twist, this recruit approached us. Well, he approached me."

There was confusion around the table. Matilda rarely accepted applicants who approached S.E.C.R.E.T. because it was usually through an indiscreet recruit who'd broken the rules and told one of his friends. Too much eagerness was frowned upon and it threatened our anonymity.

Matilda placed the envelope in front of me.

"Cassie, would you please open it?"

Why me? Maybe this time I would be chief fantasy facilitator! Maybe I was going to Paris! I snatched the envelope off the table and impatiently ripped it open. Out slid a glossy black-and-white headshot of a handsome new recruit.

What followed happened in a few seconds, five tops, but time seemed to slow. I took in the recruit's studied stance, and the way he leaned against the rough cement wall. I thought, *Hmm, he's very good-looking. But I know this guy from somewhere.* Three seconds in, I realized this man was famous. But for what? Then, in the space of time it took for me to inhale and exhale, it dawned on me: this recruit *wasn't* famous. It was just that his face was so deeply familiar, he felt famous.

I was looking at the face of Will, *my* Will, his brooding features in quiet repose, his dark blue eyes relaxed but serious, a kind smile playing across his lips. He was wearing that black shirt with the French cufflinks from the other day. He stood with his hands in the pockets of those flat-front slacks. He looked sexy. Very, very sexy.

The room was so quiet I might as well have been completely alone with my screaming thoughts. When I went to open my mouth, the only thing that came out was a strangled word that sounded like "No."

"Let me see that," Angela said, snatching the photo from my fingers. Seconds later, she slapped a hand over her mouth, her wide eyes meeting mine. She mutely passed the photo to Kit, who did the same thing. The game stopped at Pauline, who had never met Will and didn't know why everyone was so shocked.

"Who's this?" she asked.

"This recruit's name is Will," Matilda explained to Pauline. "He is . . . a friend of Cassie's."

"*Friend?*" I said, altogether too loudly. "He's my *ex-boyfriend*. And my current business partner."

Oh my god, am I going to faint? I'm going to faint.

"He's also a man," Matilda said to me, evenly, "who I think would suit our Solange perfectly."

Is this really happening?

"Well, this *is* interesting," Pauline said, spinning the photo into the center of the table.

"He came to me a few days ago," Matilda continued.

Will? Came to her?

Matilda proceeded to tell the story of one man's awakening, Will's, which had happened after he almost lost someone he loved because of certain conscious and unconscious prejudices some people held about women and sex. I thought she was talking about Will losing me, but he had meant Claire, whose vicious slut-shaming had been equal parts baffling and infuriating to him. Matilda described how Claire's victimization had left Will feeling utterly powerless. And it also exposed attitudes he hoped to correct in himself. He came to Matilda, she said, because he wanted help. He wanted to do something constructive, maybe make a donation to some of the charities highlighted at the event at Latrobe's, the very venue he had stormed out of after fighting with me.

"And that's when I suggested that he become a recruit, as a way to open his mind and to change his attitudes about women and sex."

"*You* suggested this to Will?"

"I did, Cassie. I explained that our organization works to remove sexual stigmas from women, one interlude at a time. And we do that with one another's help, but also with the help of a few good men who are also changed for the better by their involvement with us."

"*You* asked Will to become a *recruit?*" I repeated, trying really hard to contain my anger.

"Yes, Cassie," she said, matching my near-hysteria with an enormous amount of gentleness. "I asked him to consider it. And he said yes. If we'd have him."

I harrumphed, my arms wrapped tightly around my torso, my chin down. I was the physical embodiment of teenaged poutiness.

"He does know that I'd find out, right?"

"Of course. I told him that in order to be considered he'd have to pass muster with the entire group, including you."

"And he didn't care?"

"Of course he cares, Cassie. Trust me when I say this, he cares a great deal. Especially about you."

"Ha!" I said. That outburst was followed by the sickening sense of my own emotional limitations. But it was hard to see the altruism in all this.

And yet, the more Matilda talked about recruiting Will for S.E.C.R.E.T., the more the rational part of my brain began to light up and take over.

"Will made it very clear that if you were against this idea, he'd decline," Matilda said. "He feels that this might be a way to make . . . amends. To us, to you, to women in general, I guess. That's how he put it."

I had to laugh. And so I did.

"The way he makes amends to me is by fucking some other woman? That is amazing."

The approbation came swift and sure.

"Cassie Robichaud, that is not a reaction befitting a member of S.E.C.R.E.T. The 'some other woman' you speak of is our Solange, our sister in S.E.C.R.E.T. And last I checked, your romantic and sexual ties with Will were no more. And you, my dear, seem to be enjoying the many benefits of S.E.C.R.E.T. membership. Are you not? Besides, Will is going to start having sex again with other women regardless. What's wrong with him starting here, where it's just his body in the game and not his heart?"

I kept looking around the table for someone to side with me, but Kit, Pauline, Angela and the rest of them had slowly sunk in their seats, watching this like it was a tennis match on a big screen. My mind spun wildly, careening from anger to fear, to those darker places where rancid jealously brewed. Then clouds began parting on reason and a different thought occurred to me: If Will participated in S.E.C.R.E.T., saw all the wonderful things this crazy little institution offered, maybe he'd see that he'd been acting like a knucklehead all along. He'd see what sexual expression and liberation could mean to the soul. To be angry with Will was to be the hypocrite I accused him of being. To prevent his participation in S.E.C.R.E.T. because of some old fears was to admit I'd learned nothing. And it would be tantamount to admitting I still held out hope that there was a future for us. In fact, allowing him entry into S.E.C.R.E.T. fixed so many things between us: it evened out the playing field, it gave us a common experience, and it acknowledged that S.E.C.R.E.T. was a place that helped, even healed, not just women, but men as well.

I gathered up Will's photo in my hand.

"Matilda. Everyone . . . I won't, I *can't* offer any objections to this recruit. This recruit is, in fact, ideal for S.E.C.R.E.T. He's a good man. He's incredibly sexy. He is an amazing lover. And he truly adores women. So if there are no other concerns, then I see no reason to prevent moving this to a vote. You have mine."

"Wonderful. I knew you'd see reason. Any other objections? Can I get a vote?" Matilda said.

One by one, hands shot up in a counterclockwise display of yes.

"Great. We will move forward with this recruit," Matilda said.

That wave of nausea had barely subsided when another potent question surfaced, this time from Pauline.

"Who's going to *train* Will?"

The room fell silent again.

"Any suggestions?" Matilda asked.

Crazy how a good idea can quickly become a bad one. Angela's hand rose. Of *course* she would volunteer! And Will would find out what great sex really was! My blood roiled beneath the surface of my skin.

"Um," said Angela, "I would like to excuse myself from volunteering."

What? Did I hear her correctly?

"Why is that, Angela?" Matilda asked.

"Well, like, I *know* Will. And also, because . . . *Cassie.*" She winced.

"I can't do it either!" Kit blurted.

"Me neither!" said Michelle, Brenda adding, "I really can't."

Maria, Pauline and Amani's tight expressions said everything.

"So, let me get this straight," Matilda said. "We *all* agree Will is a perfect recruit. We are overwhelmingly unanimous on that front. And yet *no one* wants to train him?"

More silence. I felt my nails dig into the tops of my thighs. Were they exhibiting loyalty or fear?

"Well, in that case, I guess we can't go forward with—"

"I will!" I said, a little too loudly. "I'll do it. I'll train him."

Matilda looked at me. "Pardon me?"

"I can do it, Matilda," I said.

Matilda glanced around the table once more. Everyone had turned into owls, sitting still, eyes wide.

"Will might object, Cassie."

"I'll deal with that then."

Matilda eyed me carefully. "You can't keep him, Cassie. After you train him, you have to let him go."

"I know. I've done it before. I can do it again."

Matilda sighed. "Okay then. Will Foret is our unanimous choice. And Cassie Robichaud will be his trainer.

We'll discuss the scenario at a later date," she said, placing the folder back into her bag.

I glanced around the table. The women looked variously impressed, worried and a little stunned. Of course it was risky; isn't it always when it comes to sex? But deep down in the most secret part of my heart, the part I wouldn't even reveal to myself, I hoped that by giving Will permission to join S.E.C.R.E.T., by showing him how to please another woman, then setting him free to do just that, maybe, just maybe, it would bring him back to me.

SOLANGE

The guilt I felt when I said good-bye to my sweet boy in front of his dad's building was especially potent. I had left him before, for more than a few days, but never for such an odd, decadent reason. I had told Julius the truth, kind of. I told him I had landed a coveted interview with Pierre Castille and had secured a promise from *New Orleans Magazine* for a cover story. The magazine was thrilled and even offered to cover expenses.

"Pierre Castille? You mean that rich dude who owns my building?"

"He does?" I said, forgetting momentarily that the Castilles owned half of the Warehouse District.

"I have a question for him," Julius said. "Ask him when he's going to upgrade our elevator system."

"I'll be sure to put that on my list."

Watching Julius with Gus on the sidewalk, the both of them waving good-bye through my driver's side window,

I felt that pang again, that awful mother's guilt that struck me like a low-grade fever.

Later that night, while packing, I burst into tears before finally pulling myself together. *It's just for a week! You deserve this little break! This is an adventure. You've snagged the mother of all interviews. Be . . . brave. It's Paris! In the springtime!*

And indeed, when I arrived, big, fat buds were bursting pink and white from the tiny trees outside the window of my unbearably plush suite at the Hotel George V. I glanced around the room in disbelief. With its dense red carpet, upholstered walls covered in gold damask and four-poster king-size bed, it might have been the nicest hotel I'd ever seen, let alone stayed in.

The first thing I did after checking in was to call Gus. It was late at night for me, but dusk for my boy. Julius answered from the eighth hole at the Audubon golf course.

"Hey there, just a sec," he whispered. I could hear a *whoosh* in the background and some gleeful high-fiving. "Oh man, you should have seen that *swing*. The boy's a natural!"

"You think we have a Tiger Woods on our hands?" I said, choking up. I missed them. I missed them *both* just then.

"Let's hope. Then we can both retire in style, right, Gus? You got in okay?"

"Yeah, I did. It's really beautiful here," I said, playing with the curly phone cord, staving off the guilt.

"I bet. I've been picturing you there," he said. "Walking the streets. The light on your skin . . ."

Things got quiet for a second, oddly so.

"Put Gus on for me?" I asked. Gus's ebullience helped break the potent little spell that hung over his dad and me for a second.

"Mom! I sunk the ball in four shots! Dad says that's amazing for my first time. Can I take golf lessons? It's so cool you're in Paris! I want to go next time. Maybe I should learn French. I know, I know, Spanish is important, but it's not so different and besides . . ."

Gus always seemed charged with a special kind of energy when he got to spend long stretches with his dad. Boy energy. I loved it. After a good talk, we hung up, my heart a little less heavy.

Everything came to a quiet halt for a second as I sat on the edge of the downy bed. *Be here,* I told myself. *Don't be in New Orleans, be here. Gus is fine. He's with his dad. Let it go. It's only temporary.*

I was wrapped in a towel waiting for the bath to fill. I would soon be eating mussels in wine with a nice Chablis, my feet encased in slippers. Matilda had told me whatever I needed was on the other end of a phone, answered by someone who would say, *"Bonsoir,* Madame Faraday!" (I didn't have the heart to correct them; it was *Mademoiselle.*) What if I knew exactly what I needed but just couldn't articulate it yet?

I padded to the marble bathroom and shut off the taps, stripping down to my skin. I turned to take in my body in the full-length mirror behind the door. There I was, my whole story staring at me through the mirror—my barely perceptible yet strangely symmetrical stretch marks just below my rib cage, my smooth, firm thighs from my jock days. My arms were good arms, my breasts were beautiful breasts. My hair was shiny; it was a good cut. In a few months I would be forty-two, and I had never felt more alluring. S.E.C.R.E.T. had given me that. It had quieted that internal critic, giving me this newfound sense of my womanhood, even adding dimensions to it. I was grateful and too tired to soak in a bath for long, so I got out, wrapping my damp body in one of the comfiest bathrobes I had ever completely passed out in.

A knock on the door woke me from what I thought was a brief nap. It was the bellhop bringing me pastries and coffee, for *breakfast!* Turned out I had slept the night. A thick card was perched on the tray between the butter and the sugar. I opened it like it was a Christmas gift to see the word *Curiosity* carved in elaborate scroll on one side and underneath, a handwritten query: *Curious about what it would be like to go back in time?*

My do-over step! I shivered, excited, nervous. I tried to take my time, to enjoy my breakfast in front of the Juliet balcony: café au lait, fresh fruit, bread and jam, but I was too excited to see Paris to linger long over food.

Just after the sun came up, I threw on a sweater and comfortable walking shoes and stepped out onto the Rue George V, where I passed a flock of nuns in traditional black garb funneling into the American Cathedral next door.

The air was balmy and sweet, and it clung to my skin like a hug. Armed with a good street map, I decided to trek towards the Louvre, through the Tuileries, backtracking over to the Centre Georges Pompidou, a building I had once read wore its "messy skeleton of pipes and ventilation" on the outside, on purpose, "to leave room inside for all the art." I remember grabbing that as a metaphor for the kind of life I wanted to live, back when I thought I was going to be a glamorous lounge singer, before the practical concerns of life kicked in. I'd see the sights later; today was just for getting the lay of the land.

Strange to see for the first time a place that's familiar to you only from books and movies. I don't remember even wondering how Parisians actually lived, or about the price of real estate, or what their suburbs looked like or what kind of commutes these people would have or what the public school system was like. But that's what I was thinking about that day, marveling over the riverside balconies, imagining life in some grand six-room apartment overlooking the Seine and the Eiffel Tower, throwing open the windows while wearing a white silk robe and sipping my coffee before waking up Gus for his bus. But would he take a bus in Paris? Or would I walk him to some ancient gorgeous building with old piping and stained-glass windows? Or would he be safe on his own? Would he make friends easily here? With other Americans? Or would I insist he make French friends?

Stop it, Solange. Be here now.

Sigh. Paris might be the only place in the world where you could fall in love with a room, a view, a street, or a neighborhood the way you would with a real person. That's what was happening to me. My skin was flushed, my heart racing. I made a vow that we needed to bring Gus to Paris, and soon. Well maybe not *we*. *I* needed to bring him before he got too old to want to travel alone with his boring, old mother.

I was never much of a shopper, but I could see how Paris could ruin a woman. I started to covet things I had never looked twice at before—dramatic hats, expensive purses, even a stunning cream-colored wedding dress with lace sleeves and a satin sash that was the same price my dad paid for our house on State Street, back when he bought it in the '60s. It was all too much, too beautiful and too heady.

I grabbed lunch at a café under a vivid yellow-and-white awning. Next to me was a table of shopgirls on break, smoking and gossiping in French. How was it possible that Parisian women could make such a filthy addiction look so damn chic? All day it was hard to find a woman in Paris who *didn't* have it going on, whether it was a perfectly placed scarf, or good bangs or just the right shoes. Women here seemed to enjoy and know how to be women. Even the older ones I saw laughed loud and long, their wide-open mouths displaying a crooked tooth here and there. Gray hair abounded, lipstick was smeared, shoes were scuffed, and yet they all seemed so feminine and so beautiful. Could I do that? Could I have the courage to age beautifully and honestly without Marsha's frets about being a woman working in television and struggling to remain young-looking forever? I hoped so. Again, I thought about the women in S.E.C.R.E.T., marveling at Matilda's striking agelessness and that of the other women I remembered from my induction, none of whom seemed the type to lose much sleep over wrinkles or gray hair.

On my way back to the hotel, this time taking the crowded Champs-Élysées, I wondered what Gus and his dad were doing and if Gus would go to bed without a fuss. I missed them, and yet slipping naked between the cool sheet and the heavy duvet, I couldn't have felt more serene.

~⌒

The serenity didn't last. After that decadent nap and a long bath, the kind I hadn't enjoyed since before Gus, there was a knock on my door. This time it wasn't the bellhop but a tiny, very pretty black woman with a short red afro. She looked vaguely familiar, standing there holding heavy garment bags slung over one arm, and in the crook of the other, a big doctor's bag of sorts. If she let go of either, she'd tip over.

She screamed by way of saying hello. "Ahh! You probably don't remember me," she said in English, stepping around me into the room.

I did recognize her. She was followed by a bellhop rolling in a tray of cheese, bread, fruit and champagne on ice.

"Oh, you have a *suite!*" she squealed. "Not that I'm complaining about my room."

She hoisted the bags onto the bed, then turned and noticed my mouth was still agape.

"Jeez. You *don't* remember me." She handed the bellhop a fist of euros, and waited for him to disappear before continuing in a dramatic whisper. "I'm Bernice. We met when you—I'm from *S.E.C.R.E.T.*, hon. I'm here to prep you. For *tonight!*"

"*Right!*"

I could have kissed her. It was so nice to have someone from "home" here, and I was enveloped by an overwhelming sense of calm. She hung up the garment bags, then threw open the valise.

"Makeup and hair now, dress later. I brought a few for you to choose from."

"What's the scenario?"

She made a sad face. "Oh, Solange. We've had to warn you about so many of your fantasies ahead of time, because of your job and being a mom and everything. Let's have *some* surprises, shall we?" she said, lowering me to the seat in front of the dressing table mirror.

I'd had hair and makeup people hovering around my head for most of my professional life, but it had never felt like this, so loving and caring. I was Bernice's personal work of art, and my hair and makeup wasn't just a job or a task; it was her artistic mission to make me beautiful.

Normally I wore my hair in a conservative kind of bob—"newslady hair," Julius affectionately called it. It wasn't the sexiest choice, but it was good for work and easy to maintain. But Bernice asked me how I used to wear my hair back in my college days.

"Big," I said, making a motion to indicate *out to here*.

"*Yes!*" she said, wetting and spraying and teasing and cultivating and curling my hair into a masterful homage to Miss Ross herself. My hair was so big and wild when she finished I swear she added weight as well as height to my dense curls. I hadn't worn my hair like this in decades, and it seemed to shave years off my face.

"Now, let's pick the dress. Then lipstick. Yeah?"

There were a half-dozen couture dresses and they all fit perfectly. The low-cut navy number was made with this shimmery Lycra material that felt incredible on my skin, but I was all nipples and ass in it. You could even see the outline of my *belly button*.

"Nope."

The gold lamé minidress made me gasp it was so unbearably sexy. But then I bent to check how much it covered while sitting.

"That's gorgeous, Solange."

I gave her my best *are you fucking kidding me* face and strutted back to the bathroom to change. The silver dress was too *Dynasty* in the shoulders, though I loved how it scooped down the back. Both the little black dress and the puffy pink one did nothing for me. Last was a deep red satin gown that didn't just fit, it *encased* me. It *held* me. It made my body appear taller and stronger than it really was, my arms longer, my legs endless.

"*Stunning*," Bernice said, adjusting the spaghetti straps, zipping the dress up the back.

The finishing touch was red lipstick so glossy my mouth looked like it'd been dipped in a pot of slick candy-apple glaze.

The front desk called to tell me my limo was waiting. I turned to Bernice.

"Here we go."

"Knock 'em dead, Solange," she said with a wink, hugging me good-bye loosely, not wanting to crush any aspect of the glittery masterpiece she'd created.

Clacking my thousand-dollar heels across the magnificent marble foyer towards the ancient revolving doors, I caught a glimpse of what it would be like to be famous—not local-weekend-news-anchor famous, but notorious-famous, globally famous, whispered-about famous, gawked-at famous, Beyoncé famous; I was turning heads faster than I was passing them and it felt amazing. The driver lowered me (and my hair) into the back seat, and off we sped.

Paris at night was a lurid parade, and my eyes danced wildly around, gathering all the details: the young couples walking hand-in-hand, the lit-up shops, the monuments and marble, the artists hawking their work, people selling prints and books from stalls lining the crowded sidewalks. We passed a cluster of cafés dotting four corners of a crossroads, the street we turned down so narrow that the buildings on either side became a white marble tunnel with no roof. We pulled up to a fancy place called the Chez Papas jazz club, where my driver lifted me out of the back seat to my uneasy feet.

"Welcome," said a doorman, his accent odd and undetectable. "Your table is waiting."

Inside, a tiny woman holding a tinier clipboard whisked me past the crowd encircling the stage, past the shiny wineglasses and the fur stoles, to a small table off to the side where I was seated with some fanfare. A maître d' appeared to my right, arm slung with a white cloth, pouring me water and taking my drink order.

"Campari and soda, *s'il vous plaît*."

Just then the room went black, and a curtain rose to a quartet of young men, one holding a double bass, one a horn, one on drums and the fourth a guitarist who kept his back to the crowd while he adjusted his strings. When the guitar player turned around, I gasped. It wasn't Julius, but if you had frozen Julius in time twenty years ago, *this* is what he would have looked like: that sweet, sexy, wide-open face, slight gap between his teeth, brown skin burnished with that masculine vigor, all offset by the trademark goatee. This was Julius's smile, his face with no worries, no sleepless nights, a face not etched with endless disappointments, divorce, failure, stress. It was as though S.E.C.R.E.T. had cloned my ex, bringing him back to a time when he was young, happy, confident, *mine*. Back when we were perfect.

It all came crashing back to me, those late nights, the low pay (the big hair!), Julius watching me adoringly from behind his turntables. It was fun while it lasted. But then late-night rehearsals cut into my study time. My grades suffered and I had to make a choice. I know I made the right one—I gave up dreams for goals, a hobby for a career. I had to, and I never regretted it. I never looked back. And yet, I had left something vital behind, a part of me I hadn't thought I needed anymore or missed, until right now.

My posture corrected as the singer's hands circled the stand, bringing it more comfortably between his legs. He adjusted his guitar, strumming a few bars, his band following his lead. He brought his beautiful mouth to the microphone, his top lip snarling a little like Elvis's, before delivering an aching rendition of "My Funny Valentine."

I felt the room turning towards him the way flowers lean heavy towards the sun. He couldn't have been more than twenty-five, maybe thirty, this young man, but he sounded as though he'd been singing for decades, even through a war or two. His jazzy take on "I Can't Make You Love Me" had me snapping and bobbing. Then he started up some banter with the crowd. He wasn't French after all. He was American, *Southern* like me, which was at once incongruous and a bit of a relief.

"Ladies and gentlemen, I'm going to need some help with the next song," he said, strumming his guitar. "It's one of my favorites."

A hush came over the crowd.

"Where is Solange Thompson?" he asked, using his hand to shade his eyes from the glare from the lights. "I think she's here."

Solange Thompson? I didn't register at first that he was talking to me, about me, *at* me, because he was using my maiden name. Then I felt someone's hand on my upper arm, lifting me to my feet: the tiny woman with the clipboard.

"You weel be so kind as to join Alain for a song?" she said, pressing me towards the stage.

"Oh, no, there must be some mis—"

"There she is," Alain said, the spotlight finding me.

"I'm flattered, b-but—" I stammered, trying to resist the woman's prodding, but unable to resist Alain's urging. "I haven't done this in so long—"

My protestations were to no avail. I was ushered closer and closer to a grinning Alain and his inviting quartet, one of whom was now plunking a stool right in front of the microphone.

"Ladies and gentlemen," Alain said, extending his hand to help me up the steps of the stage. "Please welcome Solange Thompson."

Over applause, I began apologizing ahead of time for what would no doubt be a disaster. When the applause ebbed, a microphone was slapped into my hand. What happened next occurred because there was just no time to course-correct, no time to stop the band from striking up "Summertime," one of my favorites, no time to dig in my heels or flee in shock. Something took over for me, something ancient and beautiful, something embedded in my DNA. My body rose from the stool, and began to move to the opening chords, my eyes closed, my hand slapping out a gentle beat against my sequined thigh. Then I opened my mouth and sang. I sang words to a song long stored in the vault of my brain, and I sang it *well*. Alain leaned forward. We shared the mike for a few moving bars, our mouths inches apart and in complete harmony, like we'd been doing this for a long time too. Tears were stinging my eyes. But I wasn't crying. This wasn't sadness. This was old joy. And when the crowd applauded, a few in the front row springing to their feet, I could have kissed them on every one of their French mouths.

Song after song I gave them, from "I Get a Kick Out of You" to "Everybody's Talkin'," each perfectly suited to my vocals and Alain's harmony. I was *singing*. My shoulders were moving, I was smiling, *performing* for an audience in a strange city. I stood there and let them take me in. I was Solange Thompson again, the girl with all that hair, in the red satin dress and shiny lipstick, before the husband and the baby and the demanding career, before the awards and the disappointments, the tantrums and tears, the death of parents and the end of love—before everything that happened, it was just me, singing happily, in the dark.

Alain receded when the band struck up the open bars to "My Man," that lush song becoming my only solo. The lighting darkened my peripheral vision and the band gentled its tempo. The spotlight was on me and the only thing missing was a gardenia behind my ear. I sang and I sang, but this time with a heart heavy, not from missing "my" man, but from missing this part of my life, the part that had been mine and mine alone. I missed *myself.* And after I finished that song, the crowd's applause nearly levitated me off the stage and over to the table where Alain, my young Julius, sat waiting for me, the sexiest grin on the sexiest of mouths.

"You were spectacular," he said, gently bowing his head. "Thank you."

"Thank *you*," I said, warily taking the seat next to him. Was he real? He leaned towards me, his hand sliding around the back of the banquette. "And how did you know I could do that?"

"Music stays with you. Maybe it hides for a while, but it's always there in your bones, waiting to come out again."

Before I could ask him how he knew my maiden name, let alone that I sang at all, I had to get something out of the way.

"You know, this might sound strange, but you look an awful lot like—"

"Let's get out of here," he interrupted, whispering in my ear.

His voice sent shivers down my spine. He sounded just like Julius. "That is . . . if you'll accept the Step."

I turned to face him. Good lord, he even smelled like Julius. The gals at S.E.C.R.E.T. had done their research. No sooner was my hand in his than we found ourselves spilling out of the club and onto the lively street at night.

"I'll show you my Paris," he said, throwing his tuxedo jacket around my shoulders. He held my hand, tugging me towards the Saint-Germain-des-Prés station. He never let go of me, not while we were trotting down the street against the stream of crowds going in the opposite direction, not when we were navigating the gummy stairs to the damp subterranean cavern below. We came to the turnstile and he pushed in first, handing me his card to swipe myself through.

I hesitated.

I needed to take in how impossibly handsome this young man looked in his white tuxedo shirt, top button undone, the tie hanging loose around his neck like a Rat Packer. For a moment it was enough to freeze this in time, him smiling at me from the other side of the copper turnstile in Paris after midnight, looking like a vision of my best past. There was me dressed in my shimmery column of a dress, looking incongruous against the backdrop of this tired, disheveled crowd of hipsters and tourists and students heading home for the night, or just going out.

"Subway's coming!" he yelled over the underground din. "Accept this Step, Solange! Just do it!"

Could this be enough? Just the memory? To go forward was also to go backwards, and did I want to do that? To revisit all that pain and sadness?

Then I felt the urge and my whole body said: *Go!*

I swiped the card and pushed through the stile, joining him on the other side. Alain's mouth was an inch from mine, his downcast eyes hungrily taking in my ruby lips. And then he kissed me, softly at first, pressing feelings into me, sending warm memories through my body. I lifted my hands to his sides, feeling his firm torso beneath the tuxedo shirt. Someone bumped into him, jarring us out of our moment. We moved to the platform, and when the subway came, he pulled me onto it. Giggling, we collapsed into two empty seats on the uncrowded car. I felt twenty again, when every night out offered endless possibilities.

I had to fight back more tears, not from grief, but from relief, joy. We got off a few stops later and I let him lead the way up the stairs and into the warm, damp air of a different, quieter part of Paris. He told me this was the Montparnasse District, a place I knew only from stories about writers and artists. After navigating an endless maze of narrow streets, we stopped at an iron gate that he unlocked with a key as long as a pencil, which he kept on a string tied to his belt loop.

"Four stories. No elevator," he warned, quietly shutting the gate behind him.

I felt my reticence melt away at each landing. And though the building was narrow and the stairs worn from centuries of tired Parisians making this same trip, his garret apartment was neat, masculine and surprisingly roomy, made more so by the high ceilings and slanted casement windows, which offered a spectacular view of the buildings around us and the Tour Montparnasse in the distance. He had taste and style. He knew better than to take out the worn tile floors or to remove the fading wallpaper; he had just decorated around these gorgeous relics of a bygone era.

He took the coat from around my shoulders and placed it on the back of a paint-spattered chair. Then he carefully took my purse from my hand and put it on the small butcher's block next to a beautiful antique porcelain sink. He didn't have to turn on a light. The bright city illuminated the dim room. It was nothing like my suite at the George V, but a person could be happier here, I thought.

I stood in front of his wide daybed, covered in throws and mismatched silk pillows and surrounded on three sides by elaborate wrought-iron grating. I was as nervous as the girl I once was. (*You're forty-one and he's . . . not!*) But his hands on my waist stopped my fear from traveling any farther up my body to my head. He *had* me, and he knew just what to do with me.

His gaze melted me into place. He reached behind me, found my zipper, and slowly pulled it down. He slipped the straps off my shoulders. I closed my eyes as he peeled it down to my waist, reverently. I couldn't watch him watching me. I felt his hand sliding down my arm, lifting my hand to his mouth and kissing the pulse at my wrist. Then I felt another kiss at the crook of my elbow, then my upper arm, my clavicle, my throat, my lips. Then I felt my dress melt around my ankles, leaving me standing in black stockings and garters. He whispered my name over and over, his face now buried in my breasts. I opened my eyes and looked down. From this angle, in this light, he *was* Julius, *my* Julius, in Paris, with me.

What a strange, melancholy, beautiful fantasy.

My breath caught as he suddenly sent me back onto my elbows on the daybed and stood before me as he removed his clothes. He sent the loose tie sailing across the room. The shirt he practically tore off, revealing a smooth, bare chest and rippled stomach.

As I parted my knees, his hand casually circled his own gorgeous cock. I lay back on the pillows, my red-tipped fingers caressing my skin, trailing across my stomach as I watched him watch me. I knew I was wet before I touched myself.

"You're so beautiful in this light," he whispered.

He crawled towards me. He was all panther now, this young man and his young skin, his strong shoulders and firm arms. No sooner had I wrapped my fingers around his hard shaft than I was guiding it towards my eager mouth. My tongue explored the tip, the tender opening, the delicate rim, my fingers dancing along his pulsing veins. He grabbed the bedrails behind me as my hand gathered his smooth balls. He fed himself to me, his moans matching the creaky sounds the bed was making as he rocked slightly, helping me take him in all the way. My hands circled his haunches as my mind searched for a word to describe the rest of his body; *uncanny*. Even the way he tasted . . .

Just before I felt him ready to give himself over to me, he stopped abruptly, taking himself out of my mouth to bend over and kiss me again and to say my name once, twice. *His voice was just like* . . . I opened my eyes and saw it again, that flash of my past, my younger love above me. I wanted all of him inside me, *now*, and he knew it, spinning around to wrestle a condom free from his wallet. My heart raced as he returned his focus, shifting me down the bed, opening my thighs.

"I've been wanting to do this all night," he said, his head dipping down.

His mouth found me first, and he ate me eagerly, hungrily. My arms flung to the sides, I felt like I was coming apart as he licked and bit, his tongue by turns lapping and fucking me. My hips began to grind against his mouth as the climb started. I squeezed my eyes closed and then I felt it, his shaft entering me, filling me, his hips picking up on my rhythm, never losing the beat. I wrapped my arms around his strong shoulders and my legs around his lean hips as he bore into me. There was barely a warning before my orgasm shot hot through my center and out my limbs, in wave after wave of shuddering pleasure, my head thrashing. He drove into me with renewed ferocity, increasing the intense spasms. My thighs squeezed him harder as yet another plundering wave rolled over me, signaling his mounting pleasure was only beginning. As I was coming down, he cascaded over me, a look of ferocity taking over his sweet face, aging him in the sexist way. In a dark flash I saw my Julius, now, and then he was gone again and Alain was in my arms. After a few moments, he peeled his sweat-misted face off my chest and rested his chin between my breasts.

"Mother of God."

"Why do people always invoke religion at times like this?" I asked, still panting.

"I think it's all the church steeples I can see from my bed," he said, smiling. "You're so fucking beautiful. Holy shit."

"They train you to say that?" I asked, looking down at his sweet, sweet face, not even caring that my chins must have tripled at that angle.

"Did I pull it off okay?"

I slapped his ass. Hard.

He scrambled off me and reached beneath the daybed for a small box, which he carefully placed on my still rising and falling chest.

"*Ceçi est pour vous, madame,*" he said, surprising me with his perfect French accent.

"You mean *mademoiselle,*" I said.

"*Mais oui.*"

While he rested on an elbow, I opened the box and lifted out my *Curiosity* charm. It took on a burnished glow in that dim, cozy garret. This charm would remind me of my wonderment, and what happens when you let your curiosity take you back in time. I had sung again in a red dress for a crowd of strangers in a strange city. I'd rushed giddily into the streets of Paris, kissing a younger version of an old love on the Metro, turning back the clock for just one night.

The next time I opened my eyes, the sun was peeking up over Montparnasse, turning the white buildings pink with new promise. Alain snoozed while I quietly dressed. Holding my shoes, I took one last look at his face. *Uncanny, even in repose.* Then I descended the ancient stairs to the street below and flagged the first cab I found. In the back seat, I cracked open the window, taking in the smell of a city only just beginning to awaken.

16

CASSIE

After that Committee meeting, I had the sense that something had been unleashed into our little universe. Not necessarily something bad, but an unsettling energy abounded, one whose wake would probably leave my world, and Will's, reordered. And yet, I felt powerless to stop it.

The day after Will was recruited, Dell and I were in the kitchen blanching peppers for stuffing. One by one, she dipped them into boiling water. After a few minutes, she scooped them out with a slotted spoon, dropping them in ice water. My job was to wait a few seconds, then fish them out and peel them. It was strangely hypnotic work, and for a moment I forgot what I knew; I wasn't thinking about what had happened and what was coming.

Claire was popping in and out of the kitchen dropping dirty dishes on the conveyor, so for a moment I thought it was her, not Will, who punched through the doors loudly. I was about to ask her to be a little less mean to the door, but when I saw him standing there with a clutch of baguettes, his hair a sexy mess, his stubble longer than normal, my heart did its requisite tumble in my chest. I had long made peace with my body's reaction to Will; it would always jolt a little, no matter how often my brain scolded it. I could do nothing to prevent my face from burning. And instantly I knew Will knew that I knew that he had been recruited by S.E.C.R.E.T. And that we both knew things had changed, and that they were going to change some more.

"Hey," Will said, his wary eyes on me.

"Hey."

He placed the baguettes on the counter and pulled a large blowtorch out of the bottom of the bag, his eyes still on me.

"This the one you wanted, Dell?"

Dell turned to examine it. "You could repair a tanker with that thing. I just need to brown crème brûlée."

"I can't get anything right," he muttered.

I changed the subject, to give time for my nerves to settle. "So, Dell tells me the Poulet Marengo special was a big hit last night."

"Yes! And we tried it with the black-and-white quinoa. Great idea."

"That was Claire's," Dell announced, just as Claire entered the kitchen.

"Nice idea, kiddo, the quinoa," Will said as she beamed, dropping off more dirty dishes.

Dell nodded at her and she skipped back into the Café with a new lightness. She seemed to be coming out of the darkest part of the tunnel.

"Well, it was an incredible dish, Dell."

She had the same reaction to praise as she did to criticism, which was none.

Will continued. "So, um, Cassie . . . do you have a minute? I need to talk to you about . . . something important that has to do with . . . something important."

Dell looked up from her blanching, but only to stare straight ahead at the tiled wall as though to say, *Jesus Christ, please take this outside, whatever it is.*

"Be right back, Dell."

I wiped my hands on my apron and followed Will out of the kitchen, my heart pounding. *Be cool, be cool, be cool.* Once in the office, he shut the door behind us.

"I'm sure you know what this is about."

"I do," I said, as evenly as possible.

"Matilda called me this morning. I was . . . I am glad. I'm flattered. I'm not sure what to say. But I really, really need to know—are you *sure* you're okay with this?"

I nodded before speaking, trying to give myself time to knock the words loose.

"Yeah. For sure. Totally okay with it."

"Because I told Matilda if you had a problem with this, I would *never*—"

"Why would I have a problem with this?" *Did that come out too fast? That came out too fast.*

"I don't know. I mean, you said so yourself, you know, it's just sex. It doesn't have to *mean* anything."

"Right."

"So. No problem then?"

"Nope. I'm happy for you, Will. It's fun and you'll get to see what I've been saying all along, that S.E.C.R.E.T. helps people. It helps women. And I think you're doing a very good thing. For a very . . . good woman."

"Yes. Thanks. Good."

"So. Ah. Did she . . . also tell you who would be training you?"

"Yes. She did."

"And are you okay with that?" *Here it comes. Here's where he rejects me and I die a thousand deaths.*

"Yeah. Totally. As long as *you're* okay with it."

"Well, I had to be okay with it. No one else wanted to," I said, laughing at my own stupid joke, not understanding its harm until I watched Will's entire face fall.

"No. No-no-no! Will. *Jesus*, that came out wrong. I didn't mean no one wanted to have sex with you. I mean, everyone *voted* for you. They all *would* have volunteered. But they just felt that you and I . . . that maybe it would be best if I were the one who . . . Will, they're my *friends*."

He looked at me seriously. "Are you sure this is a good idea, Cassie? I mean we have a *business* together!"

"Well, if you think having sex with me again would jeopardize our business, then by all means, we don't have to do it! It's not like you signed a contract or anything. It's just sex."

"Yeah. It's just sex."

He stood there biting his bottom lip in deep consternation. Hands behind my back, I began to pace like Nixon, each of us waiting for the other one to speak first.

"Look," I said at last. "I'm a grown-up. You're a grown-up. And it's not like we've never *had* sex."

"True. True. You're right," he said. "Tell you the truth, Cass. Knowing it was you took some of the performance anxiety away. Someone I trust. Someone who knows me. I can hear it from you, you know—criticism, or direction, or whatever."

"Yes. That's what I thought. Right?"

"Have you told your boyfriend?"

"Jesse's not my . . . we don't have . . . he'll be cool with it."

"So you haven't told him yet?"

It was barely detectable. And if you didn't know Will Foret, well, you wouldn't have picked up on that bit of joy he was taking out of imagining Jesse's reaction when I told him I'd be training Will for a sex fantasy. Maybe that's what this was really about—a competition between two men, one of whom wanted to prove himself to the other. Maybe Will just wanted to show Jesse he was a better S.E.C.R.E.T. swordsman, that given a chance he'd have punched Pierre Castille at that stupid soirée many months ago.

And as much as I hated to admit it (even to myself), I was secretly happy to act as judge.

Will easily passed the physical and psychological tests, and Matilda gave us the go-ahead to book our training. We joined our calendars and found a time that worked for both of us, which, naturally, was a Monday night, the night Cassie's was closed.

"Good for you?" he asked, punching in the appointment.

"Good for me," I said.

"Good," he replied.

"Good!" I said. "See you at the Mansion at eight."

"Do you want a ride?"

"We arrive separately. My call time's earlier."

"Good. Right," he said. "You're the trainer."

"I am."

We were like that for the days leading up to that night—curt, polite. But when I finally told Jesse over a greasy dinner at Coop's, he visibly squirmed in his chair.

"Why's it gotta be you?" he said, dragging his restless hands to his temples.

"No one else wanted to. And besides, it's just sex, Jesse."

"Sex with your ex. I know a bit of what *that's* like."

I began to pick at his fries. I wondered if other owners of fine dining establishments craved diner fare or cheap takeout on nights off.

"It's not like it'll be our first trip to the rodeo, Jesse. Besides, I'm just going to give him a few pointers."

"What's the scenario?"

"I don't know yet. I find out tomorrow. But you know I can't tell you. Discretion, remember."

Funny to think that I'd once had no sex life. And even the one I had with my husband was almost nonexistent. Now, sex was a big part of my life. I guess that was progress. I guess that was the point of all this. I shook off my shoe. Then, discreetly under the table, I lifted my foot to rest between Jesse's legs. He adjusted it so my toes curled over his zipper. On cue, I could feel him get hard.

"Let's get the fuck out of here," he said, signaling for the bill.

We drove to my place, both of us silent. By the time we reached the door to my apartment, my shirt was shoved up, my bra askew. Inside, he closed the door and turned me around, lowering me to my hands and knees, while he wrestled his jeans down. Once, twice, I tried to turn around to face him, but he resisted, preferring to take me like that, bent and arched, my knees on the hardwood, my hands clutching the fringe of the area rug, pulling it towards me as I felt his mouth exploring all my darkest places, his fingers digging into me. He was growling and impatient, furious at the condom interruption, and then at my excoriations for him to be quiet, to slow down, to let me turn around.

"The sisters," I whispered, "they can hear us."

"Fuck the sisters," he hissed.

"Stop. My knee. Wait," I said, the moment bursting like a pricked balloon.

He stopped, exhaling loudly before collapsing onto the floor next to me.

"What are we doing?" he said, the palms of his hands pressing into his eye sockets.

I rolled onto my back, my jeans and panties still wrapped around one of my ankles, my shirt still shoved up. I had never really seen the ceiling from this angle. Was I looking at new cracks, or had those been there the whole time and I just hadn't noticed them before?

"I don't know," I said. "Maybe this part of our relation-ship . . . maybe it's done."

He rolled onto an elbow to look at me, his eyes smiling.

"I think you might be right."

"What do you think happened?" I asked, genuinely curi-ous. "I mean, we had something, didn't we?"

"We did. We do. But maybe it's not enough to conquer what we had . . . with other people," he said, caressing my face.

He was talking about Will without really talking about Will. I had no reply. Funny, when things run their course there's no fight left, no questions unanswered, no resent-ments. There was just this lovely release.

He pulled on his jeans and did up his belt, crouching down in front of me so our eyes were even.

"We are good friends," he said, as though newly noticing something new and interesting about me.

"Always," I said, smiling.

He leaned forward and kissed me on the forehead. "S.E.C.R.E.T. makes some damn good women," he said.

As he stood up and left, closing the door behind him, I fell back onto the floor, throwing my arms wide, blinking into the living room ceiling for a few minutes. Dixie padded over to me, tapping her nose on mine. When she realized I was perfectly happy lying there, completely surrendered, she curled into my armpit and went to sleep.

⁓

Whenever I felt like I was in the middle of a transition, unsure of my next step, I did what I always did, what always worked. That night I got up off the floor, took a hot shower and made the hour-long trek across the city to the Coach House to talk to the one person who knew me well, who would know what to do, who'd always tell me the truth: Matilda. My training session with Will was a few days away. I needed to go into it with a clear head and an uncluttered heart.

It was late, almost nine o'clock, but sure enough the lights were on in Matilda's office, though it was odd to see the red door ajar. I stepped inside, preparing to scold her for leaving it unlocked. The Garden District was a pretty safe neighborhood, but still. I heard a male voice coming from inside her office. This wasn't terribly odd. Though training always happened at the Mansion, we interviewed and tested recruits here all the time, well into the night. A few steps closer and I could make out Matilda's voice sounding more emotional than I think I'd ever heard her. I was about to make myself known when I heard the male voice speaking again, this time loud enough for me to recognize that it was Jesse.

Make yourself known, Cassie. Now's the time. But my feet felt suddenly welded to the oak floors. I was trapped between two horrible options. If I left now, I'd risk getting caught running away. If I stayed, I might hear something not meant for my ears. By the time I heard Jesse yell with genuine ache in his voice, "Of *course* I adore her! But it's *you* I love," it was too late.

"Why won't you just let me in?" he continued. "I don't care about age, for fuck's sake! How many times do I have to tell you, Matty? I just want to be with you. I miss you. Finn misses you."

Matty? Finn? The closest I'd come to meeting Jesse's son was watching him sleep that night.

"You don't care about our age difference now, Jesse, but I do. *I* care. When I'm seventy, you're going to be in your fifties. It's ludicrous. And I told you I won't have sex with you so long as you and Cassie are still involved. It's wrong and unfair. I love you both. In fact, you should not even be here—"

"We're done. Cassie and me. We're just friends. That's all we ever were, really. That's all we were ever meant to be."

Before I heard anything else, I quietly, calmly, regained the strength in my legs and staggered out and back to the sidewalk. The facts followed after me. *Jesse adores me. Jesse loves Matilda. Jesse is my friend. Jesse wants to be Matilda's partner.* I thought back to his drunken little tantrum on Christmas Eve, and of all the ways Matilda had probably thwarted Jesse's plans to be with her by placing me in their path, hoping I'd go from being an obstacle to a genuine reason they couldn't be together. I thought of what he'd just said to me that night, how people from our past were in the way of anything we might have in the future. I was so arrogant to think that Jesse wasn't carrying around his own burdens. Oh, the hearts we break to avoid heartbreak.

What a crazy, sad little circle, I thought, warm tears flooding my eyes. I searched for my anger because it had to be there somewhere, but strangely, as soon as it surfaced, it disappeared. Then fear rose up. But fear of what? Of rejection? Fear couldn't find any purchase either, and it drifted away. It seemed like there was nothing for these old, bad feelings to cling to. I wiped my eyes with the back of my hand and made my way down Third. At Magazine I flagged a cab, too tired to walk back home.

After a good cry, I slept better that night than I had in a long, long time.

SOLANGE

I got out of the car and stood at the foot of Rue Foucault in the Trocadéro, holding my Step Eight card between shaky fingers. Poking my head out of the back of the limousine, I double-checked the directions, noting the word *Bravery* etched into the heavy paper, and beneath that, a note from Matilda.

Even if you decide not to accept this Step today, know you've already earned your Bravery charm. With great admiration, Matilda. P.S. The car has been instructed to wait for you. Please proceed with caution. And call me when you get back to the hotel.

I walked up to the imposing Moorish door of the four-story mansion, a dozen Juliet balconies above facing the street. Technically it was a townhouse located at the end of a stretch of sumptuous buildings dating back to at least the 1700s. Before my knuckle could strike the ancient wood, the door eased opened and a very tall, very old butler bowed deeply before me. He straightened and his arm swept me into an all-white marble foyer almost as big as the one at the New Orleans Museum of Art.

"*Nous vous attendions, Mademoiselle Faraday. Puis-je prendre votre manteau?*" he said.

Manteau. I knew that much French. I wasn't sure what to wear to an interview-masquerading-as-a-sex-fantasy, so I had just dressed the part of a reporter—cream slacks, silk scarf and fitted navy blazer over a white blouse. As I handed him my blazer, my arms suddenly felt chilled.

The butler led me down another long, white hall, the gallery of windows to one side framing the Eiffel Tower in the distance. *My god. This is his view.* We traipsed through two more sets of fourteen-foot double doors before the white walls gave way to dark brown paneling surrounding a stand-up stone fireplace with lion heads on the cornices. It was clearly the den or the library; books covered one wall, and on the other were large black casement windows, burgundy velvet curtains on either side cascading to a pile on the marble floor. In the middle of the room was a long mahogany desk centered over a beautiful oriental rug, behind which was a black high-back chair and another spectacular view of the Eiffel Tower. I was just catching my breath when a man behind me cleared his throat.

I spun to face Pierre Castille himself. Plain and simple, this was a handsome man.

"Solange Faraday. How nice to see a familiar face. You've certainly come a long way, from my TV set in New Orleans to my little place in Paris. I hope you didn't have any trouble find-ing me," he said, his smile genuinely warm, his hands extending to clasp one of mine in both of his. He had the barest of Bayou accents and was dressed casually in faded jeans and a light blue linen shirt, half tucked, the color setting off his intense green eyes. His hair was darker, shorter too, than the last time I'd seen him. And he was sober, maybe even somber. But that didn't take away from his incredible presence; he had the kind of sexiness that, dare I say, even rivaled the MMS's.

"Thank you for agreeing to . . . meet with me," I said, surprised at my sudden butterflies.

"You have been very persistent. And I was very curious," he said, walking past me to the bar. "What can I make you?"

"Scotch, neat. Please," I said.

"Hmm, a grown-up's drink."

As he made our drinks, I looked around. "You have a beautiful home."

"I'm glad you like it."

Like it? I felt my shoulders drop, my jaw loosen, my knees melt.

"What does it do to a person to wake up seeing the Eiffel Tower every morning?" I asked. "Do you grow to appreciate it, or does that just get old?"

Still smiling, he approached me and handed me my drink, then took in the scene from where I was standing. The house seemed to be built on a curve, the courtyard acting as the crisp green foreground to the famous mon-ument in the distance.

"Truth be told, it never gets old," he said, corralling me towards one of the two leather club chairs in front of the desk.

He was a man who moved with ease, a man thoroughly comfortable in his own skin. We talked about Paris, where he was born and lived as a boy before his American mother brought him to New Orleans for his formative years.

"They wanted to scrub any vestiges of socialism from my blood before I took over the family business."

"They seem to have succeeded." This was my in. "You know I came here for an interview about you, your family business, its history in the city, your plans for the future of New Orleans, in particular that land down by the French Market. As one of the city's biggest developers, are you—?"

"Yes, we'll get to that part, I promise, Solange," he said, waving his hand as though to clear my words from the room. "But first *I* have a question for you."

Here we go.

"Shoot," I said, trying to sound calm.

"How does S.E.C.R.E.T. seem to lure such exceptional women into its fold?"

I hated that—when men, particularly powerful men, changed the subject to something frivolous and flattering when a woman asked a tough question. It was such casual sexism it almost went unnoticed, and if you complained, you were labeled humorless and, god forbid, unsexy.

"Well, seeing that you're a former recruit, I'm assuming you understand something of S.E.C.R.E.T.'s mandate."

"Former and hopefully current recruit."

I gave him a tight smile. I didn't know how to reply because my mind was suddenly churning with doubt about this adventure. A minute ago I might have been persuaded. Admittedly, I was almost swept away by the grandeur of this place, and Pierre's considerable charms. But I knew even he could sense the chill in the room brought on by my sudden withdrawal.

Pierre shook his head as though pressing some sort of internal restart button, his voice turning buttery and conciliatory. "Before we proceed, I'm sure you're well aware that you've caught me in the middle of a most unsavory year, Solange, during which my behavior has been less than stellar. Especially with your benevolent group. My mother, rest her soul, raised me to be a better man. In fact, I was quite surprised—delighted, even—that you deigned to consider including me in your . . . adventures."

The more he talked, the more that chiseled jawline, the white teeth, the lock of sandy hair across his forehead began to disassemble into features that were no longer handsome; in fact, they were turning downright menacing.

"Yes, well, we made an agreement, didn't we? I would be allowed to ask you some questions, and then you'd get to ask me yours."

"So you first, and then me, is that what you're saying?"

There was something unmistakably dark bubbling below the surface of his voice, and my defense mechanisms were on high alert.

"Yes, I'd prefer that," I said.

"Besides beautiful, you're also a savvy one, Solange."

Okay. Mind made up. I can't accept the Step. Time to wrap this up and get the hell out of here. But he walked towards me, freezing me in my tracks.

"Now, Solange, let's save the interview for later. The only question that really matters now is this: Do you accept the Step?"

I nearly choked on my Scotch. Suddenly, even this so-called feather in my journalistic cap wafted out the window and down the streets of Paris. He wanted this story on his terms, not mine, killing any remaining enthusiasm I had for this fantasy.

"How old is the house?" I asked, trying to change the subject. I crossed the room, moving away from him, acting the part of a bored tourist. I casually maneuvered over to the casement doors that led to the courtyard outside.

"Parts of it are more than three hundred years old. Can you imagine? What our lives would have been like three hundred years ago?"

"Well, I certainly wouldn't be sitting here talking to you," I said, looking around. "I'd likely be out in that court-yard with the other servants, boiling sheets."

"I wouldn't be so sure about that. The men in my family have always had excellent taste in women," he said.

Sickening.

I looked through the windows at the Eiffel Tower, trying not to seem like I was scanning the grounds for any other living soul. My inner voice told me to open the patio door and just start walking. But when I reached for the handle, Pierre placed his hand directly over mine. *Shit.*

"I'd be thrilled to take you on a tour of the grounds . . . after. Now once more: do you accept the Step, Solange?"

I pulled my hand away and faced him. *Be brave.* I met his gaze, speaking as evenly as I could without letting the fear bleed into my voice.

"Thank you for asking, Pierre. I'm flattered. But in the end, I don't believe I can accept the Step. My apologies for taking things this far and for pressing you for an interview that you still seem quite reluctant to give."

My heart was pounding so loudly I could feel it beating through the soles of my shoes.

"So . . . if you don't mind, please call your man. Tell him to bring me my blazer. I think it's best if he shows me out."

He looked at his watch, disappointment on his face. "Ah well, I'm afraid Charles has gone home for the evening. We'll have to fend for ourselves. I get to ask one final time: do you accept the Step?"

"As I said, I didn't really come here for this."

"Here's the thing, Solange," he whispered, placing his hands on my upper arms and slowly walking me backwards. I inhaled sharply. "You did come here for this. You, a high-profile member of the media in our beloved city of New Orleans, are also, don't forget, a member of a group that arranges discreet sexual encounters for a few lucky ladies. And the nature of these encounters can vary, can't they? Some are soft and lovely and gentle. Still others take on a darker hue; they're risky, dangerous. They can get a little rough. They can take odd, interesting turns. These ones, I think, satisfy very deep urges that we *all* have, but few are brave enough to give in to. In fact, these are the kinds of urges that can lead some women to cross an ocean to satisfy. You came for this, Solange. You came to play dirty."

He had me pressed firmly against the cool glass of the casement windows, his eyes liquid menace, his hands tight around my upper arms. I felt his groin against my thigh, his arousal unmistakable. I'd always wondered what I'd do in a situation like this. Would I take flight? Would I freeze and crumble? Never in my life had I been threatened or cornered. So how would I know that beneath my terror-stricken surface was a bloody-minded warrior? Calm washed over me, my adrenaline forming armor over my body. I waited a beat to reply, articulating the only word I needed, using my whole body.

"No," I said, with a spray of spit and a lightning-fast thrust of my knee to his groin.

His face flashed before me as he buckled over, his expression that of sheer astonishment, because he knew in that moment that I would fight like a crazed animal if he pressed me any further. He groaned dramatically before bolting back upright, his hands still covering my target.

Then he started laughing. *Laughing.*

"Oh, Solange, that was . . . I'm just trying to think . . . which TV station should I give the scoop to, yours or your competition's, when I tell them all about S.E.C.R.E.T. and its star candidate?"

That's when *I* laughed, the warrior in me speaking now very carefully. "Is that a threat? Because if that's a threat, Pierre, this will not go well for you either, on any level: personally, professionally, legally or physically. Don't forget, I'm a journalist."

His eyes were suddenly dead in their sockets. "You think I would hesitate for one second in making a big goddamn deal about what you just did because of some threat that you'd reveal my involvement in S.E.C.R.E.T.? Unlike you, I've done nothing to be ashamed of. On the contrary, it's a great story and I can't wait to tell it."

Could he tell I was bluffing?

"So here's the thing," I said. "I suggest you let me leave before this goes any further. And I suggest you do it now; otherwise I will hurt you in several more surprising ways."

His reasoning brain seemed to kick in, replacing the reptilian one that had formerly been in charge. He dropped his hands to his sides like surrendered weapons.

"Of course. My apologies. You are free to leave, Solange. I won't stop you."

I kept a wary eye on him as I headed towards the exit, snatching my purse off the desk as I passed. Without looking back, without retrieving my blazer, I kept walking down the gallery, punching through two sets of high, white doors, out the front gate and onto the street where my limo still waited. I climbed in. Several blocks later, my heart rate slowed to normal; several more and my knees stopped knocking.

Back at the hotel I immediately called Matilda, who picked up on the first ring. I explained what had happened with Pierre, without getting into the gory details. I was happy not to hear an "I told you so" in her voice, only concern.

"Are you safe now?"

"I am."

"This will probably inflame Pierre even further, so get to the airport. We'll fly you home as soon as possible. And brace yourself, Solange. We have no way of knowing how he'll retaliate for this, but he will. He'll have the last word if it kills him."

I packed and got on the next available flight home, to my city, my boy—and my man.

CASSIE

Every woman's sexual awakening is different, Matilda always said. Some are quick to occur, some slow, and a few, sadly, never really happen. S.E.C.R.E.T.'s mandate was simply to create the circumstances for an awakening, using fantasies to achieve it. That's why for Solange's Step Nine, it was decided that Will would learn how to let her dominate him. She was ready for that, Matilda said. That's where all her previous steps seemed to be leading.

"I think when she returns from Paris, she'll be feeling pretty assertive, more in command of her destiny. She'll be ready to . . . take charge."

My job was to train Will to submit without being submissive, an important distinction. And I was told I was perfect for the task since, like Solange, I was also new to this particular scenario.

Thankfully, Angela came by to give me some last-minute pointers, this scenario being a specialty of hers. Last year, she had trained my recruit, Mark Drury, in a session I got to monitor. So like her, I chose a white wraparound dress and high heels. She helped me pin my hair up on my head in a sexy, messy pile.

"It's a red lipstick kind of night, Cassie," she said, regarding me in the mirror.

"It is."

"Nervous?"

"Very."

"Good. That means it'll be great," she said, putting the finishing touches on my makeup. "Worry when you're *not* nervous."

She handed me a tangle of thick, red satin ribbons.

"Use these," she said. "I have a feeling you'll need to restrain him quite early in the session. And remember to enter that room like a boss. Handle that man like you own him. That's Solange's fantasy. Show him exactly how to let her."

Oh right—Solange. I'm doing this for her.

I thanked Angela, giving in to a powerful urge to hug her. She let me for a long time, returning the warmth.

"Thank you," I said, over her shoulder.

"Thank *you*," she said, not one for a lot of mushiness. "He may very well be S.E.C.R.E.T.'s last recruit, Cassie. So teach him well, and make us proud."

I nodded, surprised at how choked up I was suddenly. *Last recruit.* S.E.C.R.E.T. had given me so much. It was sad to imagine that it could end soon, that no other woman would benefit from everything this group had given me and taught me.

Equipped with my red ribbons, I walked—no, strutted—down the long, thick-carpeted hall of the Mansion's East Wing. I pushed open the doors to the Games Room, chosen because it was bright and plush with a billiard table at one end and a large cozy sitting area at the other; I wanted Will to feel comfortable. The first thing I saw was my own reflection in the mantel mirror. I was shocked at the slash of red on my lips, the tumble of curls, the epic cleavage! *It's too much*, I thought, covering my breasts with the ribbons. But the truth was that my breasts looked spectacular in this dress! And my shock was soon replaced with sheer delight. I stepped closer to the mirror, placing the ribbons on the mantel. The woman in the mirror was definitely a version of me, one of a few that S.E.C.R.E.T. had helped me uncover.

Turns out I was a multifaceted woman with layers and complexities and there were still more versions of me to discover. I was a widow and a waitress. I was a friend and an adventurer, a boss, a caregiver, a co-worker, a S.E.C.R.E.T. member, a business partner, a mentor, and a lover (a good one at that!). I was all of these things. And now I was this woman too—a trainer, a helper, a giver, a leader, a guide. But at the very core, I'd always be Cassie Robichaud, the girl from Michigan.

I heard the knocks. One, two, three . . .

I braced myself against the purple velvet divan in front of the fireplace.

"Come in," I croaked.

The door opened and there stood my Will, a man who knew every version of me, now including this one. But here was another version of Will, too, at first a nervous version who, while taking me in head to toe, seemed to become a gob-smacked teenager.

"Holy shit, Cassie!" he said, slapping his chest. "Look at you. You look so . . . I don't even know what to say . . . except *wow*."

I fought off the urge to grin and blush. I had to remember I was training him to be dominated—"without feeling emasculated," Angela stressed.

"Thank you, Will, that's very sweet to hear," I said before turning stern. "But I need you to go back outside and try that again, okay? This time you have to be . . . you have to hold back a bit. Smolder. Try to forget it's me. Try not saying anything at first. Just take me in. Let it kind of wash over you."

Wow. I said all of that, and he listened *so* intently I almost climbed over the divan to grab his face and kiss it, he was that cute.

"Smolder. Okay. I got it," he mumbled, exiting the room and quietly shutting the door behind him.

I waited for the knock. And I waited. And I waited. Ten seconds later, I heard his voice through the door.

"Cass? Am I supposed to knock again?"

"Yes, Will!" I yelled. "Knock again."

"Knock and come in? Or knock and wait for you to answer the door this time?"

Oh, this isn't going well.

"Just knock and enter!"

"I don't know if I can enter *and* smolder. I'm wondering if it might be more . . . uh . . . smoldery if *you* answered the door and I'm just, like, standing here. Smoldering."

He yelled all of this through the door crack and I wondered how many people in the Mansion were listening and giggling, because I could barely contain myself.

"Will, just come in, okay? We can skip the smoldering entry."

He whipped the door open and stepped in, his face flushed. "Sorry about that. Maybe I can work on that at home. Where do you want me?"

"Why don't you come sit here and just . . . try to relax," I said, indicating the blue velvet armchair next to the divan. I was surprised at how calm I sounded, how soothing my voice was, how I seemed to exude competence, how goddamn *sexy* I felt.

As he crossed the room, I stood with one fist on my hip, the other arm hanging casually at my side, my breasts lifting ever so slightly with my breath. Will made his way to the armchair, never taking his eyes off my dress, my breasts, my face. As he got closer, he looked like he was experiencing a kind of warm remembrance, his whole body easing up. *That's it*, I wanted to say. *That's how you do it.* But I didn't want to make him self-conscious.

"Here?" he asked, pointing to the chair, eyebrow up.

"There," I said.

He lowered himself, his legs parting slightly. Cocking his head, he regarded me with something like bemused pride.

Yes. Finally he was getting it.

Now it was my turn.

I took a few steps towards him, teetering ever so slightly in my heels, until I was almost standing between his legs. *I am doing this*, I thought. I bent forward, placing my hands on the arms of the chair.

"So, Mr. Foret," I whispered, bringing my glossy lips to within inches of his. "How shall we play today?"

I saw him squirm, his Adam's apple rise and fall.

"I'm happy to do whatever you think is best."

His right hand automatically rose to touch my breasts. I sprung upright, realizing exactly why Angela was right. The restraints were the only way to go. I couldn't have Will's hands on me. To let that happen was to lose control of the session. And myself. I turned and walked to the mantel for the red satin ribbons, then returned to Will, who was now anxiously massaging the arms of the chair.

"With your permission . . . these will help you concentrate better," I said.

He watched with fascination as I bent to secure him to the chair. Around and around I wrapped his arms, tying the ribbons not too tight, not too loose, avoiding eye contact, but the heat off his body, his breath on my shoulder as I leaned over, was almost too much to bear.

"Do I have to tie your ankles to the legs of the chair or do you think you can manage to keep them still?"

"I . . . I think I can manage," he said, tugging slightly to test the binding around his arms.

I took a step back and looked down at him, desire building inside me like a small storm.

Locking eyes with him, I took my fingers and traced the crisscrossing lines of the wrap dress, down to the side knot. Will watched my fingers and made a small sound in his throat as I worried the knot free and let the dress drop open. Beneath it I was naked.

"Cassie," he said, almost involuntarily. "I—"

"Shh! It's not your turn to speak."

I shrugged the dress off my shoulders and let it fall to the floor; I was naked, my taut breasts before him, my nipples sensitive and alert.

Will took a long inhale, and I watched him grow erect through his jeans, both our eyes following the movement. I bent forward, placing my hands on his forearms, and agonizingly lowered myself to my knees before him. I brought my face to his bound hand, rubbing across it like a cat, keeping my eyes on his eyes, noticing how his hands twitched, longing to touch my hair. Then I took his index finger deep into my mouth, calmly encircling it, sucking it hard. He threw his head back and let out a low groan, that signaled this was all too much, that just me sucking his *finger* was already killing him.

I let my other hand travel up his leg and firmly across his thigh until it was over his erection. Then I rubbed through the denim until his eyes registered an aching disbelief at this great, great fortune. I untucked his shirt, undoing it one button at a time, spreading both sides back to see his beautiful torso, which wasn't as cut as it had been while he was doing the renovations, but I loved how this added layer bulked him up, made him seem more manly and vulnerable at the same time. I let my hands linger across his pecs, moving them over his skin the way you touch something you might only get to hold once.

"Your hands on me, Cassie, feels so . . ."

"Shh. Don't say anything, Will." I brought my mouth in front of his. He lurched forward to kiss me but I thwarted his attempt. *Not yet*, I thought, *I need to be stronger.*

I worked the buttons of his jeans until they were all undone. He lifted for me as I used some muscle to pull them down and off his legs. His beautiful cock pillowed out of his boxers and unfurled into my warm, ready hands. Bringing my face to it I rubbed it across my cheeks, all the while watching his reaction. I could feel him thrust slightly, lifting himself towards my face, wanting, *aching* for some relief, for me to take him in my mouth.

"Fuck, I *can't*," Will moaned.

"You can't what, baby?" I teased, the tiny tip of my tongue circling the opening of his hard cock.

"I can't handle not being able to touch you," he said, twisting in the chair.

"You're doing a fine job, Will. In fact, I'm going to give you a reward."

I reluctantly let go of his erection and stood before him, letting my hand travel down to tease myself.

"Do you want to see what you do to me, Will?"

"Oh god, yeah, please," he said, his eyes on my fingers.

I kicked off my heels, and in the manner of the beautiful Angela, I lifted my foot and placed it on Will's naked thigh. Lazy smile on my face, I let my thigh fall open so he could watch me circle and thrust into myself, my own finger a substitute for everything he wanted to be doing to me, my clit so hard and fat I winced at this new level of pleasure.

"Do you want to kiss it, Will?"

He nodded, his eyes ablaze. When he brought his mouth closer, I guided him by the chin, the feel of Will's mouth on me like flashes of heat and fireworks, and as he licked me hungrily, gorgeously, I ran my fingers through his thick hair, feeling something akin to joy. I pulled his face closer, deeper. It took everything in me not to throw my head back and let this man make me come hard. But Matilda's words rattled in my head: *You can't keep him. After you train him, you have to let him go.* Just before I felt the build deepen, I saw it, I saw Will, I saw him doing this with Solange, *to* Solange. I saw my Will making Solange go mad with desire. That scene flashed before my eyes, and I gasped, pulling away, stepping just out of Will's reach to catch my breath, instinctively covering my breasts with my hands.

Will lunged, bringing the chair a few inches with him.

"Don't go away from me, Cassie, don't. I have to touch you. This doesn't feel real if I can't touch you. Please untie me. I need to feel your skin . . ."

I looked at him helplessly bound like that, his shirt flapping open, his erection heavy across his taut thigh, his lips glistening with me.

"I can't, Will," I said, feeling the moment slide away and the tears stinging the corners of my eyes. "I can't do this. Not with you. I'm sorry."

I ran to him. My fingers shook as I untied him, and his head hung in quiet disappointment.

"Don't apologize, Cassie," he said softly, as I liberated each of his arms.

Before I could dress and flee, he stood and looped one of his arms around my waist, pulling me hard to him. I squirmed. He gently tucked a lock of my hair behind my ear.

"Don't ever apologize to me again, Cassie."

"I feel so stupid for thinking that I could—"

"Can it be my turn to talk now?"

He took his thumb and rubbed what must have been smudged makeup off my cheek. Then he kissed my mouth, sweetly, firmly. Both arms now wrapped around my waist, he held me so tightly he squeezed the tears right out of me.

"I feel like an idiot. This was supposed to be sexy. It wasn't supposed to end in tears."

"Um, believe me, Cassie, that was . . . what you did, that was . . . seriously sexy."

He kissed my forehead.

"Do you think you learned enough?"

"For what?"

"To pull off the fantasy?"

"Right. The fantasy. Well, this is no criticism of you, Cassie, because you're a great teacher. But I'm a lousy student. So I don't think I was able to learn enough to successfully graduate to full-fledged fantasy man."

"No?"

"No. So you're going to have to bench me, unless I can get some more training. Maybe there's some special tutorial session for dummies. Do you guys do that here?"

"I could ask," I said, realizing his joke.

"'Cause I'm really no one's idea of a fantasy man."

"Well . . . you are mine."

He kissed me for that, once, twice.

"So what happens to us S.E.C.R.E.T. rejects? Do you have to kill me or something?"

"Yes, unfortunately."

"Can we at least have sex one last time?"

"Yeah, but not here," I said, looking around. "It's beautiful, this place, but I want you to take me home."

Before I could finish my sentence, he flung my dress at me and gathered up his pants. We dressed faster than a couple of firemen called to a five-alarm emergency. He extended his hand and in one swift move threw me over his shoulder, and I kicked and laughed as he carried me down the hallway and out the front door of the Mansion.

It was the last time I'd set foot in that place for several months. And even then, I wouldn't be alone. We'd both return, for a different kind of fantasy altogether.

The truth came out that night in bits and pieces, between sex and kisses, between bites of pizza and a bottle and a half of wine we took from the restaurant and drank while sitting on my kitchen floor, where we had sex one more time before the sun came up. We both knew we'd be wrecked the next day, but two of us hobbled by hangovers had to add up to at least one stellar restaurateur.

He came out with it first.

"It's been awful not having you in my life, Cassie. And by life I mean my heart, my side, my bed. So I had secretly hoped this would happen. That's the real reason I volunteered with S.E.C.R.E.T. I meant everything I said before about the good I think the organization does. I was wrong before. But I hoped I'd either make you jealous if we didn't get paired up, or make you crazy for missing me if we did."

"So you were never going to go through with the fantasy?"

"Well, let's put it this way: I wouldn't have gone through the training with anyone else, and I knew I wouldn't want to be with anyone else if the training was going to be with you."

"Mission accomplished," I said, leaning on his shoulder. "I was surprised you volunteered with S.E.C.R.E.T. I thought the whole thing disgusted you. I thought *I* disgusted you."

"You've *never* disgusted me. The truth is more embarrassing than that. I felt . . . threatened. I was an idiot."

Will threw his arm around me and pulled me closer. My hand slid down his warm, familiar stomach, then farther down, and I softly cupped my hand over him, making him erect again.

"I thought you were dating up a storm. I thought you were happy. And then when I discovered your ... I don't want to call it a 'secret life' ... my first thought was not *What a slut*, but *I can't compete*. I couldn't take being dumped *again* for a better guy, for someone more ... I don't know ... powerful, I guess. You *saw* Carruthers. His watch is the size of a fucking six-pack. You saw the car he drove, the job he has. Guys pay attention to that shit—the things we aren't, the stuff we don't have. I may not have been madly in love with Tracina, but I was geared up to be her partner and a parent and a provider, and when I was thrown over for Mr. Fucking Big, it hurt. I mean, you know me. I struggle. Then your boyfriend with the great left hook shows up and does what *I* should have done to fucking Castille. *He* stepped up when I should have." He paused. "By the way, are you still seeing him? That Jesse guy?"

Dixie came over and nestled between us like a fur island.

"No. We're just friends. We've really always been just friends."

"You're not in love with him?"

"Never was. And he's not in love with me. He loves someone else. And so do I," I said, beginning my aching assault on his body.

The thing about Will was that he had no idea how sexy he was, which is precisely what made him so sexy, even when he struggled. *Especially* when he struggled. On the floor of my kitchen, we unspooled our legs from the sheets we'd dragged there, moving the cat over in a loving but firm way. Will laid me down on that floor at dawn and entered me again while kissing me, saying my name over and over, holding my face between his hands, while I clutched his gorgeous ass and pressed my knees back, opening myself to him, inviting him all the way inside.

While he thrust into me, reintroducing himself to my body, it felt like we'd never been away from each other. I shifted my hips and reached back to press the cupboard doors so I could arch for him. He felt so right, so perfect inside me, our bodies formed just for this.

"How's this for a fantasy," he whispered. "Sex with me on your kitchen floor."

"This is the only fantasy I've ever really wanted. The only one I ever hoped would come true."

SOLANGE

Having fantastical, dramatic, exquisite sex with gorgeous strangers reminded me of what was potent about having great sex with just one good man. That wasn't the goal of S.E.C.R.E.T.; that wasn't even my goal. But that was my epiphany on my flight home, as I shook off the sickening Pierre interlude with every mile I put between us, rocking my body to make the plane go faster. I had people waiting for me. My people: my boy and my man.

I almost steamrolled everyone at the arrivals gate, everyone keeping me away from Gus a second longer. My need to grab my son and smell him and squeeze him was so overwhelming, I was worried I'd break him. And there, standing behind Gus, was my impossibly handsome ex-husband, his smile full of questions. *Why are you home early, Solange? Why did you insist I pick you up at the airport? Why are you wearing your hair the way I love? And why are you looking at me with those brown eyes as though you're seeing me for the first time?*

The answers to those questions would naturally surface

over the next few weeks and months. But that day, I didn't have words for my feelings, which is why I said very little on the way home. I just stole glances at Julius from the passenger side of the food truck. He had had to park the truck far away because it was too tall for the short-term airport garage. Instead of feeling frustrated, hypervigilant and over-competent, I let that man carry all my luggage. I let him be the man he wanted to be, instead of molding him into the one I had thought he should be. It is a strange revelation to look at someone you know well and see a whole dimension you have been blind to.

While Gus sat buckled in the trundle seat behind his dad, playing a game on my phone, Julius caught me up on his business, which had expanded yet again for Jazz Fest.

"Three trucks total. After Jazz Fest, two are fully paid for so it's all profit from now on. It's crazy, Solange. But I'm thinking of opening a small, permanent kiosk off Jackson Square. I've been talking to other franchises to see if we can share space."

"Congratulations, Julius. You found your niche."

"It took me a while. But yeah, I did."

"It takes what it takes."

He looked at me, on his face another unspoken question: *Who are you and what have you done with my hyper-critical ex-wife?* I was noticing how happiness made him even more handsome, and how success had made him sexier. It wasn't that Julius was now worthy of my attention because he had found some confidence and security. It was that he finally seemed worthy to himself. And for some reason, this . . . relaxed me. I would take a bumpy, lumbering ride in a glossy food truck over a carriage ride in Paris any day.

When he pulled into my driveway on State Street, he was as shocked at the invitation to stay for dinner as I was when he accepted. We ordered pizza. We chatted about the week, what they did, what I did, what Paris was like, what I was like in Paris. I told them I sang, that it was a lark and a fluke, but it was something I needed to try to do again, even just for me. And I told Julius the truth, that the interview with the elusive, infamous Bayou Billionaire was a total bust, that it hadn't yielded what I had hoped it would.

"Turns out that the man doesn't have much to say. Not much worth listening to anyway," I said, tossing crust into the pizza box. The truth might come out, and it might shatter my world. But all I felt in that moment was gratitude and confidence. And at least for now, all my secrets were still safe.

After Gus went to bed, my ex-husband stood in the darkened doorway of my childhood home saying good night to me for far too long. At one point I was laughing at something he said, unconsciously hooking my index finger in the waist of his jeans, an intimacy so automatic it was like breathing.

He looked down at my hand with a note of alarm and I pulled it away like I'd touched a hot flame.

"I should . . . *go*," he said, looking slightly concerned.

"Okay."

"Good night then." He turned.

"Right," I said, waving to the back of his head. He was hurriedly making his way to his food truck parked in front of the house. I was the one who had ended our marriage. I had to remember that. Trust wasn't going to come easy. And Pierre was a loaded gun. Once he exposed my involvement in S.E.C.R.E.T., a reunion might be out of the question anyway. Julius may not judge me, but the revelations wouldn't endear me to him either. Still, I had come to a kind of peace with that on the plane ride home. I decided I had meant the words I said to Pierre; I had done nothing to be ashamed of; this was a great story with a happy ending, regardless of whether Julius and I reunited. Over time, I came to realize that mine was a story that mirrored the experience of every woman in S.E.C.R.E.T. We were all made better for its existence, me, Cassie, Dauphine, Matilda, Angela, Bernice, all of us.

In fact, far from being diminished or tarnished by S.E.C.R.E.T., our lives had been greatly enhanced.

If I was to be exposed, so be it.

If there were consequences, I'd face them.

If I lost my second chance with Julius, I might as well find out sooner rather than later.

⌒

A week later I received a package at work, special delivery from Pierre Castille. Inside were two envelopes, a thin one with my name on it and a thick one addressed to Matilda.

I headed to the Coach House after work with a heavy heart.

Matilda and I sat across from each other at her desk. I went first, opening my envelope, which contained a note and a loose charm that dropped from its folds, a Step Eight charm, *Bravery* scrolled on one side.

Dear Solange,

I apologize for my abominable behavior. Should our paths ever cross again, I can only hope to exhibit an ounce of the bravery you showed that day. By the way, your secret is safe. It's your story to tell.

With head bowed,

Pierre Castille

I looked at Matilda, whose eyes were saucers behind her thick stack of papers. "I can scarcely believe it," she said, her voice cracking.

"Open yours."

She ripped the envelope open and removed a letter, then passed it my way.

"Read it to me, Solange. I'm vibrating from nerves."

I scanned the words on the cover letter, written in the same neat penmanship as my note.

"He's returning something called *Red Rage*," I said. "It'll arrive tomorrow by special freight."

"He's *what?* That's . . . that's the painting he bought from us in Buenos Aires. What else does he say?"

I cleared my throat and read.

" *. . . the painting was never mine to begin with, Matilda,"* I read. "*In fact, I can't look at it without thinking of my ungentlemanly actions towards Cassie, towards Dauphine in Buenos Aires, and I'm sure you've heard about Solange in Paris. I'm a man unused to hearing no, to being denied what I want. I've decided to make amends by returning the painting. My hope is that we can keep all of this matter a 'secret,' as it were, now and in perpetuity. I hope this gift will guarantee many more healthy years for your group. Yours remorsefully, Pierre Castille.*"

We were both quiet for some time.

"Well, this has been a very interesting day," Matilda said, staring into the middle distance. "What exactly did you do to that man, Solange?"

I told her about what might have been his moment of clarity—my well-placed knee to his groin.

"Well, you certainly had an impact. I am so sorry you went through that. All I can say is thank you. This means that S.E.C.R.E.T. is not only alive and well, but we have the means to make your last fantasy a really, *really* good one," she said.

"Truth be told, Matilda, my time in S.E.C.R.E.T. has been incredible. And I want to thank you for each and every one of my fantasies. But they've also given me a whole new appreciation for my reality. And there's one staring me straight in the face. I can't ignore it any longer."

I told her about my renewed feelings for Julius, that they had come almost out of nowhere.

"Does Julius know?" she asked.

"I think he suspects something's up. But I was the one who ended things with him. So he's rightfully wary. Any advice on how to win back your ex?"

"I wish I knew myself, Solange," she said wistfully.

Just then, we heard the grinding sound of the front gates opening. Through her office window, we watched a limo ease through and turn towards the Mansion's front portico.

Matilda looked at her watch. "Sit back in your chair for a tight second. Your recruit has just arrived for his training session."

"You can probably give him the night off," I joked, resisting the urge to sneak a peek.

"True. I could do that," she said, her eyes still on the limo, a sly smile playing across her lips. "But I think I'll just let the training session proceed. Why not? It's just sex, right? That's the easy part. It's love that vexes."

❧

Gus had been looking forward to sleeping at his dad's that night, and I was looking forward to seeing Julius, so we were both a little disappointed when he texted to say that his deep-fry guy and the cashier on one of his trucks both called in sick.

When I told Gus his night with his dad was canceled, instead of sulking, he said, "Why don't we go help him?"

"My brilliant child," I said, kissing his face a bunch of times. He resisted me, but only a little.

We headed up to the Freret Street location dressed to serve. I was a natural with that fry basket; Gus made a champion coin roller. Some people recognized me from the news, and I joked that I was moonlighting so that I could spend more time with my men.

"Great team effort," Julius said at closing time, locking up the truck and drawing back the awning.

"The Formidable Faradays," Gus added.

"That's us, baby," I said, my eyes lingering on Julius.

I hadn't packed an overnight bag for Gus, so Julius had to drop us off. I invited him to stay for a late bite, and he took off his shoes at the door and didn't leave. We ate together, and laughed together, the three of us at one table. After dinner, after I cleaned up, and after he tucked Gus in, Julius found me standing at the bottom of the stairs looking up at him, hopeful, expectant, adoring.

"Are you coming down? Or . . . am I coming up?" I asked, a quaver in my voice.

"Let's meet in the middle," he said.

I slowly took those stairs one by one, carefully stepping into his broad arms.

"Is this for real, Solange?"

I looked up at him and nodded. He kissed me full on the mouth and for a second he felt all new to me—his hands, his lips, his taste. He broke free a minute later only to pull me up the stairs with him. In the bedroom with the door shut, his body became a place I had been to before and knew so well and missed so much.

He stripped me with the concentration of a doctor removing bandages from someone almost fully healed. I let him. The T-shirt that still smelled like the food truck came flying off. My bra he kept on for a second, admiring it. I had picked out my lingerie carefully this time, hoping there was a chance this could happen. His knuckle traced the shape of my breasts beneath the lace, knowing once it came off there was no turning back; the sight of my breasts had always made that man crazy.

He pulled off my jeans, one leg, then the other. He did it reverently, disbelieving his luck, half waiting for me to stop him, to say, *This is nuts; this can't ever work again.* I couldn't speak, I could only marvel at his sinewy body, my fingers taking ownership with every inch they touched. This stomach, *mine.* These arms now bracketing me as I lay across the bed, *mine.* This back my nails are lightly dragging across, *mine.*

I was so wet by the time he entered me, and he was so hard, so insistent, saying my name over and over in my ear, his voice catching, making me dizzy with every thrust of his body, all I could think was: *Mine. Mine. Mine again.*

～

CASSIE

When it came time for the wedding, Matilda told me to spare no expense.

"Seriously?" I said, too excited to contain myself. "But it's during Mardi Gras week. Everything's going to be more expensive."

"Spend whatever it takes, Cassie. What's a wedding but one big fantasy, the fantasy of a lifetime?"

On an unseasonably warm February morning, the skies unbearably blue, the wind sweet, the city getting ready for its big party, Will and I headed down to the French Market at the crack of dawn to pick out the fattest lobsters and the juiciest prawns, which would go into making the biggest backyard jambalaya ever seen in New Orleans. It was Dell's idea to boil the corn and potatoes over three cauldrons built into the concrete hot tub, drained just for that occasion.

The whole garden behind the Mansion was festooned in ribbons and flowers, Mason jars stuffed with early magnolias, pink-and-white streamers draped off picnic tables, in between which Gus and Finn ran around with the other children over grass strewn with white and purple petals and beads. We wanted this wedding to be perfect and we threw ourselves into every detail, from the dress that Dauphine Mason helped me source and ship from Paris, to the music Mark Drury volunteered to handle, to the cake that we commissioned from Jesse Turnbull.

Claire had been up half the night helping Jesse put the finishing touches on the cake and learning all there was to know about making marzipan roses. But when it came time to help Jesse lift the five-tiered masterpiece out of the back of the van, the only person I'd entrust with that task was Will. To watch those two men cooperatively, carefully, gingerly, tenderly follow me around the side of the Mansion to the table, carrying a wedding cake the size of a small person, was to really know friendship and joy, forgiveness and love.

I'll admit I was surprised when Solange Faraday pointed to *this* dress as the one she'd always dreamed of, but when she stepped out of the dressing room at the Funky Monkey wearing it, we all fell in love too.

"You think?" she asked, holding out her long arms covered in creamy Spanish lace. "I saw it in Paris. It's not too much?"

"It's *definitely* too much, but that's the beauty of it," I said, laughing at how ridiculously stunning she looked in her off-the-shoulder couture confection, which cinched her tiny waist and flared out in a cloud of pale cream tulle.

"Jesus Murphy Jones and his sister Martha," Dauphine

said, placing her hand over her chest. "Solange. It's . . . perfection."

"It also costs more than my car," Solange said. "I don't know if I can accept all this."

"You should have thought of that before you accepted our Step," I said, moved to tears by the sight of her.

Weeks later, in the pool house before the ceremony where we all gathered to privately toast the bride, Matilda had attached Solange's Step Nine charm—*Exuberance*— to her bracelet.

"There. Something new," she said. "And you can borrow my old blue handkerchief to cover all the other bridal criteria."

There was never any question about whether Solange would stay in S.E.C.R.E.T. and take the Tenth Step. Once she reunited with Julius, this was always going to be her final Step, the one fantasy we all wanted to help facilitate. Watching her walk down the aisle at dusk to remarry Julius, the love of her life, their young son giving her away, and watching Julius lift her veil before reciting the vows they had written for each other, my heart burst wide open. And I knew it would never close again.

I scanned the crowd for my lovely assistants: Angela, Kit, Bernice and Pauline were all dabbing tears. Behind them, Jesse casually stretched his arm behind Matilda's chair. She shifted a little uncomfortably, still trying to get used to his public displays of devotion. After the ceremony, I sidled up to her while Jesse went to get us all drinks.

"What do you think?" I asked.

"It's a beautiful wedding. We might have stumbled on another source of income. Not that we need the money anymore," she said, referring to the returned painting. She took my hand. "So, do you miss us, Cassie?"

"I miss you and the girls. Though, if we do decide to cater events here, we'll see a lot of each other."

Mark Drury's band, The Careless Ones, wrapped up its first set, Mark handing the mike over to Solange to serenade Julius. The groom beamed from the back of the garden, a beer in one hand, his other arm around Gus's shoulders, both of them completely love-struck.

"Hey, babe," I heard behind me.

I turned around to gaze into my own man's face. Will handed me a glass of champagne and clinked his against mine. He had asked me to bring him a suit to change into once the party was in full swing, but he was so sexy in his jeans, his mis-buttoned tuxedo shirt, the bow tie stuffed into his back pocket, his sunglasses askew on his head. We both drank from our flutes, never taking our smiling eyes off each other.

"Well," he said, wiping his mouth with the back of his hand and slinging his arm around my shoulders. "I think our first wedding went really well."

"Could be a good side gig. We could hire catering staff, a couple of assistants for Dell, maybe put in a real cauldron for cookouts."

He looked at me. "Have I told you how fucking beautiful you look tonight?"

"You did," I said, smiling down at my cornflower blue sundress.

"Have I mentioned how brilliant you are at all of this?"

"Uh-huh, a couple of times already."

"And have I told you how much I love you?"

"Yup, earlier today, when you pulled me under the trellis and kissed me in front of all those people."

"Ah. Yes. I do remember doing that."

We stood there, swaying to Solange's beautiful voice.

"Should we cater our own wedding, I wonder?" he asked. "Or hire another company so we can relax and enjoy ourselves?"

My eyes widened as I fought back tears. "I didn't realize we were having a wedding."

"I mean, if you don't *want* to marry me, I'm happy to keep on being your number-one fantasy man for the rest of your life. It *is* a big step."

I finally turned to face him, my eyes spilling tears. "Yes, but I accept that step. I accept it wholeheartedly."

"So it's a yes?"

I nodded vigorously, too overcome with joy to do anything else but kiss him for a long time. *I picked you and you picked me.*

The band struck up the marching song "Street Parade" and broke into a little procession. I wiped my eyes and we grabbed our drinks and each other's hands and everyone shimmied and sashayed behind the musicians, all the way up Third Street to St. Charles Avenue.

We were just in time to catch the tail end of the big parade, me leaning back into Will, his arms wrapped around me, as the sun finally set on this crazy, beautiful city I could finally, truly call my home.

ACKNOWLEDGEMENTS

Right from the get-go, I had the support, encouragement, guidance and leadership of my editor, Nita Pronovost. I couldn't have embarked on this adventure without her, and everyone at Random House Canada, especially my publisher, Kristin Cochrane, Scott Richardson, Zoe Maslow and Adria Iwasutiak, publicist extraordinaire. Thank you Suzanne Brandreth and the Cooke Agency for being incredible international advocates. I have the best agent in the business who also happens to be an intuitive reader and a friend: Christy Fletcher and her stellar team—thank you—especially Rachel Crawford, Melissa Chinchillo and Kevin Cotter. And a big shout out to Gregg Sullivan for introducing me to so many passionate new readers.

To my best friends and first readers, thank you Lisa Laborde, Cathie James, Sarah Durning and my sister, Susan Gabriele—you each consistently elevated the material with your thoughtful queries and smart suggestions. Thank you so much. Finally, and mostly, I wish to thank every single reader that embraced this series and spread the word in more than thirty countries by pressing these books directly into their friends' hands. Thank you for making room on your crowded bookshelves for a different kind of love story. Thank you, thank you, and thank you again.

A READER'S GUIDE TO

S·E·C·R·E·T
REVEALED

1. There is a common theme for our main characters in the S.E.C.R.E.T trilogy. Prior to their transformations, Solange, Dauphine and Cassie have each lost touch with their sexual sides. Can you identify how each loss registered differently for each woman and how each woman recovered that aspect of herself?

2. In *S.E.C.R.E.T. Revealed*, we meet Solange Faraday, the beautiful, successful New Orleans news anchor. Her first fantasy involves a mysterious, attractive handyman. Despite her attraction, Solange stops herself from flirting with him because of her status as an older, professional, divorced mother. Why do you think she feels these attributes hold her back sexually? Have you ever talked yourself out of flirting or behaving sexually because of similar perceptions?

3. In the prologue of *S.E.C.R.E.T. Revealed*, we find Cassie and Will still madly in love before that fateful night at Latrobe's. Cassie laments that in one week she went from being a "sex goddess" to a "dirty slut." The notion of a "slut," what that is and isn't, is a common theme throughout the S.E.C.R.E.T. trilogy. How do the various characters in S.E.C.R.E.T. respond to the use of that word? How do you feel about that word?

4. That word "slut" also plagues a teenaged character, Claire, who is taunted by friends with dire results. Why do you think this issue still lingers? What can be done to cope with or prevent this kind of bullying?

5. Cassie is struck by the positive changes she sees in herself as the result of her participation in S.E.C.R.E.T. She feels she can now stand up for herself and go after what she wants. She is bolder and surer of herself and is no longer clingy and afraid. In what scenes in *S.E.C.R.E.T. Revealed* can you really see these changes in Cassie?

6. At one point, Solange frets: "What if I'm bad at sex?" Prior to accepting a Step, Solange has that private battle in her mind with her fears. What is at the core of those fears? Can you relate?

7. We learn that a contributing factor to Solange's divorce was the "falling away of sex" after her son was

born. But what else contributed to the death of their sex life? What changes between her and Julius, her ex, by the end of the book?

8. When recruiting Solange, Matilda, in her usual direct manner, explains that S.E.C.R.E.T. provides the opportunity for sex "relations," not relationships. "These relations I speak of are purely sexual. Fun, free, safe, anonymous encounters. Ones you're entirely in control of. Ones *you* define. They don't define you. Sexual scenarios you come up with, executed exactly the way you want them to be executed. How does that sound to you?" Well, how does that sound to you? Do you feel in control of your sexual experiences? What would it take for you to feel more empowered sexually?

9. Solange meets the Committee of S.E.C.R.E.T. and is quite impressed. "These women were of an age; not pretty young things, not girls but women, women who looked me square-on, who glowed with a kind of sexy self-assurance I had long abandoned for professional polish. They wore their femaleness fearlessly, comfortably, alluringly." Besides physical appearance, what qualities make a woman sexy? What does it look like to wear your "femaleness fearlessly"? How might an older woman's sexiness differ from a younger woman's sexiness? What do you think are Solange's sexiest traits?

10. The first sexual fantasy on Solange's wish list has a domestic twist to it and resembles a stereotypical male sexual fantasy, where the man comes home from work to find a sexy woman cleaning or cooking for him. What does this fantasy say about Solange? Out of Solange's sexual fantasies, which one would appeal to you the most?

11. Cassie says, "Since S.E.C.R.E.T., I had discovered that I had been wrong about a lot of things." Can you give an example of something she was wrong about that improved her life?

12. Matilda says that some men (and women) don't think that a woman's sexual appetite is as important to satisfy as a man's, or they feel that a woman's sex life shouldn't be as varied, complex and interesting as a man's. Have you ever faced these perceptions in yourself or others? How does this perceived attitude affect Solange? Cassie? What do they do to defy it?

13. When in pain, Matilda says, the best remedy is to "work hard. Try to be of some service. You can't do anything about how he feels or about how he sees the world. But you can change how you look at yourself. Don't let this stall all of your great progress." What are some actions Cassie takes to follow these suggestions? Can you think of situations where Cassie and Dauphine

let their men stall their progress in life? Would you ever apply Matilda's advice in your own life?

14. For Solange, the anticipation of her next sexual fantasy is heightened by the fact that she doesn't have to "work for it." She enjoys the freedom of not having to worry about rejection, primping, flirting, dating, jeopardizing her reputation, and introducing anyone to her son. Do you find the idea of having all that work taken out of your sex life appealing? Why? Why not?

15. "Beauty in business distracts. The more beautiful you are, the less, it seems, you're taken seriously." Throughout the book, Solange struggles with her need to be taken seriously as a professional woman and therefore plays down her sexuality, creating obstacles when it comes to S.E.C.R.E.T. Do you think she is right about women, beauty and business? Have you ever had experiences that either prove or deny this theory? How does Solange resolve this, if at all?

16. During her photo-shoot fantasy, Solange becomes more confident with each passing moment. She wonders: "What is it about a stranger that makes you abandon all your rules and regulations?" Why does the lack of emotional intimacy seem to allow Solange (and Cassie and Dauphine, for that matter) to abandon herself to the moment? Have you had

any experiences with strangers where you had a similar reaction?

17. At the opening of Cassie's, Will agrees to invite Tracina, Carruthers Johnstone and baby Neko. Cassie, now a friend of Tracina's, insists that Will forgive her. Did this surprise you? Do you think Cassie was right? How is forgiveness important for Will's transformation in *S.E.C.R.E.T. Revealed*? How good are you at forgiving people?

18. By the end of the book, Cassie and Solange end up in love with men from their real lives, not men from their sex fantasies. In your opinion, what keeps Cassie and Jesse apart? Is it harder or easier for a relationship that begins with sexual chemistry to transform into something more intimate? What makes it possible for Cassie and Jesse to walk away as friends? What sustained Cassie and Will's relationship, even when they weren't sexually involved?

19. Tracina was born with a natural comfort and confidence in her sexuality. "Be mysterious," she tells Cassie. "Be busy, date. You really want a guy? Behave like you don't." How does Cassie follow this advice? What is your philosophy when it comes to attracting someone?

20. Cassie lists facets of her life developed through her involvement in S.E.C.R.E.T.: entrepreneur, lover, business partner, boss, mentor, friend. Do you think she could have developed all of these aspects of herself without the organization's help?

21. In your opinion, what really brought Cassie and Will back together?

22. Looking back over all three books in the trilogy, can you see other times when Jesse's feelings for Matilda (and vice versa) were apparent? Or did that turn completely surprise you, as it did Cassie? How did you react to this relationship, considering the age difference and other factors?

23. What major lessons does Solange learn by the end of *S.E.C.R.E.T Revealed*? What is at the heart of her transformation? Beyond her reunion with Julius, what else has she achieved?

24. Why did it take Solange's participation in S.E.C.R.E.T. to bring her and Julius together? What did she need to let go of to make room for this reunion?

25. S.E.C.R.E.T. is a fictional society dedicating to helping women achieve a sexual awakening. What are some ways you can create your own personal sexual awakening?

The perfect threesome. . . .

Read the bestselling
S·E·C·R·E·T series

"Enticing."

"Riveting."

"Smart."

"Sexy."